ALANNA KNIGHT has written more than sixty novels, three non-fiction titles on R.L. Stevenson, two true crime books, numerous short stories and several plays since the publication of her first book in 1969. Born and educated in Tyneside, she now lives in Edinburgh. She is a member of the Scottish chapter of the Crime Writers' Association, and a founder member and Honorary President of the Scottish Association of Writers and of the Edinburgh Writers' Club.

www.alannaknight.com

Deadly Legacy

ALANNA KNIGHT

Allison & Busby Limited
12 Fitzroy Mews
London W1T 6DW
www.allisonandbusby.com

First published in Great Britain by Allison & Busby in 2012.
This paperback edition published by Allison & Busby in 2013.

A CIP catalogue record for this book is available from
the British Library.

10 9 8 7 6 5 4 3 2 1

ISBN 978-0-7490-1238-0

Typeset in 10.5/14.2 pt Sabon by
Allison & Busby Ltd.

The paper used for this Allison & Busby publication
has been produced from trees that have been legally sourced
from well-managed and credibly certified forests.

Printed and bound by
CPI Group (UK) Ltd, Croydon, CR0 4YY

For Jenny Brown,
Helen and Morna the Mulgray Twins,
with love.

CHAPTER ONE

Autumn 1901

Anyone out walking on Arthur's Seat that Sunday morning, breathing in the September sunshine and bold enough to stop and stare into the kitchen window of Solomon's Tower, would have found their curiosity rewarded by a scene somewhat familiar in many Edinburgh suburbs. A scene of tranquil domesticity.

While I frowned over a book, Detective Inspector Jack Macmerry solemnly read a newspaper, and a dog, larger than normal, occupied the rug in front of a cheerful log fire.

But all was not as it seemed; there was much that was not revealed by that first glance at this picture of married bliss. Not least that we weren't married, except under the Scottish law of 'marriage by habit and repute'.

Writing up Rose McQuinn's last case in my new logbook, I had not yet lost my sense of excitement at setting foot, as it were, in a new century. The last night of December 1900 had seen a terrible gale sweep nationwide across Britain, leaving a trail of destruction violent enough to bring down one of the ancient stones at Stonehenge.

Despite the Astronomer Royal's assurance that numbering begins at one, not zero, to many that storm was an omen for the new century, especially as rumours had drifted from the Isle of Wight that Queen Victoria was approaching the end of her sixty-three years' reign, described by some as 'glorious'.

Her death on 22nd January shocked an entire nation, destroying delusions of her immortality and prayers for her survival, which were not shared by her son and heir, who had given up hope of ever being king while his stubborn old mother ruled over him (as well as her subjects) with a rod and will of iron.

However, this royal drama made little change to the war with the Boers, an event paled to insignificance by Her Majesty's funeral cortège followed by the crowned heads of Europe, most of whom were close relatives. All recorded on what promised to be a new marvel of our age: moving pictures, viewed by thousands for the first time.

But to return to that domestic scene in Solomon's Tower. Another look at DI Macmerry would have revealed that his anxious frown was not caused by whatever changes the reign of the new king, Edward VII, might bring to the Edinburgh City Police. He was in fact much more concerned regarding the welfare of three-year-old Meg, his motherless daughter, visited far too rarely in Glasgow and now to be even more inaccessible, having recently moved with her adoptive parents to a rural area of Perthshire. Added to that was the seed of doubt in his mind as to whether the child really was his, or whether he had been trapped into marriage by the oldest trick in the book.

As for the dog by the fire, Thane was not in any sense a domestic pet, but a very large deerhound whose origins lay within the mysterious depths of that extinct volcano Arthur's Seat, from which he had emerged to become part of my life and my protector when I first arrived in Edinburgh six years ago.

On this particular Sunday morning, Jack tried to put his concerns about Meg out of his mind and was engrossed in an article concerning the anniversary of the Battle of Prestonpans, Prince Charles Edward Stuart's successful prelude to the disaster of Culloden.

It was a well-known local fact that during his 1745 campaign laying siege to Edinburgh, the prince had lodged down the road from Duddingston while his army, their cannon trained conveniently on the city, had camped on Arthur's Seat and most likely in this very house, Solomon's Tower.

This possibility was substantiated when Jack and I came across the existence of a secret room at the top of the spiral staircase. Besides past centuries' accumulation of dust and spiders' webs, evidence of human occupation was indicated by a uniform cloak hanging behind the door and the abandoned fragment of a yellowed and almost illegible map on the table. These tokens gave no hint as to the identity of the occupant – Jacobite or Hanoverian deserter – who had presumably left in a great hurry with his pursuers hot on his heels.

Jack and I decided to close the door on that incident in history and the room had been reopened by me, two years ago, for another fugitive fleeing from the law. A secret refuge and a tragic incident that I did not want to remember but found hard to forget.

To return to Prestonpans. The secret room and that long-ago battle, all would have remained part of Edinburgh's history had not Thane, on one of his rambles with Jack on Arthur's Seat, unearthed a rusted sword, identified by a military antiquarian to be of Jacobite origin.

This find was a turning point for Jack and had him delving into historical accounts, where more interesting and alluring facts emerged than twentieth-century police files offered. Such as the rumour of French gold, which had followed the prince to Scotland to assist in his campaign but had mysteriously vanished and, in doing so, had intrigued historians ever since. That it might have reached the prince in Duddingston preparing for battle led Jack to the intriguing discovery that Arthur's Seat had a hundred hidden caves suitable for buried treasure.

Because of his profession of solving murders, the existence of an unsolved mystery on our doorstep, so to speak, was irresistible and, with Thane, walks on unexplored sections of the hill became Jack's favourite leisure pursuit.

Had Jack been a Highlander loyal to the Stuart cause, I might have understood, but he was a Lowlander, his duty owed, his oath of allegiance given, to the Queen, a direct descendant of the House of Hanover.

As this new hobby coincided with our discovery of the secret room, Jack now saw himself in the role of military historian, declaring that perceived wisdom held that most successful battles were fought in summer, when there was food for men and horses, while in the autumn Highland chieftains were unwilling to call their clansmen to take up arms, leaving harvests to rot and families to starve in the bitter winter – a theory disproved, Jack pointed out, by the springtime disaster of Culloden and the autumn victory at Prestonpans.

Now each September Jack and I would go on a carriage drive, allegedly for a breath of fresh East Lothian air, but in reality a pilgrimage, a walk across the old battlefield with Jack making encouraging noises to Thane, hoping that he would unearth a treasure greater than the King George II coin, his sole discovery to date.

Hopeful for something larger, like the Jacobite sword, all he ever received from Thane was a look of reproach that said plainly he was not that kind of animal. Besides, it was certain knowledge that this particular ground had been traversed and trampled across by souvenir hunters for a hundred and fifty years and what Jack was expecting was a miracle.

I refused to be convinced about the Stuart cause, and Jack, completely failing to understand my lack of excitement and enthusiasm, looked at me in amazement.

'I thought that Bonnie Prince Charlie was every Scotswoman's hero.'

I shook my head. 'You've been influenced by too many tales of Flora MacDonald. He certainly wasn't mine.'

For me, the past was gone and I was content

to bury it along with the very recent past which had confirmed my widowhood. Now it was the present affairs of Scotland, along with the whole rapidly changing face of Europe and worldwide events, that engrossed and concerned me.

I didn't much care which king or queen ruled over us as long as they understood that women were no longer men's chattels, playthings or breeding machines.

Women's suffrage was my burning issue, rather than a royal prince, a pretender to the English throne whose family exploits were a historical disaster. I refused to regard as a hero the incompetent misguided prince who had cost so many loyal followers their lives, and the terrible disasters wrought by Butcher Cumberland on the survivors. Indeed, I considered the Jacobites initially responsible for the Highland clearances.

My battles were with the times in which we now lived, and I was deeply involved with the Women's Suffrage Movement in Edinburgh – my 'obsession' as Jack called it – since I had lately been appointed chairman of the committee which met each month, and we were shortly hoping to welcome the great Emily Hobhouse herself.

My fellow campaigners were amazed that men could be so blind to the Boer War, which had exposed every kind of social weakness in Britain, in particular malnutrition, poverty and ignorance. Even the newspapers had seized upon the fact that in every big city, almost a third out of eleven thousand volunteers for the war would be rejected as physically unfit.

The census figures were most revealing, showing a budget lingering on tariffs and refusing to consider welfare in a country where middle-class families now had an average of four children, while in labourers' families the figures of infant mortality and child bed-deaths had changed little since the Middle Ages.

Our movement was supported by mothers, sisters and wives of all classes. We demanded not only for the right to vote, but radical social reform. Out of four million women, over one quarter were domestic servants – overworked, underpaid slaves of employers, where ostentation and drudgery went together.

Since the death of Queen Victoria, no one knew what to expect of the future reign of King Edward VII. 'It seemed we stood on the edge of a precipice,' Jack said, little guessing that in fact his life, mine and that of the child he rarely saw were indeed trembling on the brink. In a few days the whole scene of our domestic life would be irrevocably changed for ever.

CHAPTER TWO

As with most major events in one's life, there were no dramatic signals, only a chance meeting in Jenners with one of my elderly clients, for whom I had sorted out a very minor domestic problem regarding a missing watch she suspected had been stolen by the window cleaner. After an exhaustive search and extensive enquiries it was later discovered by me on my hands and knees in the shrubbery, having fallen out of the window when it was opened by the maid.

For some reason she remained grateful to the extent of even acknowledging my presence in company – not at all usual with most of my clients, who were usually eager, or had good reason to wish to forget the painful incident which had led them to commission my assistance.

On this occasion I had been in the toy department looking for a suitable present for Jack's wee Meg. I had little experience of such matters, but possibly a great deal more than Jack, and feeling triumphant over the purchase of a small pretty doll with a spare set of clothes, I made my way upstairs to the restaurant.

And there was Mrs Lawers. 'I saw you entering the toy department when I was on my way upstairs and . . .' She paused. 'Do please join me, that is if you haven't an engagement and can spare a few moments.'

I took a seat opposite, and ordered my pot of tea, putting down my new purchase on a vacant chair.

I said, 'A doll for a small girl.'

'Might I take a look?' Smiles of approval followed and she said, 'I have been similarly engaged – a pretty dress for a friend's granddaughter in London. The good Lord did not oblige me with children of my own.'

I regarded her thoughtfully; it did not take any great flight of imagination to realise that there was something more significant heavily at work in Mrs Lawers' mind than polite rejoinders concerning Edinburgh's weather and the inevitable change of royalty, which all loyal citizens seemed to feel obliged to include in their conversations.

Mrs Lawers had aged considerably since our

last meeting. I noticed the walking stick, and at my enquiry regarding her health, she sighed.

'I have chronic rheumatism and the physicians say there is little hope. It is very sad as I am almost unable to travel any more.' Tears had welled in her eyes; she touched her breast in the region of her heart. 'I fear I am not well or long for this world, my dear; my only wish is to see the only kin I have, a cousin never met since childhood, to pass on to him some valued family items, including documents, long in my keeping.'

She paused and looked at me, biting her lip. 'I am almost afraid to ask this question, an impertinence really and one you may not even consider. My cousin's family home is at Lochandor, in Perth. I have never visited them, but believe it is a fine old house.' Another sigh. 'And that is where I wish to travel.' Leaning across, she placed a hand on my arm and said hesitantly, 'I wonder . . . could I possibly engage your services as a travelling companion, to see me safely there, my journey – my mission – fulfilled?'

I recognised 'engaging my services' as the polite way of hinting that a fee was involved, but the request seemed odd. She must have seen by my reaction that this was a curious request. Surely she had servants who might accompany her.

Smiling sadly she shook her head. 'I know what you are thinking, my dear – this is what is required of one's personal maid. But there is a problem. I have no one who I can trust; my dear Hinton is as old as I am and equally infirm. There is no one else. A solicitor is too busy and would not even consider such a request, but I wondered . . . that is, if you were not busy with a case at the moment . . .'

An anxious frown, then she brightened. 'And when I saw you I decided that the good Lord had given me a sign, had sent me an angel.'

I hardly saw myself in such a role, but I was intrigued and sorry for the old lady. Still it did not quite make sense until she leant over the table again and whispered, 'I must have someone I can trust, you see. These packages I will be carrying have long been in my family's possession; they are a legacy handed down through the generations.' A sigh. 'As the last direct descendant I have been trustee of the legacy all my life.' A sad smile. 'Now my life is drawing to its close, the legacy's safekeeping must not be imperilled. It is essential that I go to Lochandor and see it handed on in person, delivered to the remaining member of our family.'

Watching me intently as I refilled our teacups, she said, 'I am aware that I am asking a great deal and you must have time to think about it and to make any necessary arrangements. But as you are a young lady on your own . . .'

She left it unfinished. She must have been one of the few who did not know of my scandalous existence as the common-law wife of Jack Macmerry.

I could not refuse her request face-to-face, but it was true I needed time to consider, to discuss it with Jack. I promised to let her know shortly.

She frowned. 'Do not leave it too long. I must leave by the end of the week.' Looking over her shoulder as if she might be overheard, 'There is . . . danger, danger for me,' she whispered, 'if I do not leave soon. There are others who wish to lay their hands on . . . what I am taking to Lochandor. Will you call upon me when you have decided – tomorrow perhaps?'

I promised to do so and escorted her to her waiting carriage. Since she lived in Duddingston village, her road led via Arthur's Seat and I would be dropped off at Solomon's Tower.

She was silent on the short journey, sitting back with her eyes closed, pale-looking and seeming utterly exhausted. I already had misgivings about what a visit to rural Perthshire with this frail old lady would involve.

As the carriage drew up at my home, she handed me the leather bag which she carried. 'Will you take care of this for me?'

I was startled. It looked ancient and shabby but I presumed it was a favourite and long-treasured handbag. As I had not said yes to her request I replied, 'If this contains the valuables you mentioned, surely I am not the proper person; it should be with your bank.'

She shook her head. 'This satchel never leaves my possession, day or night, but alas I have reason to believe I cannot keep its contents safe in my own home a day longer. There are dangerous signs around me, my dear. They are no longer secure under my roof,' she added, staring in the direction of the loch, 'and for that reason I now feel they will be safer with you in neutral territory.'

And taking my hand, 'I hope and pray most earnestly that you will decide to accompany me. It will merely be two days, to see me safe to my family, that is all I ask, and you will of course be a guest at Lochandor.'

I left her, wondering what on earth I had let myself in for. What would Jack say? And what did this bag contain that was so precious?

Jack's response wasn't as mocking as I expected. His immediate interest was the fact that Mrs Lawers lived in one of the Duddingston houses associated with Bonnie Prince Charlie. And that satchel, he declared, was exactly the kind officers carried during their troop manoeuvres in 1745.

Had I been inside her home? What did it look like? I assured him that it looked merely ordinary, the sitting room low-roofed, the windows small.

He seemed disappointed, obviously having expected something a mite more grand and dramatic.

'Lochandor did you say? Is that her destination?' And unrolling one of his maps, pointing to the district, he traced his finger down an inch or so to the west. 'Tarnbrae – now that is a coincidence, it's where Meg is living now with her aunt and uncle.' Taking out his wallet, he removed an envelope. 'Here it is; Joe has taken a position as clerk to the local laird.'

I had to confess I knew very little about Meg's adoptive parents. 'Remember I told you, Joe worked in the shipyard on the Clyde, but his health has been poor, and he applied for this job, apparently got it too. Pam said it would be good for them to get away into the country for a change.'

Putting down envelope and map, he regarded me triumphantly. 'Well done, Rose. Yes, by all means, I think you should take up Mrs Lawers' offer. Gives you a chance to look in and see how Meg is settling down. And you can give me a full report.'

I said, 'I was thinking about Meg – in fact that's how I came to meet Mrs Lawers.'

Showing him the doll, he nodded appreciatively. 'You can give it to her yourself, that's even better.'

He sighed and shook his head sadly, and I

heard in that sigh echoes of guilt for his neglect of his daughter, the wee girl he had seen no more than for a duty visit once or twice a year since the day she was born, who had been gratefully adopted by her childless aunt and uncle.

'I would love to go with you, but there are matters at Central Office. I am in court, we've got witnesses from Glasgow, a murder investigation on our hands . . .'

There was to be another, nearer at home, quite soon.

CHAPTER THREE

A month had passed since Jack and I made the annual pilgrimage to the battlefield at Prestonpans. Now the first leaves had changed colour; a riot of yellows, reds and oranges had replaced the massed greens of summer. This annual scene of earthly beauty was breathtaking but transient; already storms were growling over the Firth of Forth, unleashing heavy rain clouds, driving across fields and gardens, while the first icy winds swept down from Arthur's Seat, hiding its lofty lion's head under a swirling shroud of mist.

My proposed journey with Mrs Lawers would involve travelling by train to Perth, then by coach across a rural area, to me a virtually unknown and curiously alien land. I hoped that the never-reliable weather wouldn't mean an early snowfall, bringing with it the yearly closing of the Highland glens and inaccessible travelling conditions. Even close to towns, winter journeys were always hazardous and subject to long delays.

'The autumn colours will be superb,' said Jack encouragingly. 'Only wish I could go with you,' he repeated. 'I am so anxious for news of Meg. Tell her I promise I will visit her next summer. Maybe earlier, it all depends,' he added vaguely.

How far away summer seemed. Sometimes I wondered if his new obsession with the Jacobite Rebellion was his escape from the present, from feelings of guilt for the neglect of the daughter born of that swift unhappy marriage to her mother on the rebound of my rejection. A marriage made in anger and revenge for my refusal to become his wife.

And if this supposition was true, then I too had a share in his guilt: my lame excuse for not agreeing to marry him – that Danny McQuinn might still be alive – had resulted, directly or indirectly, in his hasty union with Meg's mother, and now I felt a responsibility towards this unwanted child I had never met.

The day of my departure with Mrs Lawers approached. In reply to my acceptance I received a very substantial fee with a note that a hiring carriage would take us both to Waverley railway station.

My absence promised to be brief indeed; merely deliver Mrs Lawers to Lochandor, call on Meg in her new home, perhaps spend the night with her adoptive parents, and return the next day.

Jack would be home each night and Thane was in charge of the Tower as always in our absence. We never locked the kitchen door once he'd learnt how to lift the latch with his nose. He would feed himself, returning to hunting as he had done long before he came into my life. I had no idea how old he was at that time. He seemed young and hadn't aged at all, so I tried not to remember that a dog does not live for ever and that the lifespan of large breeds was even shorter than small ones.

Except that Thane was more than a dog. I would close my eyes and simply hope that this strange creature did not obey the natural canine laws. He had survived more 'deaths' than a cat's nine lives, a fact that neither of us could explain, and if I ever wondered out loud as to Thane's background, Jack merely shrugged, shook his head and said, 'Thane is Thane. That's all we know of him or ever will. We must satisfy ourselves that we need never expect to know more about him than we do at this moment.'

And so I prepared to leave, heartened as ever that it would take a very brave burglar to face this particular and peculiar resident of the Tower.

At last I was ready, and as a cautionary measure, remembering Mrs Lawers' fears for her life and safety, however irrational, I decided to be prepared for any emergency and took out of my study desk a small derringer and checked it for bullets, thankful that Jack was not observing my actions.

He would have been scandalised. I had learnt to use guns and rifles from Danny McQuinn in our pioneering days in Arizona. I was even rather a good shot, although I hoped that I would not have to prove that once again. I was prepared only to use this ultimate deterrent in direst necessity.

My small travelling case normally served as my carrier. Jack had devised and made it for me some time ago, to leave my hands free for the handlebars of my bicycle. It fitted comfortably on to the back of the machine and was considerably easier to carry with a shoulder strap than the rather unwieldy large suitcases and hatboxes now considered fashionable by most ladies.

Jack had already departed for the Central Office when I heard the carriage arrive. To my surprise, the woman who emerged was not Mrs Lawers. This must be Hinton, the maid whom I had never met, since she had been away at the time of the missing watch incident.

Looking past the maid, I expected to see Mrs Lawers already seated. But the maid was alone. She came forward rather tearfully and introduced herself. 'I have sad news. Alas, my mistress is very poorly this morning.'

'I am sorry to hear that. The journey is to be delayed, then?'

'We cannot delay,' was the reply. 'This is a matter of utmost urgency and you are to proceed immediately as planned to her destination. My instructions are precise; I am to accompany you and I have acquainted myself thoroughly with her map. I know exactly where we are bound for.' She hesitated and looked at me keenly. 'You have the small satchel she left with you in safe custody. I am to take charge of that also.'

I looked at her. Mrs Lawers had stressed that it was not to leave my possession and it was now firmly locked away in my carrier across my shoulder. I said, 'It is safely packed.'

'Please hand it over, then.'

Remembering my promise, in Mrs Lawers' absence I felt the momentary stirrings of unease. Something was not quite right.

'Later, miss,' I said. 'It is not very convenient here. Wait until we reach the station.'

She glanced at the travelling case, frowning, as

if doubtful about the reliability of such a piece of insubstantial luggage, and as the swaying coach hurtled down the steep hill towards the Pleasance, I added, 'Has Mrs Lawers someone taking care of her in your absence?'

'A kindly neighbour will look after her.'

As she spoke, sitting opposite I had a chance to take a good look at the maid Mrs Lawers had described as elderly and infirm like herself. Miss Hinton certainly did not look old, in fact she looked scarcely older than myself. Slim and youthful, apart from somewhat prematurely white hair, glimpsed under the felt bonnet, she was wearing a smart navy-blue costume and black boots, the garb of a lady's maid. And then there was her cultured accent.

'I gather you have been with Mrs Lawers for some time.'

'I have, madam.' Avoiding my gaze, steadfastly looking out of the window, she seemed nervous, eager to reach the station as we were held up by a cart which had shed a load of coal. As a delay seemed inevitable, I decided to ask how she had met Mrs Lawers.

'We met in the usual way of a servant applying for a situation.'

'But you are not from these parts. You are a long way from home.'

Turning her attention away from the commotion

outside, she gave me a startled glance. 'What makes you think that, madam?'

'Your accent. You are from the Highlands, are you not?'

'That is so. I was brought up near Inverness.' A frowning look. 'But I believe I lost my accent long ago.'

'Your accent, perhaps so. But your natural language gave you away – there is no "yes" or "no" in Gaelic. Am I right?'

She smiled wryly. 'That is correct. You are very observant, madam.'

We had reached the station and as we alighted she stretched out her hand for my bag. 'Allow me to take that, madam.'

In answer, I slung it over my shoulder. 'Not at all. I am used to carrying it. It isn't heavy.'

She stood firmly in front of me. 'But I insist, madam. Let me take it for you.'

I shook my head equally firmly. 'Thank you, miss, but I would not dream of letting another woman carry my luggage.'

Ignoring that, she stretched out her hand in an attitude of command.

'Thank you. But no.' And glancing past her, 'I notice we are in good time for the next train. While you purchase tickets, I shall take the opportunity of adjourning to the ladies' waiting room and avail myself of the toilet facilities.'

I walked ahead, aware of a tightening of her lips, a frown of impatience. My insistence had annoyed her and as we walked into the waiting room and I headed towards the cubicle marked 'Ladies' she remained at my side. 'No need to take your travelling case, madam, I will look after it.'

I pretended not to hear her, went inside and locked the door. There was something about her determination to lay hands on my luggage that made me uneasy. Undoing the carrier's lock and opening it was quite difficult in such a confined space. I unfastened the strap on the old leather satchel, revealing its contents as a small sealed package.

I remembered my conversation with Mrs Lawers and gathered that it had been in her family's possession for a long time, handed down generation to generation. It was certainly very old, yellowed with age; the writing on the outer parchment, a faint sepia faded with time, confirmed its value – even if this was purely sentimental, since Mrs Lawers was herself now old and infirm. But that it had some other value to someone else, particularly to her maid Hinton, seemed obvious by that woman's odd behaviour, her determination to wrest it from my possession.

I had a sudden idea how to ensure the safety of its contents. Transferring the package to the voluminous pocket of my travelling skirt, I concluded my ablutions and returned to the café carrying the satchel to where Hinton waited seated by the window which overlooked the platforms.

Relieved to see me again, the maid's eyes were immediately drawn to the satchel, and pointing to two cups on the table, she said rather impatiently, 'So there you are, at last. I decided that as we still had time, we should refresh ourselves, so I purchased tea from the refreshment counter over there.'

I looked in the direction of a small and unprepossessing serving hatch, where a surly-looking attendant operated a tea urn and hovered over some tired-looking scones.

I thanked Hinton for her consideration, however, and she shrugged. 'Better drink up. You took longer than I thought. We don't want to miss this train. I presumed that you take sugar?'

I didn't normally but thought it rude to complain, glad to have even a drink that was oversweet. Watching this enigmatic person, who was perhaps more used to dealing with old ladies, I was somewhat amused by her attitude towards me. I wondered if she was always bossy, used to treating her employer in this manner, especially when she contemptuously declined my offer to pay the few coppers involved for the cup of tea.

The Inverness train for Perth steamed into the station and we took seats opposite one another in an otherwise empty carriage which Hinton had chosen on the grounds that it is nicer for ladies travelling together to have some privacy.

Once inside, I settled down in my corner while she offered to put my two pieces of luggage, carrier and satchel, on the rack above our heads.

'Thank you, no. It is a short journey, we have plenty of room.'

'As you wish.'

My movements watched intently and with palpable disapproval, I slung the strap of the carrier over my arm and entwined the satchel over my wrist before settling back and staring out of the window. It was a grey weary day and after a few minutes I discovered that I was feeling very weary too.

My companion was silent. I studied her from narrowed eyes, observing again that her description failed to meet that of 'old and infirm' – she appeared to be both young and healthy and had rather large hands and feet. She was also quite tall – but so are most women compared to myself, a couple of inches under five feet.

Eager to learn more about Hinton, I considered polite conversation, but the words refused to assemble; suddenly it was too difficult to summon the energy to talk, and my eyelids were growing heavier, heavier.

I yawned and thankfully closed my eyes. After

what seemed like only a minute, they opened again with utmost reluctance as the train jerked to a stop halted by a signal ahead.

Hinton was watching me. She smiled. 'Did that waken you?' And when I lied and said that I wasn't asleep she replied, 'You seem very tired, madam. You might as well take the opportunity to rest. I will wake you when we reach Perth, then we will take a carriage from the station.'

I found myself hardly listening, yawning again. This overwhelming desire to close my eyes and fall asleep during the day was quite extraordinary. It was only eleven-thirty in the morning and I had a desperate need for only one thing.

All my senses commanded: *Sleep*!

CHAPTER FOUR

I knew no more until air blasting in from an open door forced open my eyelids, still agonisingly heavy. What on earth was happening to me?

I was being held by Hinton. She was a strong woman, towering above my small stature, her arms grasped firmly around my waist.

I panicked, confused.

'What's happening? Has there been a crash?'

Clinging to me, she didn't reply.

I struggled in vain. Had I been dreaming, opened the door for fresh air and was now in danger of falling out of the moving train?

And then—

And then I was suddenly alert. I was in danger indeed. But not from falling.

I was being pushed – pushed forcibly out of the open door.

Through the smoke, a steep hill, and as the train slowed down to round a corner I was in mid-air – my feet dangling above the rails.

I struggled with Hinton, calling for help.

No one heard me, and suddenly released from her iron grip, I flew through the air and hit the ground, tumbled on to a grassy verge, and began to roll steadily down the hill, my progress accelerated by agonising encounters with small stones, then halted momentarily by a series of tall weeds and shrubs.

In desperation I found one and clung on. Looking up back at the railway track far above me I called again for help. In vain.

The noise and smoke of the train had been replaced by silence as I hung there, trying to sort out my bruises and addled wits.

I was still so tired. There was no sign of the satchel which had contained Mrs Lawers' legacy at the start of our journey. My travelling carrier, however, had accompanied my fall and I saw it lodged some ten feet away.

I wanted to reach it, but discovered I was too weary to make the effort. All I wanted was to close my eyes again, confident that this was just some terrible nightmare.

Soon I would wake up again. I always did.

Suddenly, my face was wet; I struggled to open my eyes. My face was being licked by . . . Thane!

No, that wasn't possible, although the grey hairy face at close range might well have been his. A large dog was at my side, and hurrying up the hill, rifle in hand, a middle-aged gentleman dressed like a gamekeeper.

He rushed to my side. 'Pilot spotted you, miss. What the devil has happened? Are you hurt?'

'I don't know. I can't remember – I think I must have fallen off the train.'

He lifted me to my feet, very gently. 'I'm a doctor, miss. Let's make sure you're all right. Let's see, now. Can you walk a few steps?'

I managed, clinging to his arm and stumbling down the hill where he retrieved my carrier and pronounced my progress was excellent.

'Arms and legs not injured. Excellent. A few bruises, I dare say, but they'll soon mend,' he added cheerfully. 'Fortunate that you fell down a grassy slope. Excuse me a moment.' He stopped. 'Would you mind . . . er . . . breathing on me please.'

I did so and he nodded grimly. 'Just as I thought, miss.'

He said nothing more until we were safely on the footpath below, the deerhound, so like Thane, walking at his side.

Releasing my arm, he asked how I was.

'My shoulder is rather sore and my knee. I think it is bleeding.' I could feel it sticking to my skirt.

We were in a village street and he pointed to a little cottage, some fifty yards distant, almost concealed by trees. 'That is where I live. I have my surgery there, and once we have attended to your cuts and bruises, I'll get the carriage out and take you to the railway station. Where were you heading?'

I told him Perth and he nodded. 'You're nearer Edinburgh than Perth; this is Kingmere.'

A brass plate on the door declared its owner was Dr Hugh Everson. The interior was neat and pretty, suggesting that the kindly doctor was no bachelor, confirmed by family photographs on the sideboard.

'My wife is away visiting a friend in Kirkcaldy, who has been ill,' he explained, his arm supporting me and leading the way into a small but well-equipped surgery. Removing my cloak, he bathed and bandaged my cut knee and gently examined my arms and shoulders.

'All present and correct, madam. May I know your name?'

'Mrs McQuinn,' I said. 'Thanks to you, Doctor, I've survived – I don't know what I would have done if you hadn't come along.'

He smiled. 'Your thanks belong to old Pilot here.'

And before I could tell him the coincidence of Thane he stood up and regarded me sternly. 'One more thing I must ask . . .' He hesitated a moment. 'Tell me, Mrs McQuinn, are you on some kind of drugs?'

'Drugs? Of course not.'

'You are absolutely certain. No kind of medication?'

'No. I assure you I am perfectly healthy.'

He nodded but looked rather doubtful. 'Very well. If you have any problems, then you can consult your own physician when you return home. Meanwhile I will make us a restoring cup of tea before you continue your journey – in safety this time.'

Dr Everson placed the cup of tea before me and proffered milk and sugar, which I declined. The first sip and the mists of confusion began to clear.

'I was perfectly fit until I boarded that train for Perth. But I have not the slightest idea why I required fresh air, opened the door, and fell out of the train.'

Now as I said the words, the pieces of the puzzle began to fit together. Those last moments – the maid Hinton's strong arm around me, my cries for help unheeded . . . and the thought came sharp as a knife: did I fall or was I pushed?

'Your questions intrigue me, Doctor. Is there

some point to them? Do I look as if I might be an opium addict?'

He smiled. 'Far from it, Mrs McQuinn, but many ladies take laudanum for relief from pain – our late Queen set a lamentable fashion.' He shook his head. 'As I lifted you, it was not opium or laudanum I detected on your breath but a substance much more dangerous.'

And as I raised the cup again to my lips, I thought of that other time in Waverley station. Hinton with the two cups of tea.

'Then I know the answer to your question, Doctor. I was travelling with a woman who tried to rob me.' I told him about the refreshments and he said firmly, 'It is obvious that she put something in the tea to drug you, and when it took effect, she pushed you off the train. What did she steal?'

'Nothing. I felt uneasy about her from the outset of the journey, her insistence that she should carry my bag I found rather odd.' And I told him of how I had taken the precaution of removing the package from the satchel in the ladies' lavatory at the station.

'I have the packages she wanted safe here,' I added, indicating the large pockets of my skirt, an invaluable necessity for the convenience of a lady cyclist, but I omitted any mention of the derringer I also carried which I had had no opportunity to use.

Dr Everson listened, his expression grave.

'This is a very serious matter, Mrs McQuinn. Attempted robbery and assault. A matter for the police for immediate investigation.'

He sat back and looked at me. 'This woman is a dangerous criminal. She tried to kill you. You must inform the police. At once,' he repeated.

'I shall do so when I get home, Doctor. My husband' – how odd the word sounded – 'is a detective inspector with Edinburgh City Police.'

The doctor gave a sigh of relief. 'Then he will know what to do, although I fear by the time you get back to Edinburgh it will be too late to catch this woman. She almost got away with murder.'

And that was all she got away with, I thought triumphantly, imagining her anger when she opened the satchel and discovered the small doll, intended for Meg's birthday, which I had substituted in the ladies' lavatory for the sealed package.

I was considering continuing my journey to Lochandor, but on my feet again, I realised that I was still severely shaken.

A glance in the mirror produced a very dishevelled image; in general I looked awful, with dusty clothes and wild hair, never easy to control at the best of times, clearly sending a message to all the world that I had been pulled through a hedge backwards. Which, in fact, was not far from the truth.

I had tried to restore equilibrium. The doctor had provided soap, a towel and a clothes brush, but when I reappeared he would not hear of my plan to continue my journey, insisting that doctor's orders were that I return to Edinburgh immediately and inform my husband of the attack made on me and allow him to begin investigations for my attacker's capture.

I had to agree with him. Even disregarding my appearance sorely in need of repairs, I did not feel like going to Perth, making my way to an unknown destination alone and travelling on to look for Meg in her new home.

I had to feel stronger than I did at this moment, and there was something else . . .

Considering Hinton's murderous behaviour, I was seriously concerned about the welfare of Mrs Lawers. I had to check that all was well in Duddingston before I resumed my journey.

CHAPTER FIVE

As the doctor and I sat in his carriage at the local station, awaiting the arrival of the train for Edinburgh, Pilot was by his side and I asked the doctor about the deerhound.

'I have one almost exactly the same at home. How did you come by him? Tell me – how old is he?'

'Maybe fourteen or even older. Since he came to us fully grown, I couldn't tell you exactly.' He shook his head. 'It is a long story, Mrs McQuinn.'

The dog looked up, knew he was being talked about and seemed to smile.

Dr Everson patted his head. 'He has shown no signs of ageing. He is as active as he was in those first days, which we thought of as near puppyhood.'

'Indeed, he looks remarkably young,' I commented and told him that Thane had been with me for six years.

The train was late, delayed at the signals. When it arrived ten minutes later, I said goodbye gratefully to my rescuer, and having exchanged cards with him, sat by the window in a compartment with several other passengers. I was taking no chances this time. Looking out of the window, I went over what the doctor had related in the waiting room about the strange origins of deerhounds.

'These hounds are the oldest breed in Britain, and, along with their cousins the wolfhounds of Ireland, they were certainly here at the time of the Druids, and the Romans knew them. Legend has it that the Irish princess Deirdre had a deerhound always at her side when she lived in the Highlands, in Glen Etive. Their roots probably go back to man's earliest arrival, and it would seem that magic was involved. They were first heard of in the wilds of Argyll and live there still, a wild pack of them, seldom seen, roaming the hills, and people fortunate enough to persuade one to become domesticated and live with them never see their deerhound die.

'When death is approaching they grow restless, refuse to eat and seem to be listening, waiting. Then a day comes when their pet disappears.

Time passes and the whole household agrees that he has died out there somewhere. Then one morning they open the door and he is back again, as if he had never left.

'Is this the same dog? For he has the same characteristics, recognises them, takes on again where he left off, as if he has been away for a day or two, and behaves in every way like the same beloved pet reborn.' The doctor had finally added, 'Perhaps you did not realise, but something very odd happened this afternoon. The pack seem to have a universal telepathy transcending time and place. They seem to know when some human to whom they are devoted is in danger.'

And looking at me very intently he continued, 'As you were today. Pilot got the message from your deerhound. It all happened quite suddenly for me, sitting by the fireside enjoying a quiet moment before my afternoon visits. We had had our walk for the day and I wasn't intending taking him again, but he was quite insistent, rushing back and forth to the door. I have had him long enough to realise that something was bothering him and that he needed me. So I followed him, and as the train was approaching, he bolted up the hill. What the devil was he up to? I was alarmed and yelled at him to come back.

'But as the smoke faded, I saw him bending

over an inert figure, halfway up, someone lying injured.' He sighed. 'The word had been spread and he had found you, Mrs McQuinn.'

By the time we reached Waverley and I left the train it was raining hard. My bruises and cut knee made themselves painfully evident and rebelled against that two-mile walk to Solomon's Tower, so feeling rather reckless and extravagant, I took a carriage home.

Thane bounded out to meet me. Remembering the doctor's strange stories, I could have imagined that there was relief in that welcome.

Jack would be in shortly and, preparing a meal, I wondered what he would make of my terrifying experience.

I was not to find out that day. There was a note on the table that he had been called away to a court case down south as a witness, and as it might drag on, I was not to expect him back for a couple of days. He was looking forward eagerly to my meeting with Meg and hoped that I had found her well and happy. I groaned. Unless he was considerably delayed while I made my second foray to Tarnbrae, he was in for a disappointment.

The rain was fairly lashing down now and, too tired and achy to bicycle, it was quite out of the question in my present state to walk even the short distance to Duddingston to see Mrs Lawers.

A warm bath in front of the kitchen fire was a wise move but more beneficial than I had intended. I sat by the fire, had some of the soup I had left for Jack, and opened my eyes, to find the room in darkness. I had slept for two hours and it was now too dark and, as the rain continued unabated, too wet for Duddingston. The visit to Mrs Lawers must wait until tomorrow. I would go quite early, and having made sure that all was well with her, resume my journey to Lochandor, deliver the package and proceed to visit Jack's little daughter.

With cuts and bruises still troublesome and with some added misgivings, the result of nightmarish dreams about train journeys, bicycling was a painful experience. I was glad to dismount at Mrs Lawers' house, one of four in a little row, very old but well preserved.

A knock on the door followed by a long delay added to my growing disquiet. At last, I thought, the twitch of a curtain, the shuffle of footsteps, but the door remained closed.

'Is that you, Mrs McQuinn?' It was Mrs Lawers and I gave a sigh of relief. 'I cannot open the door to you, the doctor fears that my influenza is highly contagious.'

She remained invisible, her voice a hoarse whisper, interupted by a fit of coughing: 'I am being well cared for. Thank you . . .' she gasped, 'we will talk when I am well enough to receive visitors.'

A further bout of coughing terminated any further attempts at conversation and I was left there, standing helpless, unable to tell her of the terrible events of yesterday or warn her of Hinton's duplicity while reassuring her that the package was still safe with me.

I was mounting my bicycle again when the next door opened and a handsome middle-aged woman with dark curly hair emerged carrying a large basket. I hesitated and she waved to me and hurried over.

'I saw you at Mrs Lawers,' she said and began to tell me about the influenza, that the basket was for provisions for her sick friend. So that was true.

'I am taking care of her as best I can; she has but to knock on my wall and I will come to her, although she will not let me enter the house.'

'What about her maid?'

'She's away visiting a friend . . . I think,' she added vaguely. 'Most unfortunate at this time, although Mary – Mrs Lawers – is pleased; she wouldn't like her to take the influenza. Has a bad chest, poor thing; they are both getting on a bit, rather frail.'

A vision of the strong Hinton came sharply to mind as the cheery-faced neighbour said, 'I'm

Amy Dodd, by the way. Pleased to meet you.' She smiled. 'Mary and I have been chums since I first came here four years ago.'

Introducing myself, I wanted to hear more about the missing Hinton but Amy rushed on, 'I have no fears for myself, except that my two grandchildren may be coming to stay and I wouldn't like them to take ill. Hinton will be returning tomorrow; we hope by then that she will be out of danger of passing on the infection.'

I left her, feeling relieved and dismayed both at the same time. Mrs Lawers had been too ill for me to distress her further with what had happened along with my suspicions regarding her maid. She believed I had been successful in delivering the package and I realised that I was morally obligated to carry out the mission for which I had been paid so generously. I had another urgent reason – seeing Jack's daughter in her new home and setting his anxieties at rest, I would be able to return with good news for him as well as cheering news for my client.

Returning to the Tower, doubts crept in. Jack could not have been absent at a more crucial time. If only he had been here, he would have known what to advise. But this was always the way, and always would be. One of the disadvantages of being a policeman's wife: they were never at hand when most needed. 'Married to the job' was an easy way of putting it.

I decided not to leave a message. Best that he did not know of my sinister adventure, and hopefully I would be home again before his return.

So I gave Thane a farewell hug and instructions to take care of everything in our absence, which he seemed as always to understand – I have no idea why, but a communication between Thane and myself certainly existed. This had been confirmed by Doctor Everson and I wanted to ask Thane if he was acquainted with a deerhound called Pilot – but that was nonsense and I still found the doctor's story hard to believe.

I made my way to the station in time for the Perth train and prudently took a seat in a carriage with four other passengers. There was safety in numbers and I had a book by my favourite authoress, Jane Austen, but found my mind drifting away from Emma's trials to the scenes outside the window – the fascination of rapidly appearing and quickly disappearing countryside beneath the train's fast-moving wheels through the clouds of steam, and the small villages and occasional stops at stations on the way.

But mostly my thoughts were fixed on that last journey and the murderous attack by the woman who called herself the maid Hinton, an impostor, and deeply involved in a plot to steal Mrs Lawers' package.

There must have been some intriguing story

regarding its value but I could not imagine from that faded writing on the exterior what was inside, merely that the contents were very old and valuable enough for the bogus Hinton to be prepared to commit murder to gain possession of them.

I went over her behaviour step by step. Obviously she intended that my death should be reported as an unfortunate accident. I knew the sort of story that 'Hinton', if questioned, would have ready: the lady, unknown to her, of course, a fellow passenger, felt faint, opened the door for fresh air and fell out. What explanation would she give as to why she had not stopped the train by pulling the communication cord?

None of my possessions remained on board the train, except for the satchel, and I would have enjoyed seeing her face when she saw the package's replacement.

Making enquiries regarding a carriage as I left the train at Perth station, the porter said:

'Lochandor, is it? There's a local train, miss.' And consulting the clock. 'This platform, in ten minutes. Cheaper than taking a carriage, miss,' he added, his wry look taking in my shoulder-carrier and lack of elegant attire, suggesting that I would be well advised to count each penny and avoid unnecessary expense.

I purchased a ticket for one shilling and half an

hour later alighted at Lochandor, indicated only by a lonely platform. No village or hamlet, no visible sign of habitation. Nothing in sight beyond a couple of hiring carriages awaiting the train's arrival.

Ahead of me, two passengers from other parts of the train were moving rapidly in their direction. Two ladies who from their polite acknowledgements of one another were unacquainted and had travelled separately. Both heavily veiled. A quick scrutiny suggested they were young, well off and in an interesting condition. As each claimed a hiring carriage and had her luggage boarded, I wondered how long I would have to wait until the next carriage arrived. One of the drivers looked in my direction and, leaning forward, had a brief conversation with his passenger.

Whatever he asked I heard only a strongly negative response and a rather shrill, 'I think not, driver, please proceed.'

With a sigh he called across to me, 'Back in ten minutes, miss!'

CHAPTER SIX

It was a fine day and the delay did not bother me as both carriages drove swiftly away up the hill and I took in my surroundings, still at a loss by the complete absence of any habitation.

The driver, true to his word, was back in ten minutes.

He grinned; a friendly soul, he thought an apology was needed.

'Sorry about that, miss. Thought as you was going the same way, the lady might have shared with you. Less costly. Looked as if she could afford it right enough, but it would have saved you a shilling.'

I sat back, certainly not as well dressed or well luggaged as the two ladies, but did I look so shabby and poor? Concentrating on the empty road ahead, in a few minutes we turned into ornate gates, and headed down the drive to the entrance of a large mansion.

Suddenly it all became clear and I realised that Lochandor was not a village but a large estate. Mrs Lawers' distant relative, a wealthy landowner, possibly the local laird, had decided with the advent of the railways to have a halt on his land, particularly for goods and guests from the south, sparing them and himself the inconvenience of being met at Perth, the nearest railway station.

'Front or back entrance, miss?'

'This will do very well, thank you.'

From his chatty manner and my unprepossessing appearance, he had concluded that I was a servant. He looked almost apologetic as I alighted, paid my fare and proceeded up the steps between their fierce-looking rampant lions.

As the door was open, I rang the bell and went inside to discover a large hall with an imposing-looking desk and a lady receptionist. As I approached, the veiled lady in green velvet who had declined to let me share her carriage was ascending the large staircase, preceded by servants carrying her luggage.

Without looking up, the receptionist asked, 'When are you due, madam?'

'I have only just arrived.'

She shook her head. 'That isn't what I meant, madam.' Frowning, she consulted a list which obviously perplexed her. 'What name, madam?'

When I said Mrs McQuinn, there was a further search of the list. 'And is that the name you are using?'

I was utterly confused, but before I could explain my business, she held up a hand and said, 'Very well. But we were not expecting you so soon,' and regarded me closely for the first time. 'May I enquire when is your expected delivery date, madam?'

I shook my head. 'I am here to deliver a package to Mr Lawers.'

Her face reddened. 'Oh forgive me, madam. I thought you were booking in for your baby's arrival.'

She stood up. 'Come with me, please.' I followed her to a window. 'Mr Lawers no longer lives in the house, madam.' And pointing to a path down the drive hidden by trees she added, 'You will find him over there. The lodge near the main gate.'

I would have asked more, but a bell rang noisily and she rushed off. I walked in the direction indicated, through overgrown shrubbery, and emerged at a small cottage with an almost non-existent garden, whose walls had completely vanished under the onslaught of very determined and invasive ivy, the visible door badly in need of a coat of paint.

Mr Lawers thankfully was at home, a middle-aged rather portly gentleman whose somewhat seedy appearance suggested that he had seen better days. Having once owned the magnificent house, it was obvious to all the world that he had fallen on ill times.

He was not in the least pleased to see me. I thought the door was to be closed in my face before I uttered my first words.

He sighed. Remaining memories of gentlemanly behaviour decreed that I be invited in, however reluctantly, and as I followed him, he cleared his throat and said brusquely, 'Thought you were selling something.'

I bristled at this comment, again a tribute to my travelling costume, adapted for cycling rather than train journeys for wealthy clients. Indicating a seat on a sagging leather armchair, he grimaced when I produced the package that had been entrusted to me.

'From Mary Lawers? And what on earth am I supposed to do with her precious legacy? I have no family to hand them on to.' An exasperated sigh. 'Do you know what this contains?'

When I shook my head, he said, 'Utterly worthless, madam. Letters between Prince Charlie and my ancestor Justin Lawers, who was with him before the battle of '45. And a piece of jewellery. None of it is worth a scrap. You've made a long journey for nothing, madam, for a mad old woman's whim.'

The remark made me angry. I thought highly of Mrs Lawers and she certainly was not mad.

I stood up preparing to leave and said stiffly, 'I have delivered my message according to Mrs Lawers' instructions.'

'Oh, do sit down, you've come a long way. Let me at least conform to the rules of hospitality and offer you a cup of tea. I had just made one for myself when you arrived.'

I guessed that Mr Lawers was apologising for his rudeness and was doubtless a rather lonely man. I could hardly refuse, and indeed my curiosity was aroused. He walked with a stick, and I guessed from the photographs and medals on the sideboard, doubtless demoted from the big house, that he had been an army officer.

I learnt in the course of conversation, now eagerly supplied by Lawers, that his family had owned all this vast estate for generations.

Some parts of the house were very ancient and were a refuge to the loyal followers of Prince Charles Edward Stuart during their campaigns and after the disaster of Culloden and Butcher Cumberland's vengeance on the Highlands.

He ended sadly, 'My father, alas, gambled

away all our fortune, and when I returned wounded from fighting the Boers a couple of years ago, he had died and all I inherited was a list of debts outstanding. There was nothing else for it but to sell the house as a convalescent home for gentlewomen with respiratory illnesses.'

I concluded that Mr Lawers did not have very good eyesight, or was simply unaware that there was another more secret purpose behind the convalescent home.

As I was about to leave, he took the package from the table and handed it to me. 'Be so good as to return this to Mary Lawers with my compliments.'

When I looked surprised, he said sternly, 'I have never met this remote relative since childhood and I have no one to hand these on to.' He shrugged. 'The existence of this family legacy is not of the slightest importance to me; I do not care what becomes of it – it is a matter of complete indifference to me. I have greater problems in my life, and as a matter of fact, between us, Mrs McQuinn, I will immediately consign them to the fire here, as soon as you leave.' And taking the poker he stirred the flames.

Here was a quandary indeed as he thrust the package into my hands. What could I do but accept his decision, although I did not relish the prospect of explaining the situation of his reception of the package and its intended fate to Mrs Lawers. There was no possible argument; I realised he was quite adamant. At the door we shook hands and he enquired as to whether I was returning to Edinburgh. When I told him of my next destination, he added an apology for being unable to take me to Tarnbrae, on the neighbouring estate some three or four miles distant. He knew little of its present circumstances as there had been a lasting feud between the two families for several generations.

We said farewell and I walked down the drive in no good or easy mind. Although my mission had been accomplished in the legal sense, I could not consider that in any sense my fee had been earned. Nor could I be indifferent to the fate of this family legacy, allowing it to be destroyed by an uncaring relative when it was of such great value and importance to my client – she having been its guardian for her lifetime – and, for some reason as yet unknown, of considerable importance to her bogus maid, who was prepared to commit murder to gain possession of it. That it had almost cost me my life was an added incentive not to abandon what I now knew as historic family documents sentimentally protected over the generations.

The railway halt was deserted. How on earth was I to reach Tarnbrae other than on foot? And which direction? Here was a dilemma indeed. I was studying the small map of the area that Jack had drawn when the sound of a carriage came clattering down the hill. It was my old friend, the driver. 'Didn't keep you long, miss. Did ye no' get the job?'

I shook my head vaguely and he tut-tutted. 'I need to go to Tarnbrae. Can I get a train from here to the nearest station?'

He laughed. 'You just get aboard, miss, and I'll take you there – I have a lady friend who lives nearby and she will give me something to eat. It's a good excuse to call on her while her man is at work. Do you want to sit inside or would you enjoy the fresh air?'

I decided on the latter and he gave me a hand up to the seat beside him. 'Do you go often to the convalescent home?' I asked.

'Lochandor? That's what they call it.' A mocking laugh. 'Well, miss, I have a steady job there. This is for your ears only. It isn't really a convalescent home for sick gentlewomen but a place of refuge for very rich young women who get themselves into trouble and whose families can afford to put them away out of sight for a few months.'

'What happens then, to the babies, I mean?'

'There's an orphanage in the grounds. I expect the unwanted babies are sent there to be put up for adoption. I can only say that when the young ladies no longer have a big belly – if you'll pardon the expression – I put them back on the train to Edinburgh or wherever they are going.' His laugh was loud and scornful.

Backstreet abortions were the province of the poor, crudely performed and mostly fatal, but for the rich Lochandor was the perfect disguise, the solution to an unwanted pregnancy. The two heavily veiled ladies I had encountered fitted the roles as well as the anonymity of the house.

'We're almost there, miss,' said the driver, whose name was Jim. He pointed with his whip, but we had not passed through any habitations, only vast areas of farmland, with no smoke to indicate the unseen presence of a village.

As we drove through the gates of Tarnbrae, I kept a lookout for the cottage which I imagined would be Meg Macmerry's new home. The rhododendron drive was identical to that of Lochandor Convalescent Home. This time, however, a sign proclaimed: 'Tarnbrae Golf Course. Visitors welcome.'

The driver nodded. 'They are doing very well. It's a great game, everyone's at it these days.' In my acquired role as maidservant there was little point in bringing up the subject of where I might find the cottage which was my destination.

Handing me down and letting his arm linger a fraction too long about my waist, he doffed his cap and with an appraising look he smiled. 'Been very nice meeting you, miss.' And wishing me well, he nodded in the direction of the golf clubhouse. 'They're always taking on new staff, so maybe you'll be lucky this time. And maybe we might see each other again,' he added wistfully.

I smiled vaguely and he refused my offer of a fare, pushing the coin aside. 'You keep it, miss. I was coming this way anyway and your company has been a pleasure.'

Remaining in the role of servant that he had allotted me, I thought of the married woman down the road and decided that my friendly driver was something of a flirt, if not a philanderer. Thanking him once again, I set off through this new set of gates, and as there was no lodge immediately visible I headed in the direction of yet another mansion. Slightly less grand than Lochandor, and now home to a golf course, Tarnbrae was my second stately home in one day.

CHAPTER SEVEN

I climbed the steps into the splendid oak-panelled reception area of the golf house, its opulent airs increased by a distinct and not unpleasing smell of expensive cigars. The sight of an unattached female, from her appearance certainly not of the class the gentlemen were used to, created something of a stir of indignation and a flutter of newspapers from the armchair brigade.

But before the man in charge of receiving members, who was darting towards me, could utter one word of rejection, I held up my hand and reduced his stern expression by putting on my very best Edinburgh accent and proclaiming, 'I am in search of a family by the name of Pringless. I have been given to understand that they occupy a cottage in this vicinity,' I added with a sweeping gesture taking in the grounds beyond the windows.

It was with considerable relief to both of us that he recognised the name and, leading me to the door, indicated the direction. A short distance away, concealed by a vast amount of shrubbery from the golf course itself, stood a neat little cottage, very spruce with a well-kept garden, where windows prettily curtained told of comfortable domesticity and gave assurance that I would find Meg Macmerry's welfare was in good hands.

I rang the bell, waited. No reply. Tried again, looked, listened, waited. It seemed that there was no one at home.

So frustrating. All this journey for nothing. I was sure that Jack would have sent them a letter to expect my arrival, but thanks to my earlier journey to Lochandor they must have been expecting me the previous day. I could hardly expect them to remain close at home in such circumstances, no doubt equally annoyed at my non-appearance.

With a sigh, I returned to the clubhouse, and in reply to my question the lofty gentleman who was in charge, indicating that he could not be expected to know their whereabouts or be involved in such tedious matters, summoned one of the porters returning from upstairs.

'Pringless, miss. Aye, new here they are. Moved

in recently. I've no idea where they are – out for the day, maybe,' he shrugged. 'Could be away tattie howking. It's that time of year. Always a bit of extra money to be made. Lots of folk round here go each year,' he added encouragingly, and looking me over candidly, 'If it's work ye're after, lass, I could write a note to them for you.'

I thanked him for his consideration and, in my best Edinburgh accent again, said that I could write – and read. His embarrassment was my scant reward; his face reddened and he suggested that he would see my note was delivered.

Telling him I could take care of that myself, I walked down the steps resolving to do something immediate and drastic about my appearance. My lack of interest in fashionable clothes – or indeed any, other than those needed for bicycling – had twice portrayed me as a maid seeking employment. How Jack would enjoy that when I told him.

What to do next? In no mood to search the potato-picking fields of the area in search of Meg's adoptive parents, although logic suggested that if such was their destination they would have taken her with them, I returned to the cottage, tore a page out of my notebook and wrote that I was a friend of Meg's father and hoped to find them at home on a future visit. With that Jack would have to be content.

Walking in the direction of the entrance gates,

completely dismayed by my present predicament, the prospect of the long walk back to Lochandor's railway halt and a possibly long wait for the next train home to Edinburgh, the drive seemed interminable.

I was suddenly aware that the slight headache which had been hovering for a couple of hours was gathering violent momentum. I also felt very sick indeed, my stomach churning, although I had eaten nothing since breakfast. Worse, my vision became blurred. Dizzy, I felt distinctly faint.

Needing to give relief to what I hoped was a temporary upset that would pass in a few minutes, I sat down on the grass verge. I felt really dreadful. Was this the reaction from my fall from the train that Dr Everson had warned me about? There was another terrible possibility looming. That I had succumbed to Mrs Lawers' influenza. She had looked very poorly the day we met in Jenners and it was quite possible that she already had the influenza on her and was in a highly infectious state.

My troubles had just begun. As I sat there feeling very sorry for myself, it began to rain. Wondering how on earth I was going to shelter and get to the railway station I stood up, shivering and so weak that I could hardly drag one foot after the other. Panic overwhelmed me. I felt so terrible; was I going to die out here on the drive to the Tarnbrae golf course?

At that moment, the rumble of wheels

approached from the clubhouse direction. The driver saw me, stopped and leant out. I realised I must have been a dreadful sight when he called, 'Anything wrong, miss?'

A passenger looked out of the window and asked what was the matter.

I could hardly speak but gasped out that I had called on a friend who was not at home.

The young woman looked at me. 'You can't stay out there in the rain. Come inside.' And so saying she opened the door. I was assisted up the step, ushered to a seat and asked my destination.

The three passengers were a young married couple and the girl's brother, and as they made room for me, the talk was about what shots the two men had played, their handicaps and so forth. All this seemed to give them cause for fierce argument.

Thankfully ignored, I leant back, eyes closed, and heard the young woman whisper to her companions, 'She's very pale, poor thing, she looks quite ill.'

A gentle touch on my arm. 'You don't look at all well, miss.' I murmured some vague response. There was more whispered conversation as I tried to summon up energy to reassure them and failed.

'Look,' said the brother, leaning forward. 'I am going to Corstorphine. Please allow me to see you safely to Edinburgh.'

The carriage journey seemed endless. Finally the

couple were dropped off on the outskirts of the city, accompanied by cheers and laughingly rude remarks between the two men regarding the success of their next golfing assignment and the practise needed.

I tried to respond civilly to the young man's polite remarks as we headed into the city but I heard not a word of his conversation, barely able to keep my eyes open, my head pounding a fearful tattoo with every jolt of the carriage, every cobblestone like a sharp nail driven into my skull.

I expected to be set down in the centre of the town, and as we crossed Princes Street and began the slow climb up Waverly Bridge I said, 'You have missed your road.'

My escort, whose name was Eric, smiled. 'You are in no fit state to travel anywhere, miss, and it is my intention to see you safely home.'

When I protested that this was taking him out of his way, he held up his hand. 'I am taking you to your own door, miss, so if you will kindly give me directions.'

Five minutes later Arthur's Seat hovered above us, shortly followed by Solomon's Tower, at the base of Samson's Ribs. I blessed this man and his kindness, for as he handed me down from the carriage, my legs were shaking. I was in a state of collapse as he took my arm and led me to the front door.

'What a lovely house. Have you someone to take care of you?'

As I was replying that I had, he took from his pocket a small sachet of powder.

'Our mother was a nurse before she married father, and as I suffered from violent headaches as a boy, this was her unfailing remedy, one I never travel without.'

I took it and thanked him once more for his generosity. Turning to leave he looked up at the impressive walls of the Tower and producing his card he smiled. 'Perhaps we might meet again and I would be permitted to call on you; we might have dinner and a theatre when you are feeling well again.'

Again I thanked him, barely able to speak, and frowning he said, 'I don't know your name, Miss . . . ?'

I gasped out, 'It's Mrs . . . Mrs Rose McQuinn.'

He bowed. 'Oh, I do beg your pardon. I had not realised – I do apologise.' And most embarrassed, he regarded my ringless hand.

'There is no need. Mr McQuinn passed away some time ago,' I said. 'I shall not forget your kindness, sir.'

I walked towards the Tower with the resolution to wear my ring in future as well as improve my wardrobe, although these were the smallest of my problems.

Thane greeted me eagerly as I staggered into the kitchen, only wishing that his attributes included making a cup of tea. Drinking a glass of water as I swallowed the contents of the sachet, I noticed Jack's note still on the table. At a time when I needed him most, he was not here.

My legs felt too weak and shaky to carry me much further and I regarded the spiral staircase with dismay. Thane was watching me anxiously and rushed to my side. He knew what was required of him as I clung on to his shoulder and eased my way step by step to the bedroom.

The sight of the bed was enough. Removing my outer garments, I had no further strength but to drag extra blankets from the press and lie down. Thane sat upright close to the bedside, alert like a nurse watching over a sick patient.

I patted him and whispered, 'Take care of me.' My last sight of him, as my eyes closed, was that oddly almost-human expression.

I felt dreadful, sure that I was going to die this time, as the fever carried me back in wakeful nightmare seven years ago to the Indian reservation in Arizona where I had waited in vain for Danny's return. I had thought then that I would die. I survived, but not, alas, our infant son Daniel. Weak as I was, that bitter memory could still, as always, set the tears flowing.

I sobbed, helpless, conscious of Thane's huge paw on the coverlet, his head on a level with my own, his gaze like that of an anxious parent. He normally slept on his rug, his place by my bedside when Jack was absent. When we were together he retired to the kitchen with almost human feelings of delicacy about invading our privacy.

Grateful for his presence now, I drifted away once more in the darkening room, a voice inside my head repeating, 'Sleep and the fever will leave you – sleep.'

I have no idea how long I did just that, in a journey through nightmares and strange dreams, a tormented sleep. Once or twice I opened my eyes – Thane was still there; he had not moved. Asleep, his head now gently resting on the covers.

Once it was dark and I saw the stars gleaming through the window, then it was daylight, then darkness again. Still I slept, night came, and then one morning, which I later calculated must have been the third of my fever, I awoke feeling desperately hungry and thirsty.

Could I get out of bed? Was it too early and I too weak? I threw back the covers.

Thane had now retired to his rug; he sat up and watched me gulp down a glass of water, wagging his tail delightedly.

I smiled at him, patted his head and realised to my astonishment that I was feeling quite fit again. I had fully recovered. The fever had left me, not shaky and weak, but strong and completely restored.

As I walked downstairs, shadowed by Thane,

my footsteps firm, I laughed. 'I'm well again, Thane. Isn't that amazing?'

He looked at me and seemed to smile with what in human terms could be described as indulgent satisfaction.

In that moment I guessed, or knew, the reason for my miraculously swift recovery. Thane. It was his voice I had heard, urging me to sleep; Thane, who miraculously had once again somehow acted as my protector. Strange magic indeed. I hugged Thane, whispered my thanks and set about boiling the kettle on that other miracle, a peat fire still smouldering after three days. Slowly I stirred into life. Bread, butter, eggs and cheese from the pantry, and my hunger appeased I noticed a note pushed through the front door.

From Jack, presumably delivered by one of his constables, while I lay inert upstairs. It was brief: 'Sorry about the delay. Be home tomorrow.'

Tomorrow? Had that been yesterday or was it today? Now with a sudden yearning for fresh air and the sunshine that caressed the world outside, I decided to ride down the road to Duddingston and report back to Mrs Lawers the dismal failure of my mission.

CHAPTER EIGHT

The day was surprisingly pleasant and mild as I rode past the loch, after my recent experiences of dour skies and rain in Lochandor and Tarnbrae. This was a day when October forgot its rightful place in the autumn calendar and made a last dash to be summer in disguise.

Much to my surprise there was a gathering outside Mrs Lawers' door, and as I parked with a premonition of disaster, her neighbour Amy Dodd, who had spoken to me earlier, ran swiftly to my side.

'What happened?' I gasped. 'Was it the influenza?'

Tearfully she shook her head. 'We don't know for sure. Mary assured me that they were on the mend as I'd been called away to Gullane to see my daughter. They've had an outbreak of the influenza there and I was anxious about the grandchildren. I stayed longer than I had intended. When I came back I went straight in to see how they were next door . . .'

She paused and took a deep breath. 'And there they were, both lying there – Mary and Hinton – both of them . . . Hinton had come back while I was away.' A sobbing breath. 'I knew at one glance . . . and the smell of death. I've seen enough in my time – buried six bairns, I have. I knew they were dead. It was terrible. I went for the doctor, along the street there, and he came right away. Came out looking very grave, very white, and when I asked him what it was, if it was the influenza, he wasn't prepared to say more than that they had been dead for a while.'

She looked round and whispered, 'Now the police have been here, taken things away. I was sure I smelt gas when I found them both. I knew there would be trouble when Duddingston was linked up.'

As she shook her head, still suspicious of this new fad, I thought how much easier it made life for folks in Edinburgh – Jack had promised me my very first gas cooker once Solomon's Tower was on the circuit.

Amy was saying, 'We don't know what will

happen, both alone in the world, neither with any family. No one to bury them.'

I thought of Mr Lawers, uncaring in Lochandor, as she went on, 'Hinton was devoted to Mary. Been with her since she was a young lass, more of a close friend than a maid.'

She looked at me anxiously. 'You'd better come inside, miss, not stand talking out here in the cold. You're not looking too well yourself.'

I was glad to follow her into the cottage, very similar to that of Mrs Lawers', in a row of ancient houses built more than two centuries ago.

Inviting me to sit down with a gesture, she said, 'Would you like a bowl of soup, just to warm you up?'

I accepted gladly. Food was scarce in Solomon's Tower when Jack was absent. Since I had been ill there had been no shopping and the pantry was almost empty.

The soup was delicious, and as I praised it, she nodded. 'Are you one of Mary's Edinburgh friends?'

'We are quite recently acquainted, so I didn't know her very well. I live along the road at Solomon's Tower.'

Amy smiled sadly. 'Mary's a lovely lady, and I'll miss her sorely, that I will. A good friend these four years. I felt quite honoured as I soon found out she doesn't abide neighbours. There's that

Frenchie fellow on her other side; he's been here years and years but she's kept him at the door, wouldn't have anything to do with him. But so kind and friendly to me – we'd meet nearly every day 'cos we share the communal garden. Through there.' She pointed to the kitchen window. 'Mary's been getting too frail and rheumatic to do much any more and her dear Hinton was never good at gardening, so as I'm strong and willing, I do most of it now.'

'Tell me about the maid. What did she look like?'

Amy seemed to find this question curious but she said, 'She was quite small.' She looked at me. 'A bit like yourself, Mrs McQuinn, not very tall. I always thought she must have been right bonny when she was young, and although she had a club foot from birth, it didn't deter her. She was quite sprightly.'

Under five feet tall and a club foot didn't sound like the bogus Hinton who had taken her place. I wanted to know more, especially as I had being doing some rapid calculations that suggested the two women had already been dead when I made my second journey to Lochandor. I remembered that I had not seen Mrs Lawers, only heard that hoarse whisper from behind the door. I felt suddenly chilled at the realisation that while I stood outside the door, they were both lying dead inside.

Who then was pretending to be Mrs Lawers? There was only one answer – their killer.

'Did they have any visitors?'

'Not often. Mary liked to meet her friends in Edinburgh. She'd take a carriage, her "little luxury" she said, a nice change of scene and a bit of shopping.'

And I remembered that momentous day in Jenners as she went on, 'It was quite an event if someone came to call, and Mary would tell me all about it. I'd even do a bit of baking, on the rare occasion there was something like a birthday to celebrate.'

'Any recent callers?'

The question worried her. She frowned. 'Yes, a strange youngish man, tall, well dressed. A gentleman. I thought he might be some sort of a solicitor. Called about a week ago, while I was visiting her. He didn't seem pleased to see me, and Mary didn't introduce us, which was odd. She was always very polite and proper about such things, well brought up, good family, y'know.' She nodded. 'I left them – I know my place. Never intrude.'

She paused, with a thoughtful frown. 'Odd that was, because she never mentioned his visit and when she had an important visitor she enjoyed gossiping about them to me afterwards.'

'It might have been private matters, of course.'

'Maybe you're right. Something urgent, because he was back a couple of days later. I saw him through the window; it was a nice warm day and I was doing a bit of gardening and gathering some vegetables, nice and fresh – they make the best soup.'

She frowned. 'Anyway, whatever it was, it wasn't nice business, he was being rude and upsetting her. Yes, shouting at her like no gentleman would. He had a loud voice, and although she was getting rather deaf and he needed to speak up, there was no need for bullying her.'

'Are you sure?'

She nodded vigorously. 'I know bullying when I hear it, Mrs McQuinn. Although I couldn't hear the exact words, I knew he was threatening her. Yes, that's what it was.' She paused. 'They were having words. And I know all about voices. I used to teach elocution.'

'What kind of words?'

'Angry ones. First time I ever heard Mary raise her voice to anyone, except Frenchie next door, telling him that he was trespassing on private property when he was looking in her back window – searching for a lost kitten, he said. Told him off properly, said trespassing applied to his cat too, using her garden as a lavatory.'

A smile of satisfaction. 'That was him put in his place, but this other fellow – it was quite a shock.

He was shouting too: "You're not listening, you old fool." I heard that, it was so loud and so rude and she was saying something about never letting him have it. Sounded as if he wanted to buy the house. But I knew she would never sell.'

'Why was that?'

'Oh, she was very proud of her cottage, said it was the one Bonnie Prince Charlie lived in before the Battle of Prestonpans. One of her ancestors had served with him. She was very proud of that but never told me anything more; she liked her privacy and was always angry and upset when nosy folk came and stared in the windows. Like yon Jacobite society or old Frenchie, who she said was always wanting an excuse to come in and have a look round. She sent them off sharpish, I can tell you.'

'This bullying man, did you see him again?'

She shook her head. 'No. Maybe he came when I was in Gullane. I came back—' her voice broke. 'That was when I found them. I'll never forget the sight – both lying there, dead. Not a mark on them, looked as if they had just fallen asleep. But I blame that awful man; everything had been fine before he came. Perhaps he had frightened them to death.'

I thought that most improbable and as she was talking I was adding up the evidence. And my own theories were grim indeed. The fact that the police had been called suggested suspicious circumstances and that the women had died by violence – the most likely suspect the man who had wanted this house so much, the man speaking behind the door and pretending to be Mrs Lawers on that last visit.

I found no consolation that I had completed my assignment for Mrs Lawers. I could have closed my eyes, put the money in the bank and walked away, got on with the rest of my life. Instead I felt that I was personally involved, under an obligation to find their killer.

I had the first clue, a certainty, that the bullying mystery man was in league with the bogus Hinton who had tried to steal Mrs Lawers' legacy by pushing me out of the door of a moving train.

I had much to occupy my mind as I rode back to Solomon's Tower, where I was delighted and greatly relieved to see Jack sitting at the kitchen table. His first words were, 'How was Meg? Did she look well? Was she happy and did she like her present? Tell me all about her – did they have a photograph of her for me?'

And alas, I could answer none of his questions.

Saying that the Pringlesses weren't at home sounded like a weak excuse. His eyebrows shot up. 'After all that distance, couldn't you have waited for them to return?'

And when I mentioned the tattie howking, his sigh was full of reproach. 'Surely that would be local and you could have tracked them down?' A pause and then he added, 'What about Mrs Lawers' precious package? I suppose you managed that.'

I nodded vaguely. He was so cross I forbore all but the minor details about Mrs Lawers' reluctant heir. 'I'm sorry about Meg, but I was feeling awful, Jack. I just had to get home,' I added weakly.

'Doesn't sound like you,' he said mockingly. 'You're always strong as a horse.' And giving me a hard look, 'You certainly got better very quickly in a couple of days, so it couldn't have been all that bad.'

I was growing weary of this inquisition, cross too, and guilty that I had let him down. I certainly didn't feel like discussing Thane's part in my miraculous recovery. Normally the almost-fatal circumstances of my first journey and the salacious details of the Lochandor Convalescent Home would have intrigued Jack, but not this time. He was otherwise involved, all his thoughts on Meg and my failure to reach her.

A moment of calm and he said, 'Well, I will have to do something about contacting Meg's folks now. So what have you being doing all this time?'

'If you mean this morning, then I've been

down to Duddingston to see Mrs Lawers. And what do I find? She and her maid are both dead. A neighbour found their bodies – I had presumed the poor souls had succumbed to influenza. She said she had smelt gas.' I paused. 'And I gather from her neighbour that the police are interested.'

He looked sheepish, cleared his throat. 'I didn't want to upset you, Rose.'

'I think you know me better than that, DI Macmerry, or you should by now,' I said coldly.

'Chief Inspector Gray is on this one, based on the doctor's suspicions, I gather. He wasn't satisfied with his findings, thought it might be more than a gas leak which had killed them. I've just heard.'

'But you weren't going to tell me! Did you think I wouldn't be interested?' I added sweetly, 'Well, I hope this doesn't put you off the idea of a gas cooker.'

I gave him a hard look and he said sternly, 'This is a police matter, Rose. You must stay out of it.'

Gray and I were old foes; his scathing comments about lady investigators still rankled. That was the moment I decided to keep my own counsel, certain that Jack would dutifully pass on the details of my almost-fatal train journey to Gray. *But what a triumph*, I thought, *if my own investigation could reveal the truth about the*

Duddingston murder. I said only, 'If you want to steal a march on the chief inspector, then have a private word with Amy Dodd, her next-door neighbour and long-term friend. They've lived in and out of each other's houses for years.'

And I went about preparing the meal trying to pretend I had accepted Jack's ruling. My mind was already racing ahead making plans for the immediate future.

As we ate together, I said, 'I intend returning to Lochandor, seeing John Lawers—'

'Even if you get the door slammed in your face again?'

'Even if he throws the package into the fire this time. I have been paid to deliver a client's dying wish. And this time, I will see Meg.'

Jack smiled, 'Fair enough, Rose. That's my girl.' And taking my hand across the table, 'That's what makes me love you.'

As we prepared for bed later, he said, 'Sorry I've sounded so uncaring. I've got a lot on my mind, just now. What with one thing and another, I think you understand – about Meg. Not knowing if she's really my child is gnawing away at me.'

I looked at him. The mother had gone and he would never know the truth. But for the child's sake, the innocent in all this, I hoped his fears were unfounded as he added, 'I've reached the stage where I am almost afraid to meet her, Rose.

It was different when she was just a baby but now – what if she doesn't know me, or even like me? That is why it is so important that you see her now, take her a birthday present, explain that I promise to come and see her in a week or two.'

Lacking any recent news of Meg, I could well understand his anxiety. He had my sympathy. Three-year-old Meg would regard the Pringlesses as her real parents and Jack would be a stranger.

CHAPTER NINE

I decided to leave immediately. My plan was to appeal once again to the irascible John Lawers, hoping that, influenced by Mary Lawers' tragic end, he would not be so dismissive this time. I might even learn from him some tenuous family link.

If he decided to put the legacy on the fire, then I must insist that it was opened first as it might contain vital evidence relating to his relative's death – or murder.

If this failed and he still refused, the only alternative was to open the package myself. I was unwilling – it would be like reading a private diary – but if by so doing I could unravel the mystery and steal a march on Chief Inspector Gray, all the better. Especially as, if I felt magnanimous, Jack could take all the credit, claim the idea was his own.

First, to Tarnbrae to see Meg. This time I must make a determined effort to track down the Pringlesses, praying that they were at home. The tattie howking was fairly local, a daily occupation from which they would return each evening.

After a visit to Jenners' toy emporium for another doll for Meg, en route to the station I met a familiar figure – Sister Clare from the convent at Newington, with a group of excited small girls. She greeted me cheerfully. 'We are off to Princes Street Gardens to gather chestnuts and leaves for our Harvest Festival fair. I do hope to see you there, my dear.'

I promised to do so and we parted with mutual good wishes.

After a mercifully uneventful journey, at Perth station I seized a carriage for Tarnbrae, which excited interest from a more than usually talkative driver, rare in Edinburgh where they tend toward the taciturn. He regarded my lack of golf knowledge as a serious shortcoming.

Informed that Tarnbrae was famous, I soon discovered the reason for his particular interest – he presumed I was heading for the tournament. Did I have a ticket? If not, he could procure one for me, at only a fraction more than the asking price at the gate, with the solemn warning that to his certain knowledge they had been sold out days ago. He was clearly disappointed at my refusal and I guessed that this was a little lucrative sideline during such events.

Paying my fare, I opted out of the drive up to the clubhouse and was put down at the ornate gates, heading in the direction of the cottage, where a wisp of smoke from the chimney brought a sigh of relief.

A tap on the door, the sound of footsteps.

They were at home. The patter of feet increased and shrill voices declared children.

At any moment now I was to see Jack's little daughter for the very first time. I took a deep breath and arranged my face.

The woman who opened the door was somewhat slatternly in appearance, very harassed, thirtyish with thin lips, brows knitted in annoyance allied with shouts and threats that boded ill for the still-invisible children.

My heart sank a little. I had imagined Pam, who I had never met, as a homely, smiling, motherly soul and this woman's demeanour failed on all accounts. But I told myself sternly that I must not make hasty judgements on first impressions, especially when it was obvious that her scant patience related to the fact she was in the later stages of pregnancy.

The door behind her opened and a noisy group of children poured into the passage, led by one screaming lad of about five, yelling about what Ned had been doing. This she quelled by telling him to be quiet, adding a sharp slap across his head which merely turned his yells into roars.

As the others huddled behind him, trying to evade the same punishment, I looked for Meg.

To my dismay I saw that all were boys. Four of them, in varying ages from eighteen months to eight in what are commonly called 'steps of stairs'. But no small girl.

Where was Meg?

'Well, what's your business?' demanded the woman.

She had shoved the boys unceremoniously back into what was apparently the kitchen, closing the door with terrible threats as to what would happen if they dared to come out again and interrupt her when she was busy. The subsequent silence suggested trembling in terror, out of sight.

I said, 'You are Mrs Pringless?'

'That's my name.'

'You are the adoptive mother of Meg Macmerry?'

'What is this about?' she demanded suspiciously. 'Who are you anyway?'

'I am a friend of Meg's father. As I was to be in the area, he wished me to call and deliver his fondest greetings to his daughter with her birthday present.'

That sounded an impossibly bad way to put it, but it was too late to withdraw the words. I saw the Pringless woman stiffen, regarding me through narrowed eyes. I added, 'Her father is naturally keen to have information regarding her welfare—'

'Then he is not up to date with what's going on here,' she interrupted impatiently. 'I am Joe Pringless's new wife, as from two months past. His first wife, who was the lass's aunt, died earlier this year.'

That Pam had died and her husband remarried was something of a shock. I said, 'We had not heard—'

She put up a hand. 'These are my four lads – I was a widow. I couldn't take on any more bairns – especially a lass with this lot; you've seen for yourself how rough and rowdy they behave, a terrible handful – even their poor father could make nothing of them.' She sighed for a moment and patted her stomach. 'And now this, another one.'

I hadn't time to wish her joy of it when a man's voice shouted, 'Who is it?'

She sighed. 'That's Joe. You'd better talk to him.' She called, 'A visitor here for you,' and ushered me hurriedly into some sort of living-room-cum-bedroom with untidy pallets on the floor – a slatternly evil-smelling place, with children's battered toys, soiled linen and a strong odour of urine.

Joe was slumped over a table, reading a newspaper, a bottle in one hand, with all the signs of overindulgence already having overtaken the man who had left Glasgow dockland to upgrade himself with a better life as clerk to a laird.

'A visitor, ye say.' Curiosity led him to turn round and try unsuccessfully to rise to his feet. He gave up and stumbled back into his chair as his wife said, 'She's here about yon lass.' With that she went out, and firmly closing the door behind her, left him to an explanation in much demand.

He indicated the chair opposite which I approached cautiously and swept some dirty undergarments on to the floor.

'Go on, miss. Sit ye down.' And lifting the bottle. 'A drink perhaps?'

I would have loved a drink of tea at that moment but a swig from his ale bottle had no appeal whatsoever.

'Where is Meg?' I demanded.

He stared at me, taking in the words slowly as if having difficulty in understanding them.

I added sharply, 'I expected to find her here with you.'

His eyes evaded me, searching the corners of

the room, as if she might be lurking there. 'Oh aye, she was here with us, until recently. Ye'll ken that her aunty, my late wife, died of consumption in the summer?' And without waiting for any response, 'Annie nursed her in the last months.'

'You were fostering other children—'

'No, just Meg then. When Pam died, Annie moved in – we're just married.'

I could see the reason for that: as well as nursing Pam she had been consoling the husband with some missing home comforts. I thought of the result – the unborn child filled in a whole lot of the story that was thankfully left to imagination.

'Where is Meg now?'

He tried looking at me, but his gaze was shifty. 'She's fine – all is well with the wee lass, I assure you.'

'Then why was her father not informed of this change of circumstances, namely that her aunt had died?'

Again he looked at me. 'We didna' want to worry him, but Annie wrote a letter. Did he not get it?'

I said, 'The last letter her father received was when you were moving here to Tarnbrae six months ago. There was no mention that Pam was in poor health.'

'Oh,' was all he could summon up as a reply, frowning, thinking hard.

'I want to see Meg,' I said firmly. 'If you will be so good as to inform me of her present whereabouts. And tell me what has happened in the meantime.'

'Aye, aye, let me explain. Annie was living here – when Pam died – had all these lads and she didna' think it a proper place for a wee lass, seeing as they were a bit rough. If ye see what I mean.'

I didn't, but it was becoming repetitious and abundantly clear from my recent witness of their behaviour.

He sighed deeply. 'As Annie's expecting another, that makes things a bit awkward. I'm out of work at present, so there's no money coming in.'

I gave the ale bottle an accusing look, no doubt the reason for Joe losing his job, as he went on, 'It was all going to be too much for Annie. The wee lass had all her own way with my Pam – spoilt her a bit, right fond of her, fair doted on her in fact, especially as we had no bairns of our own.'

He frowned, a moment's thought. 'So Annie and me thought she'd be much happier with a family who wanted her, needed a bairn of their own.' He paused. 'We decided the best thing was that we put her up for adoption.'

I was horrified. 'You did this – without even consulting her father?'

He shook his head. 'Ah, but we did. Just that exactly. Annie wrote to him.' Then looking at me very directly, suddenly quite sober, 'To be quite honest about this, I didna' ken how well you are acquainted with Macmerry, but we thought he would be quite glad not to have the responsibility. It's not as if he's a married man and could have ever offered her a home.'

As he spoke he was looking me over very candidly, as if trying to assess what position I held in Jack's life.

'Between you and me,' he added confidentially, 'Macmerry's never showed that much interest in the wee lass. Of course, I kenned from my poor Pam that his marriage to her sister had not been a success – to put it mildly. And after she died, he was right glad we took the bairn in. A busy policeman chasing criminals in Edinburgh hadna' much time to spare and didna' want to spend it with the bairn Pam believed he never wanted in the first place.'

Although I listened in shocked silence, I knew Joe Pringless made sense; he was speaking nothing but the truth. The truth I had heard in as many words from Jack himself. Now the situation was obvious. Perhaps the wily widow had seduced Joe and he had got her pregnant, but the conditions of marriage had undoubtedly been that he would take on her children but would get rid of that existing encumbrance, namely Meg Macmerry.

Again I asked him coldly, 'And where is Meg now?'

'She is being well cared for, a better life than she would have here, I can assure you,' he added almost sadly, and a quick look around that squalid room and his future expectations did not surprise me. 'We did it all proper. I had an advert put in the local paper.'

How horrible, how heartless. A child advertised like a saleable commodity, or a domestic pet urgently in need of a new home. Aware of my shocked expression he went on hastily, 'There's a lot of wealthy folk in big estates round here. As a matter of fact there's one just a few miles away and they have a good reputation – a convalescent home for gentlewomen and there's an orphanage attached.'

I thought of Lochandor as he smiled proudly. 'A real lady saw our advert and came along, said she would be glad to take such a nice pretty wee lass. Meg seemed to take to her, went over and held her hand. The lady laughed, gave her a hug and asked if she was a good little girl . . .'

I was seeing it all and my eyes filled with tears as he continued, 'The lady said we were not to worry. They would find her a good home and parents who would love her and do right by her.'

He stopped there, looked away, and I asked the obvious question. 'Was this offer free of charge?'

Embarrassed now, he said, 'Well no, I had to

pay her for her trouble. Five pounds it was . . .' And then looking at me quite brazenly, 'I hope, of course, to recover this from her rightful father.'

And that made me so furious I could have hit him. It required little imagination to realise how dreadful the effects of all this bargaining, this transaction, would have on a three-year-old child uprooted from the only true home she had ever known from which the aunt she had regarded as her mother had suddenly disappeared.

Biting my lip to contain my growing fury, and ignoring his hint about the money, I said coldly, 'If you will give me the address.'

'Here it is.' He took out a stump of pencil, scribbled on a piece torn off the newspaper. I glanced at it and saw with considerable relief that it was Lochandor.

Watching me, his relieved expression was replaced by a crafty look. 'I suppose there would be a chance of getting the money back – for bed and board and keep, like, these past years – from her father, the policeman.'

'You suppose wrong,' I said, 'and he's not a policeman, he's a detective inspector.'

He grinned. 'Why, that's even better!'

'It is not, I can assure you. And he will be exceedingly displeased that he was not consulted about this very important matter of his daughter's future.'

Joe shrugged. 'But I told you, Annie wrote a letter to him. I told her what to say. Blame the post if it never reached him.'

If it was ever written. I began to have doubts about him entrusting a letter that required the utmost delicacy to the slatternly Annie with so much else to take care of – a new husband and her own brood.

As I left, he did not rise to see me out, merely stretched out his hand for the bottle again.

Annie was digging up vegetables in the garden, the boys rushing about, scrambling and fighting and swearing at each other. She was doing her best to ignore their activities and I had for her a fleeting shaft of sympathy. Whatever she had done or had not done, hers was not an easy life, nor were her future prospects hopeful with a lazy husband whose fondness for drink had cost him the 'better life' for which he had abandoned Glasgow's dockland.

She looked up briefly as I reached the gate. 'Got it all settled, then?'

'Yes,' I said, and holding out the note, I pretended to study it. 'Your husband's writing isn't very clear. What is this word?'

She never moved. 'Don't ask me. I canna' read. Never learnt, never had time.' And looking anxiously towards the cottage door, 'But he doesna' ken. Never told him.'

Her words gave me all the proof I needed. The letter to Jack had never been written.

CHAPTER TEN

As I regained the drive leading up to the Tarnbrae golf course, I stepped aside for a carriage emerging empty from the entrance of the clubhouse. Having delivered his fare, the driver leant down and asked, 'Can I take you anywhere, miss?'

I said 'Lochandor' and climbed aboard, thankful for this fortunate encounter and no longer having to contemplate the long walk ahead.

As this driver was more of the taciturn variety I was used to, I had ample time to go over that interview with the Pringlesses and how I was to tell Jack, who would be furious as well as anxious and distraught.

Poor Jack. I hated to think of his agony when all of this was added to his already well-established feelings of guilt.

I could do no more than hope Meg would go to a childless couple longing for a child. Jack had been extremely fortunate that after her birth her own aunt had been in a similar situation.

To take a practical view, all things considered, the prospects offered as Joe Pringless related them suggested a happier future than with her real father to whom she was a constant reminder of a time he was most eager to forget. But the child was my main concern and, however reluctant, I had to consider the alternative which would be obvious to everyone except myself and Jack.

She could come and live at Solomon's Tower. But I would be a poor substitute for Aunt Pam, my life devoted to a career as a private investigator. And, alas, one whose every inclination defied motherhood. Marriage to Danny McQuinn had been marked by a series of miscarriages. After ten years we had given up hope. Ironically after Danny disappeared I had discovered that I was pregnant. This time I had successfully given birth to a healthy and utterly adored baby.

Maternal feelings aroused for the first time overwhelmed me, wrenched brutally from my heart when our baby son Daniel died in Arizona. His death tore me apart and I had, even to this day, never fully recovered from his loss, although that part of my life was over for ever. I had lost my beloved husband and my beloved baby and I never wished for another.

Happy to accept Jack Macmerry as a lover when I came to Edinburgh, I had been horrified to find myself pregnant with his child a few years ago. Marriage was arranged, but I was involved in a murder case that almost cost me my life as well as a miscarriage.

I had wept, but not a lot, resigned to the fact that Faro women had never been lucky in childbirth – my own mother had died with the son Pappa longed for. It was like a curse upon us, something to do with our Orkney origins and a selkie ancestress, or so legend told it. As for me, selfishly perhaps, I was happy with my present existence and a prospering career.

Jack had made a promise that he would take care of me, and accepted that we resume our life together, but he never again tried to persuade me into marriage. The situation suited us both – or so I pretended to believe. I retained my independence, happy to stay that way without the bonds of matrimony.

As we approached the gates leading to the convalescent home, it was with mixed feelings, remembering my last visit, that I headed in the direction of the lodge, framing the words that might influence Mr Lawers and change his mind with the news of his relative's death.

In the middle distance some ladies were taking a little gentle exercise on a well-cultivated lawn. But my reconciliatory efforts were not needed. There was no Mr Lawers and no lodge – just a burnt-out ruin, the roof lying open to the sky.

I stood back in amazement. All this in a few days. Ironically I thought of my last visit; instead of burning the unwanted package, Mr Lawers' house had itself been consumed by fire.

But what of its owner? And I made my way up to the convalescent home to discover what had happened.

It was the same woman I had met on my earlier visit but this time she received my question regarding Mr Lawers with considerable tact, and her face told me the worst.

Mr Lawers had not perished in the fire but from a heart attack shortly afterwards. The matter of his funeral and so forth was being dealt with by his solicitors in Glasgow but an enquiry brought forth the curt reply that such information was only available to members of the family, with proof of their identity.

To pursue the matter further seemed utterly hopeless. By his own admission he had no family; with his passing the Lawers were extinct, and as if fate had stepped in, my mission had been decided and the future of Mrs Lawers' package rested, however reluctantly, in my hands.

Such were my thoughts as I walked through the grounds towards the orphanage hoping to see the lady, Mrs Bourne, who had taken Meg into her custody.

The orphanage, originally the stable block, proclaimed its presence by a handsome signboard invisible from the convalescent home.

The reception area was clean and cheerful, its desk occupied by a woman with a welcoming smile.

'Mrs Bourne? She is not here at present. Can I help you?'

I explained my business with Meg Macmerry and she sighed. 'Such a pity, madam, you are too late. Mrs Bourne has taken that little girl to Edinburgh to present her to interested new foster-parents. Here you are . . .' Pausing to scribble an address, she added, 'How unfortunate, you have just missed them. They left for the train half an hour ago.'

I left feeling the bitter irony of it all. Had I come first to Lochandor to interview John Lawers, Meg at that time would still have been here. And it was a frustrating thought that we might have passed by each other on the road.

As I made my way to the station halt, I felt the tide of affairs was running against me, already more complex than many of the cases in my logbook. My main concern was how I was going to explain all this to Jack. At least having Meg in Edinburgh was a consolation of sorts. There was only one other prospective passenger waiting on the short platform, a girl carrying a shawled bundle. As I approached, I saw that the shawl contained a tiny newborn baby. The girl looked pale and tearful and pointed to the printed timetable in a glass frame.

'I have been waiting here for almost half an hour with no sign of a train,' she wailed, looking up and down the railway line.

All was silent, then a rumble of wheels announced not a train but a carriage coming down the road, heading in the direction of the convalescent home, with a heavily veiled passenger inside.

The driver signalled to us. 'No train, ladies – I'll be back shortly.'

I smiled at the girl. She merely looked frantic, and wiping away a tear, moved a little distance away, my words of consolation lost on her. A few minutes later, we were both relieved to see the carriage reappear. We went over. What had happened to the train?

'There's been an accident, ladies. A tree down and a landslide back up the line. There won't be another train to Edinburgh today.'

He looked at us both. 'You had better find somewhere to stay for the night. I dare say the line will be clear and the trains running as usual in the morning.'

'Is there a hostelry nearby?' the girl asked. She had a pleasant voice, the kind used to giving orders to servants and lesser mortals.

'No, but a little way down the road there's a public house and you should get a room there. Jump in and I'll take you.'

We sat in silence, the girl holding the sleeping babe close, occasionally wiping away tears.

'I'm sure it will be all right,' I said, words I hoped would alleviate her obvious distress. She said nothing, just shook her head and wept again. I gave up and that was the end of any communication until we reached a single street of half a dozen dingy-looking cottages, with a small shop and a public house, dark and dreary. No doubt it cheered up a bit at opening times.

The driver set us down, and perhaps taking pity on our predicament, gallantly refused the fare as he lived nearby and was going home anyway. He wished us well and I only wished he had offered to wait and see whether we were successful with accommodation. What would happen if there was none available? Being stranded overnight did not bear dwelling upon.

My travelling companion was looking anxiously towards the shop, muttering about getting something for the baby. She set off down the street and I went into the public house. Its unprepossessing interior, shabby, dirty and smelling strongly of stale tobacco smoke and beer, brought grave misgivings regarding rooms. But beggars not being choosers, I drew a breath of relief when the publican, whose exterior was a fine match for the conditions that surrounded him, said yes, there was a room.

Gratefully, I paid the modest fee of two shillings, and following his directions I was halfway upstairs when the door opened and the girl came in.

I hesitated, listening.

'No, we have nothing else. Only the one room.'

'What am I to do?' the girl cried.

The man shook his head. 'We're not a boarding house, madam. Just the one room and it's booked,' he repeated.

The baby started to whimper, the girl slumped into a chair at one of the tables and, clutching the crying infant, she looked ready to faint.

I hurried downstairs. 'You can have the room.'

'Of course I cannot have your room.' She stood up, swayed, and I grabbed her as she sat down again. She whispered, 'I haven't eaten all day.'

I called to the indifferent publican who was polishing the counter and regarding us with mild interest. 'May we have some sandwiches and a pot of tea, please?'

He didn't look enthusiastic about this suggestion and gave a reluctant sigh. 'I'll see if I can find anything.'

'If you would be so good,' I said heavily, and off he went in the direction of the kitchen premises.

I sat down beside the girl, the baby now quiet again, all her attention on its sleeping face. I murmured sympathetically, she nodded absently. In due course a plate of roughly cut sandwiches arrived containing beef slices, which the girl fell upon as if she was indeed starving.

I wasn't particularly hungry, took one and said, 'When you've eaten, off you go up to bed.'

'No . . . I cannot,' she said, doing battle with one of the thick crusts.

'I insist.'

The man came back with a pot of tea, and, perhaps observing our plight or deciding that he might as well get the extra money, he said to the girl, 'The room has two beds and a cot, so you could share – if this lady,' he indicated me, 'is willing.'

'Of course I am willing,' I said firmly.

'I could not possibly—'

But I would accept no argument and indeed the girl was too tired and distraught for any further protestations.

She climbed the stairs like one in the last stages of exhaustion, clinging to the banister with one hand. Once inside the room I inspected it for the first time; there were two beds with thin mattresses, rather hard and covered by grey-looking sheets and pillows, plus one rough blanket on each. Indeed, the setting suggested that they might have provided accommodation for soldiers used to barracks rather than women travellers.

The baby awoke, and excusing herself, the girl turned her back, and undoing her blouse, put it to her breast. Eager sucking noises struck a chord for me from long ago, awakening that brief motherhood, the wonderful joys of fulfilment, the memories of which I had firmly rejected and thrust from my mind ever since.

The baby asleep once again, I watched her settle it in the cot cocooned in its shawl.

'You have been so kind,' she said.

'A fine wee boy.' I said, with lingering thoughts still of my Daniel.

She looked up at me and said shortly, 'He is not a . . . wee boy. She is a girl and she is not mine. I have never seen her before – until a few hours ago.' Her voice rose hysterically as she choked on the tears that flooded again. Pointing to the cot, she cried shrilly. 'This is not my baby.'

'But—'

'You don't understand, nor will anyone else. It's so dreadful . . . a nightmare.' And because she had to tell someone she proceeded to unburden a sorry tale of tragic love and betrayal.

CHAPTER ELEVEN

Her name was Elizabeth Montiford – Beth to her friends and family who, I gathered, were wealthy landowners in East Lothian. An only daughter, she had met an actor with the local Portobello Players, engaged by her father to provide Christmas entertainment for his tenants and the local villagers. During that brief stay, Beth had fallen in love with the handsome Highlander.

'I had never met anyone like Adrian Dyce. He stayed at our home. I believed our love was mutual, and when he asked me to marry him, I thought only of my wonderful future.'

I was already rushing ahead, filling in the details. It sounded all too familiar a story and never one with a happy fairy-tale ending either.

When she paused, I asked, 'How old are you?'

'Seventeen. I was sixteen when we met. My father refused to even consider Adrian's proposal. Insisted that he was a fortune-hunter and too old for me. He was only thirty-five, that's not old, now, is it?'

I smiled indulgently. I certainly didn't feel old but I wasn't a man, an actor, in the marriage market.

'Besides,' she went on, 'my father had other plans for me, to marry a titled neighbour who had known me all my life . . .' She shuddered. 'Middle-aged, like my parents, and now a widower, he had asked for my hand. I was horrified, and so was Adrian.'

As she dabbed at more tears, I felt I had been suddenly transported into a novel by Jane Austen. This was the twentieth century, after all, the age of progress, hardly believable that such situations existed outside the pages of fiction as she continued.

'I offered to elope with him, run away to Gretna Green, but he said no; as a matter of fact, in all fairness he warned me that he couldn't yet afford to keep a wife, although he was hoping for acting roles on the London stage. He loved me but we must bide our time; he would write to me meanwhile. We parted and that was all. I have never seen or heard from him again. But any letters would have been carefully scrutinised and destroyed by my parents.

'I believe he still loves me as I do him,' she added firmly. 'I was distraught, heartbroken. When my parents discovered that I was carrying a child they were furious. They decided I must leave home, have the baby adopted and return to marry Frederick, their chosen spouse for me. I was to go immediately to Lochandor Convalescent Home, back there. To friends and acquaintances they said it was for the good of my health – an invented infection of the lungs – so that I would be fit to marry the following year.'

She shook her head sadly. 'My parents were not being cruel; my father has always adored me and I knew I had let him down badly. My mother is made of sterner stuff, but was prepared to overlook this indiscretion if I would obey their orders. She pointed out that although I had disappointed them by my imprudence, it was vitally important that the scandal was kept secret and they did not lose face in their circle. I was told firmly to dry my tears; sending me away was the best they could do, and I was soon to discover that with wealthy families who could afford it, sending away unmarried pregnant daughters was not at all uncommon. Adulterous wives, anxious to conceal this unfortunate condition from suspicious husbands, were also regular patients.

'My parents assured me they had made most careful enquiries and that I would get good care and live well at the nursing home. That was true, it was a lovely place, though not so grand as our own, and there were always other patients, ladies of quality in a similar condition, also under assumed names.'

She sighed. 'I thought of writing to Adrian and telling him, then I changed my mind, afraid that news of a baby would upset him when he could not even afford a wife.

'As the weeks passed, sometimes I could hardly believe that I was carrying a baby . . . Except that my clothes no longer fitted properly – I had been given a personal maid, and she was very discreet and attended the changes in my wardrobe most carefully. Then, at last, the day came.' She shuddered. 'A terrifying experience, I expected . . . wished . . . only to die, but instead it was all over and there was a baby boy put into my arms.

'The arrangement with the home was that after two weeks I would be fit enough to return home to my parents and I could put the whole episode behind me, forget it completely. The baby meanwhile would go to the orphanage and be put up for adoption.'

'That is the usual procedure at Lochandor?' I interrupted.

'Yes. And my parents would have paid them well to make sure that the scandal of my behaviour never became known.'

She sighed deeply. 'Most mothers refuse to see their babies and have them taken away immediately after the birth, but I had seen my little boy. I presumed that in those first weeks while the adoptions were arranged the babies were put with wet nurses. But I insisted on feeding mine, especially as my breasts were sore, full of milk. The nurses didn't like the idea and tried to persuade me against it, but I was quite determined.'

Again she sighed, looked at me and said, 'I was having secret hopes that since my father had no heir – I am an only child – perhaps means might be found of persuading him to accept little Adrian, as I called him.'

Wiping away a tear, she went on, 'But then yesterday, Mrs McQuinn, when I went to the nursery to collect my baby, I discovered that the one put into my arms was not my Adrian. They insisted that I was mistaken, but how could that be so? He had been in his cot at my side since the day he was born, so that I could feed him and look after his needs. '

Her voice shrill, she pointed to the cot, and cried, 'The baby you see lying asleep over there is . . . a girl – they had substituted a female infant.'

111

Her voice trembled. 'They refused to listen to me that I wanted my own baby. They said, "You wanted to keep your child, and this is it. Your time with us is at an end, so go now – at once." They had called a carriage to take me to the railway halt, then they warned me not to make trouble or it would be all the worse for me – and my family. They said I would not like the scandal of my stay with them to be made public, my name advertised – and that's what they would do if I did not abide by their rules.'

She broke down. I put my arms around her and she wept on my shoulder.

I said that it was a terrible story indeed, but there must have been some reason for this strange behaviour.

'From rumours I heard among my fellow patients, sometimes the babies are born to order. Time is of the essence. Someone needs a boy, and quickly. In one case it was a mistress whose titled lover would only marry her if she could produce an heir. Lochandor have access to many noble houses. So my little son has been sold off and I am made to accept, without argument, a girl in his place or simply have her adopted.'

'You could have left her for adoption.'

Beth smiled sadly. 'Yes, I could have done so. But conscience said no. She cried to be fed and I am not cruel; I could not reject her hunger and

112

I took her to my breast. As I looked at her, she reminded me of a baby doll I adored and lost when I was a little girl. A doll so real to me that I was heartbroken, inconsolable when she could not be found. I shed so many tears and now it seemed that I had her back again – and alive this time.' She shook her head. 'I could not abandon her. She looked at me with such pleading eyes and trusting smiles.'

In the silence that followed, her reasoning made little sense to me; I could think of nothing to add, and I realised that, exhausted, she had fallen asleep. I listened to her deep breathing, but an inhospitably hard bed, which was none too warm with its one coarse blanket, and too many problems scurrying round my mind like rats trapped in a cage ensured that I did not sleep much that night.

It must have been dawn and a baby crying that shot my fitful dozing into wakefulness. I wondered where I was. I had been dreaming I was back in Arizona, and the baby, my own wee Daniel, was awake and crying to be fed.

One moment of wild sweet joy and then alas, the present's bitter reality.

The day had begun. I did my ablutions while Beth fed her baby. Giving her the privacy of the room for a while, I went downstairs in search of breakfast, to be told there was only porridge.

I accepted gladly – for another shilling. Beth came down, we ate and left. I refused payment of her share of what had been a miserable night's lodging and hopefully we walked back to the station halt where the trains between Perth and Edinburgh stopped 'on demand' according to the timetable.

With two minutes to spare, the only prospective passengers, we found an empty carriage.

Sitting opposite, we didn't talk much on that journey. Maybe her silence, her air of preoccupation, indicated regret that she had said too much, while I was considering what sort of a reception awaited her from her unforgiving parents at the stately home; perhaps for Beth there was little left to say. She had talked herself out last night. It was the old story, so often easier to confide in a stranger on a journey never to be met again than in one's nearest and dearest.

As Edinburgh came into view, she smiled and apologised – in case I thought badly of her. I was quick with reassurances and added that if ever she needed a friend she could contact me.

'You are very kind, Mrs McQuinn, but I have been giving much thought to what will happen when I arrive home with a baby – in full view of the servants.'

I mentally envisaged the consternation and horrified whispers below stairs, as she went on, 'I have decided to call on Nanny Craigle. She took care of me from infancy and has always been a loyal servant. She now has a boarding house at Portobello – Adrian and some other actors stay with her when they are not on tour.'

She looked thoughtful, gave a wavering sigh, and I doubted whether this was a good move as she went on, 'I am going to throw myself on her hospitality. I can leave the baby with her while I approach my parents and put myself and my future at their mercy. I am sure Nanny will help,' she added in a tone of desperation.

We boarded a hiring carriage that would take her on the first stage of her journey home and deposit me en route. I was somewhat insistent about paying my share, but she laughed and assured me that she had money for the fare, otherwise she would have taken the local train.

We left the Pleasance, climbing the steep hill, and at the base of Arthur's Seat arrived at Solomon's Tower. Beth was one of the few people who did not gasp with admiration at the sight of that ancient and imposing tower. The reason was easy to guess: to someone who lived in a historic mansion on a grand estate it must have looked less than impressive.

We parted most cordially and again she thanked me for my kindness to her. 'What would I have done without you? You have been a true friend – may I call you Rose?'

'Of course. And I was glad to be of assistance in your hour of need. Truly, if you ever need me, feel free to call at Solomon's Tower.'

I hoped all would go well for her. Watching the carriage head down the Duddingston road, I thought she would remember the address without my business card, which seemed somewhat inappropriate.

Looking out of the back window, she turned and waved goodbye. I did not envy her the prospects of the immediate future, aware that I was unlikely to hear the end of that extraordinary and tragic tale or ever set eyes on Beth Montiford again.

As always, I had misjudged the workings of destiny.

CHAPTER TWELVE

As ever, Thane was waiting to greet me. Of Jack there was neither sign nor message. This was disturbing. Surely he must have been anxious when I had not returned home last night, but he had not left any word before departing for the Central Office that morning.

I was fond of remarking, 'The lot of a policeman's wife, or even his common-law wife, is not a happy one.' To which Jack always grinned and replied, 'That goes with the marriage licence.'

And it was sadly true. Unreliability was the name of the game. In my young days at Sheridan Place, my father, Chief Inspector Jeremy Faro, was never there, always chasing some criminal or other, when we children, my sister Emily and I, most wanted him. I sighed. No doubt Jack would have some fine excuse and explanation, as always, when he got home in time – or thereabouts – for supper.

Until then I had a lot to consider. First and most important I must go to the address I had been given and see Meg, knowing how delighted Jack would be that she was to be so near at hand. Later, we would discuss her future.

Then there was the matter of Mrs Lawers' package, still in my possession, its future weighing heavily upon my conscience. What was to become of it? I hoped Jack would tell me what progress had been made in the mysterious affair of the deaths of Mrs Lawers and Hinton. Should I now reveal the existence of a bogus maid and my own perils at her hands?

I was suddenly very tired. The events of the last few days were catching up on me.

Taking out my bicycle from the barn I discovered a slow puncture. And again the weather defeated me: the fierce cold wind hurtling along Duddingston Road, past the loch and round the base of Arthur's Seat, would be in my face on the hilly return journey.

At that moment it was too much. Drained of all energy, I decided to abandon the plan and bring my logbook up to date with the events of the last few days, before attending to some wearisome and much neglected domestic matters, such as ironing, before preparing supper.

The kitchen was cosy, the peat fire welcoming. I sat down in the armchair, book in hand – promptly fell asleep and awoke to the clock chiming seven.

It was growing dark and Jack had not returned. Irritation with the whole of the Edinburgh City Police became alarm when, an hour later, there was still no message.

Everything was so still outside. The hours passed slowly and the creak from a loose floorboard that had developed just inside the back door (which Jack had repeatedly promised to mend – when he had time), now influenced by the high wind, constantly alerted me to a familiar footfall that failed to materialise.

I picked up a book but, too uneasy to read, concentration was beyond me. Midnight came; a full moon illuminated the garden and the sky was full of shining stars – all so peaceful, yet I was suddenly afraid, for Thane seemed to have caught my mood and had been unusually restless, roaming back and forth to the kitchen door all evening as if he too anticipated a visitor.

I patted his head. 'Tell me what's wrong, Thane. What is it?'

Gazing at me with that familiar intense look, I felt him shiver. I repeated what I had said so many times: 'Oh Thane, if only you could talk.' And as always he raised a paw, laid it on my knee, a gesture of protection.

I went upstairs to bed. There was no point waiting any longer; it seemed doubtful now that Jack would return before morning, coming in the door with his usual cheery greeting, grinning apologetically, full of laments and excuses.

I slept surprisingly well considering, to be awakened from a disturbing dream by someone knocking on the front door. The grandfather clock struck seven, and putting on my robe I ran downstairs. Thane was already there, waiting.

I opened the door to a man in police uniform who I recognised as Con Wright, Jack's new sergeant. One look at his face, even before he uttered a word, told me that word was not good news. My heart sank.

'It's the inspector, Mrs McQuinn. There's been an accident.'

'How bad?' I demanded.

The sergeant gulped, as if he found it difficult to find the right words. 'He's been shot.'

My hand flew to my mouth. 'Is he . . . is he . . . ?'

'No, no. He's in the infirmary . . .' He looked at me, trying to think of something consoling. 'I'm sure there's a good chance he'll recover . . .'

So there was hope, then. There had to be hope.

Jack dying? No, that was impossible, but even as I whispered the words I knew that was a lie too. I had dealt enough with death to know there is no answer to its call.

CHAPTER THIRTEEN

'What happened?'

'We had a hostage situation in the Canongate. The inspector insisted on going in, reasoning with him, getting the woman and bairn to safety.' He paused. 'The wanted man shot him point-blank. In the chest.'

I was shaking. I had to sit down. 'Come in for a minute, Sergeant.'

He followed me into the kitchen, took a seat at the table, looked up at me as if awaiting comment or instructions.

The kettle had been over the hob on the peat fire all night. I hoped it was hot enough for tea. Such a silly thing to feel that was important when at this moment Jack might be dying.

Jack dying? The thought was impossible. It just couldn't happen. Not now, when I was planning to bring him and Meg together in Edinburgh.

I set out two cups, hovered with the teapot, my hand shaking.

'Let me do that, Mrs McQuinn.'

I watched him put in the milk, sugar for him, none for me.

'When can I go in and see him?'

'Well, not today. But soon. They'll let us know when he can have visitors.'

I gulped. 'That serious, is it?'

He nodded. 'For a while, maybe. The bullet . . . you know . . . have to remove it and so forth.' A pause. 'The inspector is strong as a horse, don't you worry, Mrs McQuinn, he'll pull through all right. You'll see,' he added, that note of much needed hope mostly, I felt, to reassure himself.

He drank his tea, made some conversation about Thane, what a fine dog, etc – anything to keep away from Jack perhaps bleeding to death a mile away. I interrupted, asking a question I knew was idiotic.

'Will they let him come home once they've operated?'

He stared at me as if I was mad, which I probably was at that moment. 'Well, it might take a wee while before he's ready for that.'

And carefully putting down his cup, he seized his helmet and said, 'Have to be off now, Mrs McQuinn. Anything you need, get in touch with Chief Inspector Gray.'

I closed the door, sat down and wept. It wasn't an indulgence I often allowed myself, but this morning I decided I deserved it. Thane came over and leant gently against my side, gazed at me imploringly.

I got up. 'Things to do, Thane.'

First of all I would walk across to the Royal Infirmary and talk to the doctors. I went to the barn for my bicycle and must have repaired the slow puncture automatically before setting out. The kit was on the barn floor when I returned, but I remembered nothing of that repair or of the short journey to the hospital, apart from propping up the machine outside and discovering which ward Jack was in.

The receptionist's face was so serious I was almost certain that I had come too late.

As I dashed along the corridor, there was Chief Inspector Gray talking to one of the nurses. His presence would have made me realise, if I had not already done so, the full measure of what to expect regarding Jack's condition. That he was holding on to life by a frail thread and I might already be too late.

Gray was coming forward very briskly; he

bowed and looked sympathetic before addressing me. Courteously this time. Jack would have been most impressed.

But I was suspicious by nature. This change of heart also had a hint of finality, that he was already mentally composing the funeral eulogy for his best officer. Was I to be forgiven? Jack Macmerry could have gone so much further with a conventional lifestyle, a wife and family, but a long-term mistress or common-law wife did not sit well in the personal details on the promotion report. The sanctity of the family was everything. It even outdid a brilliant mind in the echelons of Edinburgh society, where conventions and respectability decided a man's merit, rather than sheer guts and bravery.

Well, they'd had sheer guts and bravery this time, his cohabiting with a lady investigator (despised by the Edinburgh City Police and adherents) the only fly in the ointment . . . if Jack survived.

Gray was saying, 'This is an anxious time for you, Mrs McQuinn.' A grave headshake. 'Indeed, for all of us. Jack is a fine officer, the very best and we don't want to— We cannot afford to . . . to lose him.'

A man approached. White coat, serious expression and the dangling stethoscope announced 'doctor'. A door opened from the operating room and we stepped aside – a stretcher with a sheeted figure, a still white face barely recognisable as Jack.

I called his name and the doctor held my arm. At least the sheet wasn't covering his face. He was still alive.

Gray stepped forward, gave me a hard look and said to the doctor, 'This is Mrs McQuinn, a close friend of Inspector Macmerry.'

He was introduced as Mr Wainland, which indicated the rank of surgeon. He bowed, arranged his face into the right aspect of cheerful but cautious optimism. I regarded the white coat, not covered in blood, quite pristine, substituted for the butcher's leather apron or even the greatcoat, white shirt and cravat of the dandified surgeons operating before medical students in the past century.

'Is he going to be all right?' I asked. It sounded so banal but it was precisely all I wanted to know.

The surgeon straightened his shoulders and I could see how exhausted he was. 'It has been a long and delicate operation but we managed to remove the bullet without damaging the main artery.'

At this information CI Gray nodded eagerly. A lot of technical medical detail followed which I didn't understand, but was relieved to see it ended with the slightest of smiles.

'We have reasons for hope, especially as the patient has a good health record, and given a little time, should make a good recovery. Rest assured, we have done all we can. The rest we leave in God's hands,' the surgeon ended piously.

'When can I see him?'

He frowned. 'Not immediately, I'm afraid. In a day or two, let us see how he progresses . . .'

A nurse hovered. His attention needed urgently, the surgeon bowed and was gone, bustling down the corridor.

Gray was also eager to depart, consulting his timepiece in a manner of urgency. 'We will be keeping in close touch with Jack's progress and I will send someone immediately he is able to see visitors, Mrs McQuinn.'

With that I had to be content, although my inclination would be to haunt this corridor outside Jack's ward every day until I saw for myself that he was recovering.

As we walked out of the hospital Gray courteously offered me a lift in his carriage which I declined politely, indicating my bicycle. His nod contained relief, as well as faint disapproval, confirming his opinion of my eccentric and bohemian behaviour, out of keeping with the code of conduct for senior police officers' wives.

Too upset to return to Solomon's Tower and brood over my fears for Jack, I decided to continue into the town and call on Meg in her new home. That would be something to cheer him on my first visit.

Turning the corner on to South Bridge, Sergeant Wright was heading briskly towards the hospital gates. He too looked grave as he saluted me. I dismounted. He had been present at the shooting incident and I wanted to know every detail. Pointing to a café across the road, I said, 'Inspector Macmerry is still unconscious but they have successfully removed the bullet.'

Wright gave a sigh of relief as I went on, 'He is not able to have visitors, but if you have time to spare for a cup of tea, I would be most grateful to know exactly what happened.'

As we sat down and waited to be served, he said, 'The man we were after had shot his wife and her lover in a Glasgow tenement and fled to Edinburgh, taking refuge in a house in the Canongate, where he was holding the occupant, a terrified woman and her child, as hostage. He opened a window, and holding them as a shield threatened to kill them both if the police tried to take him.'

Evading my eyes and trying to keep his voice calm as he relived those terrible moments, he continued, 'Inspector Macmerry picked up the megaphone and said he would come alone and unarmed and talk about it, but first Jutley should release the woman and the child. But Jutley laughed at him and said, 'I am going to hang anyway, so what difference does that make now? I have nothing to lose. I'll count to ten and if you don't clear off and let me go free I'll kill them.'

The sergeant paused, closed his eyes as if the memory was too painful to relate. With a sigh he continued in almost a whisper, 'The inspector called his bluff. Shouted again that if he would release the woman and her bairn, who were both screaming their heads off, he would do the best he could, and promised Jutley a fair trial.' Again the sergeant stopped, looked at me and said slowly, 'Then he just stepped forward, said he was coming into the house unarmed. Jutley shouted, "I've warned you. Stand back!"'

Wright paused a moment. 'But it was no use. The inspector just started walking across the road . . .'

For a moment I thought the sergeant was going to break down. He looked away, shook his head, said slowly, 'And that was that, Mrs McQuinn. You know the rest. Jutley had to release his hold on the woman to fire and the police marksman shot him too.' A shuddering sigh. 'Spared the hangman a job.'

As he spoke, I, who never cried, found the tears rolling down my cheeks for the second time that morning. I wiped them away remembering how

Jack, in a reserved occupation with the police force, had always regretted not being eligible to join the Highland Regiment in the ongoing conflict with the Boers. Now it didn't matter any longer, one way or another, whether he had faced death as a soldier or a policeman serving his country.

Sergeant Wright was asking if I had seen the inspector and I repeated that there were no visitors permitted at the moment. He nodded and said he would come back again tomorrow.

What could I do? And suddenly I had the completely idiotic idea that I should try and smuggle Thane into the hospital to Jack's bedside. I had seen the deerhound's miracles as a healer – a boy from the circus mauled by a lion recovered without a scratch, Thane's own unscathed emergence from a death bullet. There had been other remarkable instances that I had witnessed, along with my own strange recovery from a raging fever two days ago.

There was something else too. As I bicycled down the High Street, I realised I had known a weird feeling listening to Wright's story. I was there by Jack's side, seeing it all, knowing his next words. It was as if I had been through all this before. The scene was so vivid, a kind of déjà vu.

Not déjà vu, alas, but premonition.

CHAPTER FOURTEEN

Riding down the Royal Mile, the high street in the poorer part of the town, engulfed on either side by lofty grey tenements, brought my first misgivings. Consulting the scrap of paper – was this the right address, I thought? – I parked in the stone corridor and climbed the twisting stone stair to the fourth floor.

Two bleak doors facing one another. A name: 'Bourne'.

No reply. I knocked again. A flurry of footsteps, children's shrill voices as a door opened inside.

A woman's angry voice telling them to behave – a sound, like a sharp blow, resulting in a shrill cry of pain.

The door was being carefully unlocked, bolt by

bolt and chain, like some fortress – or prison – but only opened enough to reveal part of a woman's tired angry countenance.

'Well, what is it?'

I consulted my piece of paper. 'Am I speaking to Mrs Bourne?'

A sniff, a suspicious glance. 'Aye, that's me. What d'ye want?'

'I am calling to see Meg Macmerry who, I understand, has recently been put in your care for adoption.'

A short silence followed as the woman's eye studied me as intently as she could through the barely opened door.

'She's not here . . .'

And I was listening, appalled, to a repeat though less well-educated recital of my interview at the Lochandor orphanage.

I interrupted the excuses. 'Meg is the daughter of Detective Inspector Macmerry of the Edinburgh City Police.'

This jolted her. The eye temporarily withdrew, perhaps in a state of shock, as I continued. 'I am here on the inspector's behalf to see her and deliver an account of her welfare.'

The eye returned, a rattle of chains and the door opened a fraction more this time. 'We take children from the orphanage until other arrangements are found for them. The child you mention, Meg Macmerry, has been taken by a family who want to adopt her.'

'When did all this happen?'

'Soon after she arrived, the day before yesterday.'

Trying to sound calm I said, 'Their address, if you please.'

The door opened wider. The woman disappeared and children of assorted ages, mostly girls, came into view, peering at me wide-eyed, hopeful. Their pleading expressions wrung my heart – these were not reminiscent of children, but rather of stray dogs and cats abandoned and betrayed by their owners.

At least, I saw with relief, they looked well cared for, dressed alike, in plain grey dresses, like institutional uniforms. They didn't look cold or hungry but they were well past babyhood – the youngest must have been five or six years old.

The woman reappeared, pushed them aside with a warning growl and handed me a piece of paper, the address this time in Joppa on the far side of Arthur's Seat, familiar territory and thankfully not far distant from my home.

Now that I had a good look at the middle-aged Mrs Bourne, she was well dressed too and seemed no longer hostile or suspicious.

'You were misdirected to this house.' And choosing her words carefully, 'We merely provide a stepping-off place for unwanted children, orphans mostly, to be found suitable homes, where they will in time be trained to become useful members of a household.'

A kindly way of saying that the children I was seeing were being trained to be domestic servants, their entire young lives spent as cheap unpaid child labour in the kitchens of Edinburgh's better-off houses. All they would ever get were cast-off clothes and leftover food, their futures decided for them, bleak indeed. No education, rarely even taught to read or write.

A few might be lucky enough or strong enough to escape, but, for the majority, a life of toil and deprivation lay ahead.

The woman was saying, 'The child Meg was too young, you see – three years old, they can't do much at that age. They're just a burden. And I have more than enough to take care of at the moment, without another mouth to feed.'

There was something else I needed to know before I walked down the stairs and escaped into the fresh air again. 'Am I to presume that you received a fee for Meg Macmerry's care at the orphanage—?'

She glowered at me and interrupted. 'Aye, a fee mostly passed down the line to them at Joppa – for their trouble.'

'Trouble' was not the word I would have used

to describe adoption, a business of delight and joy for a childless couple yearning for a baby.

I left with the expressions in those children's eyes following, haunting me, as well as the feeling that I had not been told the whole unpalatable truth. But at least Joppa gave me hope, as a respectable suburb easily accessible on my bicycle. And in the right direction to include Duddingston, where I was eager to discover from Amy Dodd the latest developments next door, in which the police and Chief Inspector Gray were showing so much interest.

With considerable effort I summoned up my other role, that of lady investigator. I regarded the contents of the package which had been entrusted to me, and hopefully the clue it contained which would lead to the bogus Hinton who must have been an intimate of the murdered woman. How otherwise could she have known about the legacy?

Before beginning these proceedings, which must inevitably take some time, my most urgent and immediate duty was to track down Meg and bring Jack good news of her.

As I rode towards Joppa my route took me through Portobello, much in demand as a summer playground for Edinburgh folk and a popular seaside resort for those further afield. The added attraction was a season of variety entertainment from popular vaudeville actors as well as the local Portobello Players.

Riding along the promenade, staring across the now-grey Firth of Forth towards the Kingdom of Fife, brought back nostalgic childhood memories of seaside picnics – great adventures they seemed to my sister Emily and me in the charge of our housekeeper at Sheridan Place, our dear infallible, unflappable Mrs Brook, always ready with delicious food, a hug and words of comfort.

And as all childhood memories turn golden with the years, I recalled only the warm sunny days, and never a picnic spoilt by rain and a chill east wind.

At Joppa I gave a sigh of relief as my destination revealed itself as a large and handsome villa, facing seaward, with a gate and well-tended garden, built some sixty years ago in the traditional exuberant style of the late Queen's reign.

I walked up the path and rang the bell. As it was not immediately answered, the old misgivings returned. I looked at the small box containing the new doll. Was this to be yet another wasted journey, a further frustration? At last the sound of footsteps and the door opened.

'Mrs Blaker?' I asked. The woman shook her head.

'Madam is not at home. I am the housekeeper.'

Again that sinking of the heart, as she asked, 'May I ask who is calling?'

'Of course.' I introduced myself as a friend

of Meg Macmerry's father. 'I have brought her a present from him.'

The housekeeper glanced towards the box and smiled. 'The wee girl.' And I sighed – at least I had come to the right place. Then she shook her head. 'You have just missed Sir and Madam. They are off to Aberdeen to visit Madam's sister and have taken wee Meg with them to meet the rest of the family.'

'When will they be returning?'

'In a few days. I'm not sure precisely when.'

I left my card and the doll which the housekeeper promised would be given to the wee girl as soon as she returned. And Sir and Madam would be told right away that I had called. No doubt they would get in touch with me.

With that I had to be content. At least both house and housekeeper looked promising, along with the knowledge that Meg was safe at last. In a few days I would be able to meet her and perhaps be permitted to take her to visit Jack in the infirmary.

That should cheer him; one anxiety less would perhaps speed his recovery.

As wearily I cycled homeward, my sense of relief was more than slightly undermined when I considered the effects of all these sudden and bewildering changes of environment on a three-year-old girl. First the move to Tarnbrae, which was swiftly followed by the loss of the aunt who had been the only mother she had ever known. Then the introduction into her life of a large uncaring woman, in the role of her new mother, plus a quartet of rowdy unruly boys introduced as her new siblings. But not for long; suddenly she was uplifted, packed off into a great house full of more strangers, some of them children like herself, with a new set of bewildering unfamiliar grown-ups staring down at her, followed by a long train journey to Edinburgh, a strange city full of high buildings and hills.

Would she remember being carried up all those stairs into the tall tenement, to be handed over to an impatient angry woman who didn't want her, and children who were subdued and unfriendly? Hopefully these childhood recollections and their nightmare effects would be happily supplanted with this last move to Joppa with no other lasting memory than always being the daughter of a loving family.

But no more Meg for the moment, and although I was anxious for news of Jack, I had to briefly stop at Duddingston. Waiting for Amy Dodd to answer the door, Mrs Lawers' empty house looked sad and forlorn, as if already the recent tragedy had stamped itself indelibly on its ancient walls. From the house on the further side, a curtain moved, a man's face appeared at the window and was hastily withdrawn.

I sighed – no doubt the enigmatic French neighbour who kept himself to himself. Pointless to ask him Amy's whereabouts.

I was about to leave when she appeared bustling down the street, basket over arm. She greeted me breathlessly. 'Been down to the shops. Come in.'

And seated at the kitchen table, after dealing with the usual polite preliminaries regarding health and the weather, I asked had she seen any more activities at Mrs Lawers' house.

'Just the usual policemen who seem to be looking for something. They were talking to the Frenchie. Very annoyed and upset he was. I stood at the door listening, he was protesting like mad.'

That pleased her. 'Something about a hurt bird that he was looking for. I've seen him looking in the windows again, but I didn't tell the police. Not my business.'

She looked thoughtful. 'Mind you, maybe they think he had something to do with what happened to poor Mary. Wouldn't surprise me. He looks villainous enough. Scruffy, wild hair, not like the gentleman he pretends to be.'

A pause and she added, 'Remember that man I told you about, who was such a bully to poor Mary? Well, he's been back a couple of times and

I've seen him walking round the house, staring in at the windows, as if he might be thinking of breaking in.

'Last night when he was there again, prowling about the back garden, I went out, asked him what he wanted. He kept his head down, turned his back on me. I asked if I could help and he said not unless I had a key to the premises.

'That made me right angry, I can tell you. I said of course not but what did he want anyway? And that made him angry, he swore at me and shouted it was none of my damned business. Cheeky devil!'

Giving her a moment to calm down, I asked, 'When is the funeral?'

'No one's told us. I asked one of the policemen and he said not until after the Fiscal's report. About the gas and so forth.'

What were they looking for, hoping to find? I wondered as she added, 'That big bossy man giving orders, behaves like a policeman but he doesn't wear a uniform . . .' The description fitted Chief Inspector Gray. '. . . he's been around asking questions up and down the street, all the houses. I could only tell him that we were all friendly neighbours and I didn't know if Mary had any enemies, but then we didn't talk about private affairs.'

'Didn't you mention the prowler?'

She nodded. 'I did that. Told him about the man wanting a key but he said probably a prospective buyer who wanted to put in a bid for what was a historic property – you know, associated with Bonnie Prince Charlie and the siege of Edinburgh. He didn't seem all that interested, especially as there have been other local folk wandering past and peering in at the windows, as well as neighbours like the Frenchie. Not a bit of shame, these other nosy folk from round about, the kind who dash to the scene of accidents full of morbid curiosity.'

I left her and as I headed homewards I couldn't help wondering what Gray's reactions would be if I told him about my encounter with the bogus maid who tried to kill me. Jack would say that I was concealing vital evidence.

On second thoughts, aware of Gray's low regard for my success as a lady investigator, he would probably dismiss that as circumstantial evidence. Besides, I must tell Jack first of all.

There was no message from the hospital. I breathed a sigh of relief. It meant that there had been no crisis and that Jack was still alive. And if I knew him, putting up a fight for survival.

Next morning as I made my way along the corridor, outside Jack's ward, I was intercepted by a nurse who asked for my name. I said 'Mrs

McQuinn' and she shook her head. 'Family visitors only, I'm afraid. That's the rule.'

I stood my ground. 'I am not his wife, but we live together.' And disregarding her scandalised expression I explained that Jack's only family were his parents, living at a fair distance on the Borders. They were elderly, didn't travel and Jack would be relying on me to keep them informed.

As I was speaking, the surgeon Mr Wainland had approached and obviously overheard the conversation. Recognising me, he looked unperturbed by what he had heard and, bowing, said, 'Of course you may visit.' And to the nurse standing stiffly at my side, 'Kindly inform Sister that Mrs McQuinn is to be admitted at any time.'

Turning to me again, he smiled. 'Our patient is making good progress considering the seriousness of the injury and the loss of blood he sustained. We will have a better report, hopefully in a day or two, and certainly seeing you will cheer him up.' He wagged a finger at me. 'But only ten minutes, this first time. See to it, Nurse.'

Opening the door, she ushered me inside. I went over to the bed. Jack's eyes were closed. He looked pale and wan, far from his normal, healthy, outdoors complexion.

I touched his hands on the counterpane and whispered, 'Jack!'

His eyes flickered open. For a moment dazed, like one awakened from a dream, he then smiled, a shadow of that old familiar grin. Leaning over, I kissed him.

A chuckle. 'Steady on there. I am forbidden any excitement, doctor's orders. Have to remain calm at all costs.' We both laughed, entwined fingers. Then came the question I was dreading.

'Have you seen Meg? How does she look? Have they had a photograph taken of her? I've asked for one so often. And did she like the doll I sent for her birthday?'

There was nothing else for it. I took a deep breath, and carefully editing out any mention of Lochandor and my frustration and defeat in tracking down Meg, I told him precisely what he was most anxious to hear. That she had found good adoptive parents, with a very nice house in Joppa.

'Did you see her, then?'

'No,' I had to reluctantly admit. And as Jack's expression turned to one of dismay, I said hastily, 'The housekeeper told me that the family had gone up north to Aberdeen to present Meg to her new relatives.'

The mention of a housekeeper seemed to impress and I added the reassurance that I would return at the end of the week.

If I had any misgivings, I kept them to myself.

I did not care to air them to the invalid, especially an uneasy and growing suspicion that the woman who handed on Meg via the orphanage at Lochandor was perhaps just a step away from the notorious Edinburgh baby farmer in Stockbridge and in Dalkeith Road in the 1880s, just a stone's throw from Arthur's Seat.

Jack listened patiently. 'Well, it all seems very promising. These Blakers people sound like ideal foster parents. However, the final business, signing papers and all that sort of thing – not needed when her Aunt Pam took her – that will have to be dealt with now, all made legal.' Another sigh. 'Have to wait until I'm up and about again.'

He moved gently as if to get into a more comfortable position. 'Have you told my parents yet what happened? About the accident? They're in the police records – next of kin,' he added with an apologetic glance as if it should be me. 'However, I've told the doctors about them being elderly and I don't want some local bobby charging up to their door with bad news . . .' He paused and smiled thinly. 'I said that you were the one to break it to them gently.'

I realised that 'bad news' and 'breaking it gently' meant that Jack had not expected to survive at all. I shivered and said, 'I've already mentioned the situation regarding your parents to the surgeon, so I'll send them a letter right away, just saying that you had an accident at work—'

'A *slight* accident – stress that, Rose. Nothing serious,' he put in. 'Go on . . .'

'And that you are meanwhile in hospital but making good progress.'

I felt I should cross my fingers as I said it.

'That's the ticket.' His smile twisted into a grimace, a spasm of pain, then a cough brought the nurse rushing in. Bending over him she took his pulse with a reproachful glance in my direction.

'Please go now. You've had more than your ten minutes.' And she added severely, 'Visits tire patients out, you know.'

'Is he going to be all right?' I asked.

'Come back tomorrow. We'll know better then.'

Walking towards the entrance, picking up my bicycle, I tried to fight back tears which threatened to blind me to the road ahead. Pessimism has never been one of my vices. Even in my darkest hours in Arizona when Danny disappeared and I lost our baby, I had never completely given in to despair. Once again, I had to learn to face facts, however terrible.

But what if Jack did not recover, or, what was uppermost in my mind, did recover, but was left unable to carry on his duties as a detective inspector? Pensioned off with early retirement for him would be the equivalent of dying.

And that other question resolutely forced to the back of my mind refused to be banished. What of Meg, the child for whose existence I also felt a shadow of responsibility?

Back in Solomon's Tower, I wrote to Andy and Jess Macmerry trying to make Jack's accident sound as light as possible, just a gunshot wound but healing nicely. That didn't sound exactly truthful and struck, on reading it over, a note of false cheer. I sealed the envelope firmly, cycled down to the nearest postbox, and returning considered the thorny question of that other responsibility nagging so heavily on my conscience: Mrs Lawers' legacy.

There was only one thing to do. Hopefully it contained some clue as to where its future lay and a clue as to why I had been attacked on the Perth train while Mrs Lawers and her maid were murdered to gain possession of its contents.

CHAPTER FIFTEEN

Thane was absent. The Tower seemed strangely empty, desolate without his presence; although he spent more time out on the hill during the day, reverting as he often did in autumn to being a wild deerhound, hunting, catching and eating his own food, he always returned when darkness fell to take up his role of protecting me, especially when Jack was away from home.

But at the back of my mind I knew the reason for my present unease. Thane had been with me for six years, since I first came to live here on Arthur's Seat, and despite the curious, almost unbelievable story regarding his breed which Dr Everson had told me, I could not shake off the fear that one day he might grow old and not return and I must lose him for ever.

Thrusting aside these melancholy thoughts, I went across to my desk, where at the back of the drawer lay Mrs Lawers' package alongside my derringer.

Suddenly there was a ring at the front doorbell. Praying that it wasn't news from the hospital, I opened the door to find Beth on the doorstep. A very different Beth from the pale shivering girl, so frightened and tearful, I had first met clutching a newborn baby to her heart.

'I do hope you don't mind me calling on you unannounced.' She smiled and went on quickly, 'But you were so kind to me, I wanted to say thank you again and let you know what has happened . . .'

I invited her in and we walked across the hall. 'The kitchen, I'm afraid,' I said apologetically, aware of present neglect, of floors needing sweeping and a duster vigorously applied.

She sat down, removed her gloves and smiled. 'I came by train and got off down the road, but the horse omnibuses from Portobello are also convenient for those of us without carriages. Don't you agree?'

I nodded. She didn't know about my own unique form of transport, the bicycle parked in the barn.

'Nanny and Adrian are looking after the baby—'

'Adrian?'

That accounted for the radiance, I decided, as she clasped her hands delightedly.

'Yes, Adrian! I am so happy, Rose, I just had to let you know. We have been reunited and he and his actor friend Steven are staying with Nanny just now.'

And so the story she longed to tell began to unfold.

'Adrian was so upset, I can't tell you, about my parents' foul treatment. They turned him from the door, told him sternly that I wanted nothing to do with him and refused to tell him where I had gone.'

She paused for breath and I asked what was intriguing me most at that moment. 'Is he pleased about the baby?'

A wry smile. 'A little taken aback. He had no idea, of course, nor did my parents mention that I was pregnant and that I had not found out until he was away on tour. He wants her called Lillie – after his favourite actress Lillie Langtry, who he once had the pleasure of meeting in London.' She frowned, and as I waited for her to continue, I asked, 'You did not mention that your own baby was a little boy?'

She shrugged and said firmly, 'No. He was so pleased to have a little girl – he had always wanted a girl. When he said that, I did not want to spoil it for him with a disappointment, or throw in all those horrible complications, that awful business of the substitution.'

Pausing, she shook her head. 'I just didn't know where to begin. I wanted to forget it all, just be happy together again, pretend it had never happened, like a bad dream.'

She looked at me as if for some comment, hopefully approval. I said nothing, thinking only that this situation bore all the roots of further disasters. Beaming at me, she said, 'You know, I have grown so used to little Lillie now, that I almost believe she was always mine.'

I shook my head. It might well be complicated for Adrian to understand the truth, but this attitude of building a life on such a shaky foundation was quite beyond me.

'I hope we will marry as soon as I come of age next year,' she went on. 'Adrian thinks we should wait, as I come into an inheritance from my great aunt when I am eighteen, but I lose all claim to it if I marry before that without my parents' consent. I do have a small personal allowance which keeps me going, without any luxuries, of course.'

A sigh and I thought of the thousands of young girls in poor homes who had been in a similar predicament, disgraced, thrown out by angry parents and forced in despair to end it all with a leap from the Waverley Bridge, or if they were of stronger stuff, take to the great army of prostitutes walking the Edinburgh streets, selling their bodies to keep from starving.

As for the unfortunate babies, they belonged in the chronicles of baby farmers who made a lucrative business of conveniently disposing of unwanted infants. Not by adoption but by murder – for a small fee and no questions asked.

Beth was saying, 'It isn't long to wait, especially as Adrian has expectations of his own. It's a big secret, something he cannot talk about, not even to me, but it will bring him fame and fortune. I think it has to do with a recent audition in London. Now isn't that exciting news?' Her eyes gleamed bright. 'Oh, I should dearly love to move to England.'

I smiled and said, 'I hope it all works out well for both of you.' Truth to tell, it all sounded a bit unreal, a bit too much of a fairy-tale ending and I was used to tougher reality.

'I am sure it will, and you must promise to come to our wedding. I insist on that, Rose.'

Preparing tea, I asked, 'Have you seen your parents yet?'

And that was the equivalent of throwing a bucket of cold water over her. She shivered. 'I have tried to tell them, to explain what happened and that their granddaughter Lillie is lovely – they would adore her – and that Adrian and I plan to marry.

'They were not pleased, to say the least . . . very

angry in fact. They had hoped that I would allow the outcome of my indiscretion to be adopted, sensibly put the whole unfortunate business behind me and go ahead and marry Frederick as they wished. They reminded me, once again, that if I did not obey their wishes and married against their will, I would lose my inheritance and they would have nothing further to do with me.'

She paused, suddenly tearful again, a reminder to me of the old Beth lurking below that surface radiance of high hopes. 'It is so unfair, Rose! As I was leaving, the obnoxious Frederick was driving up to the front door in his carriage. He stopped, of course, and I had to speak to him politely. He said how glad he was to see me again, restored to health once more.'

A sigh. 'He then offered to drive me wherever I wished to go. I tried to refuse but a carriage was so tempting, especially as a long walk lay ahead. The drive up to our place is a mile long. So I took a seat, and when he repeated that he was sorry about what had happened, I wondered suddenly if he knew about the baby – or guessed.'

Her eyes widened. 'Then I remembered an incident – before I knew positively about the baby. My parents and I were dining at the home of a doctor friend of Frederick's. I felt sick and, leaving the table, I fainted. I came to in the library with Frederick and his friend bending over me. They were whispering together but neither said anything to me. Excuses were made that the room was too hot but perhaps the doctor knew the true reason even at that early stage. And, after all, Frederick had been married. He is a man of the world.

'When the carriage reached Nanny's house, she insisted he came in for refreshments. I watched them, both delighted by this unexpected meeting after several years. She had been Nanny to his own children who are now married and gone their separate ways. I was ignored completely and thankfully little Lillie was out of sight in my bedroom.

'As Frederick was leaving, I followed him out to his carriage. He took my hand, said he would always have the utmost regard for me and made me promise that if ever I needed him, or any help whatsoever – he stressed that – I was not to hesitate to contact him, that I was to think of him first and foremost as a true and loyal friend.'

She shook her head. 'I knew that was true. The thing is, I liked him well enough when I was a small girl; he was like a kindly uncle. It was only when my parents tried to marry me off to him that I began to dislike him.' A sigh and a smile. 'Now it was good to hear that in my present circumstances, Adrian and I could rely on him as a trusted friend.'

I did not express doubts about the inclusion

of Adrian in her admirer's scheme of things, and as she was leaving by the front door, we walked again through the Great Hall and she seemed conscious of her surroundings for the first time.

Looking at the ancient tapestries, the high stone walls, and windows with their embrasures, she said, 'This is a beautiful room, Rose, so large and most impressive, more like a castle than a mere tower.'

I explained about the difficulties of heating and so forth and how the centre of activities had become the kitchen.

'I would feel as if I should be having a dinner party every evening here.' She smiled, running a hand along the edge of the massive table with its elegant chairs dating from the time of Charles II.

'Having to live in the kitchen premises, the servants' quarters, must be very inconvenient.' And gazing around with a sigh, 'Especially when this is so beautiful, so romantic. It must be sad for you,' she added regretfully, staring towards the stone spiral staircase. 'And I have only seen one of those before in the home of a duke we used to visit.'

Her tone was so wistful I had to show her the rest of the tower. Pausing, she looked down on the Great Hall from the now disused Minstrels' Gallery. 'Just to think of this in the old days, with music and dancing.'

I wondered if any of her imaginings had ever

happened and suspected that in those old days the residents were fully engaged in defending their property and keeping a lookout for the armies of the English kings bent on subduing northern Britain.

I opened the door to the main bedroom, a vast space occupied by a mammoth-sized postered and curtained bed.

Her eyes widened. 'Sleeping here must make you feel like someone out of a fairy tale. Tell me, how did you come by such a lovely place, did you inherit it?'

'No. And it isn't mine. It was bequeathed to my stepbrother who is a doctor in London' – I omitted the royal-family connection – 'by an eccentric old gentleman. We knew nothing of his aristocratic family connections, if he had any. A bachelor and a recluse, he filled the rooms with stray cats for company.'

I remembered the smell of them, which seemed to linger still in that master bedroom. 'We use this as a guest room. I prefer the one across the corridor here,' I said, opening the door. 'Not so grand but comfortable and easy to heat. I love my twin turrets.'

Beth ran across to them. 'So pretty, Rose. You must feel like Rapunzel looking down waiting for your handsome prince.'

I smiled wryly. 'I gave up that idea a long time ago, Beth. But look – through this one – you can see straight across Arthur's Seat.' And leading her to the other, 'There's Salisbury Crags, and see, a glimpse of the Old Town.'

The other less impressive rooms were only worthy of a fleeting glance. And I omitted the secret room from our little tour.

As we went back down the spiral stair she sighed. 'Adrian will be so envious when I tell him that I have actually been inside Solomon's Tower – "an ancient house of mystery", he calls it. He is a keen student of local history, you know,' she added, her wistful tone begging an invitation. And I was very curious to meet Adrian who believed Lillie was his child. Would meeting him reveal some facet of character that would indicate why she had not told him about the substitution for his own baby son? That made me decide.

'Then you must bring Adrian sometime.'

'May I really? Oh, he would love that.'

And I thought Jack would enjoy a chat with someone interested in his pet hobby too.

Watching her rush off again and closing the front door, I saw that she had dropped her gloves in her flight.

With a sigh, I put them aside to deliver later and, taking out Mrs Lawers' package which had caused so many insoluble problems, I sat down at the kitchen table, drew a deep breath and broke the seal.

CHAPTER SIXTEEN

Papers yellowed with age – letters inside a parchment wrapped around a silver snuffbox. Inside, a mourning ring encased in small diamonds and containing a lock of the loved one's hair. A family heirloom reminiscent of the mourning jewellery of the late Queen's reign, made popular after Prince Albert's death.

I put it aside and concentrated on the letters. One was very difficult to read, creased and stained; the ink, having faded to brown with age, was almost illegible, as were two others written in French.

Then, one of more recent fate. 'This snuffbox was given to my ancestress who bore my name by Prince Charles Edward Stuart while in this house in Duddingston. He took the ring from his finger and gave it to her. It contains a lock of his hair, his mother's and his father's, James VII, the rightful king of Britain.'

A closer look. Yes, twists of hair, brown, grey and fair, and smoothing out the parchment that had bound the package, I saw that it was in fact a roughly drawn map.

That struck a chord. It was almost identical to the map we had found in the secret room, alongside the uniform cape which Jack decided had been the property of an officer at the time of the Battle of Prestonpans and the siege of Edinburgh, when the Tower might have been used to billet some of the prince's soldiers.

'If that was the case,' I had argued, 'why was a Jacobite hiding in the secret room?'

'Possibly a wounded Hanoverian – or a spy?' Jack had shrugged. 'Too late now – we'll never find the answer to that particular riddle.'

And although we had agreed to consign the secret room and its contents to history, I guessed that it had been our discovery, this intriguing question – an unsolved mystery in our home – which had triggered off a detective inspector's interest in the period.

He would be fascinated by this new evidence. I expected to find 'our' map in the file containing the research documents he had gathered in his desk in the Great Hall; I searched in vain – the file was there but the map was missing.

That seemed odd and I wondered what had happened to it. I felt frustrated, as it seemed that Mrs Lawers' legacy confirmed Jack's theory that there was a link with ancient Solomon's Tower, the Battle of Prestonpans and the house in Duddingston where the prince had lodged and planned his campaign for the siege of Edinburgh.

Perhaps the map, rough as it was, had been drawn by the prince. I sat back, fascinated by a sinister thread, linking past and present, but most of all frustrated that the vital clue that I'd hoped to find, which would explain the reason for the two murders, was still missing.

I could hardly wait to tell Jack of my discovery and was delighted to find the nurse smiling and saying that the patient was improving each day.

'The danger is not completely over, Mrs McQuinn, although he prefers to believe so and he is proving a difficult patient to keep inactive,' she said, adding a stern warning. 'He is healing well and puts up a good front for the doctors. But you must take care not to exhaust him. He has very little strength still, much less than he imagines.'

Jack certainly looked more like himself, his colour restored, and after a kiss and the preliminary exchanges between patient and visitor, his first thought was for Meg. How did she look? Did I think she would be happy there and well cared for?

Explaining about the Blakers' absence and that I hadn't seen her yet, I moved swiftly on to tell him what I had unearthed in Mrs Lawers' package. Describing the contents, I said, 'The map. I feel there might be a link with the one we found in the secret room, so I took the liberty of searching your file of Jacobite papers—'

He shook his head. 'I could have saved you the trouble, Rose. It isn't there. I guessed it was a valuable historic document, so I took it in to the National Library. They introduced me to a reader who was in changing a book at the same time. A retired professor of history, he was very interested in the map, so I left it with him. He said a quick glance suggested that it was only a sketch, or part of a map, but promised to do what he could and consult the archives.'

He shrugged. 'I would have done it myself, but I'm so busy.' He looked at me with a wry smile. 'I could have asked you to do all this, of course, but I never felt that you were particularly interested in the old map.'

'When was all this?' I asked.

He frowned. 'Oh, months ago. If there was anything important, he would have got in touch with me, and I must confess I'd almost forgotten about it. Too many other important matters on my desk.'

That was true. I knew how these important matters frequently cut into his leisure time; small domestic matters of joinery, like broken shutters and the creaking floorboard in the kitchen – often the work of a few minutes but considered of no importance by comparison. 'When I have time' was his favourite and well-worn excuse.

As for the map, at the time of its discovery it was true that I had not been wildly interested; my leisure hours were concerned with the present and the future, particularly women's suffrage and social reforms.

Suddenly all that had been changed. I had been drawn into the web, not by the map's historic connection but its possible link with Mrs Lawers' legacy, very possibly the reason for her murder as well as the attempt on my own life.

'Perhaps your historian friend imagined you were donating it to the library archives.'

Jack shook his head. 'No, that was never my intention. I'm sure he understood. It belonged to me – or rather to the history of Solomon's Tower.' He sighed. 'Never mind, I'll track it down once I'm out of here and on my feet again.'

I sighed too. That belonged to the 'when I have time' category. It would not do. It couldn't wait that long, a sense of urgency was involved.

'Tell you what, Jack. Give me a letter of authority and I'll recover it.'

'If you think it is all that important.'

I gave him a sheet from my logbook and watched while he wrote. Then, suitably armed, I left and headed towards the National Library on George IV Bridge. One vital thing was missing – Jack had forgotten where he had written down the historian's name and couldn't recall it offhand!

I had pursed my lips, a silent reprimand. There were seldom times I could compare efficiency notes with Jack but this was one of them. As a lady investigator the success of my profession relies on being meticulous about precise details, never relying on memory alone and keeping an exact record by writing everything immediately into my logbook.

After waiting at the library desk for some time while a search ensued, the receptionist returned. Enquiries with my limited information had been made, his sigh indicating that this had been very exhaustive, until someone guessed the identity of the keen historian, a retired professor, Trevor Hayward.

'Unfortunately, we are not permitted to divulge personal details, such as an address, without permission. Would you care to call back in a couple of days?'

Cross and frustrated once again, I was gently but sternly informed that the gentleman – Jack Macmerry – should never have left an important document out of his keeping without obtaining a signature to be produced before the document was returned to him.

There was no more I could do that day, so I decided to return Beth's gloves and made for Nanny Craigle's address in Portobello that she had given me, a pleasant bicycle ride on a calm sunny autumn day, interludes to be cherished before the storms came raging in from the North Sea.

I was pleased to find the house where Beth had taken refuge in a charming road close to the sea with a glimpse of the promenade. Searching for the number as I approached the gate, I saw a man emerging from the front door.

'A moment, please – I am about to call on Mrs Craigle.'

Turning, he gave me a startled glance and said, 'Of course.' And thrusting open the door again, he called, 'A visitor for you,' bowed hastily and hurried down the street.

I stared after him, sure for a moment that we had met before. A woman came hurrying into the hallway. Smiling, she was silver-haired, with the gentle features and ample frame that must have been a comfort to her charges.

I introduced myself and handing her the gloves, explained how Beth had left them at the Tower.

'Miss Beth will be sorry to have missed you. She

has taken Lillie to meet some friends of Adrian's.'

'Adrian? Is that the young man who has just left?'

'It is indeed. A fine actor,' she added proudly. 'I have two of them boarding with me at present. Do come in if you have a moment to spare.' I followed her into a pleasant parlour, beyond the window a pretty garden.

'I have just made a cup of tea,' she added, inviting me to take a seat. 'I know all about you from my wee girl – I mean Miss Beth, I still think of her as a little lass. She told Adrian and me all about you and that old tower you live in. Adrian egged her on, wanted all the details; he loves old houses, it's all part of being an actor in historical roles.'

That was why I was sure we had met before and I told her I must have seen him at the Pleasance Theatre with the Portobello Players, where Jack was especially keen on supporting local talent.

Mrs Craigle smiled indulgently. 'Adrian will be pleased to hear that. He is very good – too good, alas, we feel for a repertory company. His ambition is the London stage. Not vaudeville,' she added hastily, 'that's too common for Adrian. He has set his heart on performing Shakespeare, like his idols.'

She paused and bit her lip. 'It's all very well, but I'm not entirely sure that being an actor's wife is the right thing for Miss Beth. London's a big city from what I hear and there's a lot of bad things go on which she hasn't experienced in her sheltered life.'

She sighed. 'And there's the added complication of having a baby to look after. Adrian loves little Lillie but how would they be able to afford a wee baby?'

Hesitating, she looked at me. 'Miss Beth confided in me that you know her terrible story – God knows it's an absolute disgrace, but let's face it, neither of them are Lillie's real parents, and to be quite honest with you, I'm deeply worried about her future.'

She shook her head. 'Miss Beth ought to tell Adrian the truth but she's scared that if he knows the baby isn't his, well, that might change his mind about getting married.' A sigh and she went on, 'Adrian is a good fellow – but what we call "deep", if you know what I mean. He doesn't wear his heart on his sleeve, neither does his friend Steven, the other actor who lives here – he's very ambitious too, harps on about his ancestral connections.' She paused.

'The two of them were always a bit wild, you know, gambling and drinking too much, the way young lads are, and Adrian was heavily under Steven's influence until Beth came into his life. Lots of young ladies but never any commitments. That's how Adrian got Miss Beth into trouble,' she added grimly. 'I blame myself for that. They used to meet here. I should have known what was going on – I'm afraid I still thought of her as a stage-struck wee lass, nothing more.'

Pausing to refill my teacup, she regarded me steadily as if trying to make up her mind about what to say next. 'As a matter of fact, I had in mind a different ending. At seventeen a lass can't see ahead like those of us who have lived a bit longer. It was a pity about the baby, but I've always thought she would be much happier staying in her own class, marrying a fine gentleman like Sir Frederick who is so devoted to her.'

She shook her head sadly. 'I've seen these other marriages between the daughter of the house and the coachman before, in my own life, and I could assure her they never end in happiness. Perhaps I ought not to be confiding all this in you, a stranger, but from what Beth tells me, I know that we both have her welfare at heart—'

This soul unburdening was cut short by a knock at the door. A neighbour for whom Nanny was doing some sewing had called to collect it.

I took my leave, meaning to ask Jack if he could remember which play we had seen Adrian in. The picture Nanny had painted of the handsome actor was not encouraging and I couldn't shake off an unhappy feeling that the prospects for Beth's future were not exactly heartening.

CHAPTER SEVENTEEN

I was busy in the kitchen when Sergeant Con Wright appeared at the back door.

'I tried the front – but you didn't hear me.'

Thane bounded to the door and, inviting the sergeant to come in, I shook my head wryly.

'The bell is somewhat temperamental.' Out of loyalty I didn't add that this was just another on Jack's waiting list of household repairs. Thane was making a great fuss of the sergeant and seemed to find his uniform intriguing. 'I expect it's all those smells of foreign places,' he laughed.

'Leave him be, Thane,' I said sternly.

'No, no, maybe he recognises me.'

'How could that be?'

Again he laughed, patting Thane's head. 'We

had a deerhound once, just the image of him, when I was a lad over in Fife. He was great with us children, and when he left us I never wanted another dog, unless I could have one like him.' He shook his head regretfully. 'But he's not quite the right breed for a single man in police lodgings in Edinburgh – are you, old chap?' And turning to me, 'It's perfect for him here with the hill and all.'

I wanted to ask him more about that lost deerhound. Had he died, or just disappeared, as Doctor Everson had told me often happened? However, the sergeant's eager expression said he had good news.

'I've just been in and he seems very much better, Mrs McQuinn. Getting along well and taking a great interest in things again. Asked me to pick up his file – he said you would know the one he meant – and to get him some nightshirts; he's sick of wearing hospital gowns.'

Leaving him to make a fuss of Thane, I went upstairs to Jack's wardrobe, took out some garments that I thought would please him and collected the Jacobite file.

Con thanked me and said, 'He's keen to get back on the job. Wants to know all the latest details about that murder enquiry at Duddingston. Especially as there's been a new development. We've traced a relative of the maid Molly Hinton.'

My heart leapt – could this be the bogus maid? He went on, 'She is being very helpful with the enquiries, was in constant correspondence with her aunty, that's how we got her address—'

'Where is she now?'

'Staying at the house next door to Mrs Lawers. With Mrs Dodd. Intends to stay until the funeral.' And gathering up the two parcels for Jack he said, 'I had better go now, sorry to have taken up so much of your time, Mrs McQuinn.' Another pat for Thane. 'But it's been great meeting you, old chap. You take me right back to happy days.' He sighed. 'All gone now, alas. Both my parents – and I was an only lad.'

He had hardly closed the door when I rushed out to the barn, took out my bicycle and headed for Duddingston.

At last, I thought, a vital clue!

Amy Dodd greeted me eagerly. 'You'll never guess . . .'

And although I was aware of the details from the sergeant, I wasn't going to spoil her excitement about the new arrival.

'Molly Hinton's kin. Name's Jane – she's out at the moment, won't be long. Just a stroll, a breath of fresh air. Keen on walking . . .' And breathlessly she added, 'So if you're not too busy, why don't you just sit down and wait to meet her.'

As those were exactly my intentions, I did so and asked, 'What does she look like?'

Amy seemed surprised by this question. 'She's a lot younger than poor Molly – a niece in fact. And a lot stronger. A quite robust young woman—'

That fitted the description of my attacker and the sound of footsteps in the passage indicated that the robust young woman was about to appear.

Going to the door, Amy ushered me into the parlour. 'I'll be making a cup of tea.'

I held my breath, waiting for this confrontation with the woman who had tried to kill me – as well as some logical excuses or explanations.

She came in and removed her bonnet, Amy hovering ready to introduce us.

We shook hands. This Miss Hinton was of medium height, plump and rosy with curly brown hair, which was enough for me to recognise instantly that this smiling young woman who greeted me bore not the slightest resemblance to the other Miss Hinton.

I was both disappointed and relieved at the same time, since how I would have dealt with the scene I had envisaged was quite beyond me. She took a seat opposite and said, 'Oh, I am so glad to meet you, Mrs McQuinn. I gather from Aunt Molly's letters that poor Mrs Lawers thought highly of your services.'

'You knew of me?' That was surprising.

'Of course; as her only remaining kin, Aunt Molly and I wrote long letters to each other.' She paused and a shadow crossed her face. 'Aunty was a bit of a gossip and she told me everything that went on in the house. Nothing much else to write about, poor soul, seeing she couldn't get about much outside, being lame.'

I remembered the club foot as she added, 'Aunty knew Mrs Lawers trusted you and that you had once helped her—'

The door opened. Amy came in carrying a tray, and Jane went on, 'The police are very interested in her letters to me – after this awful tragedy. Asked to read them.' And biting back tears, she shook her head. 'I hope they get the man who did it, but those letters didn't help, mostly just family things.'

'But she did talk about Mrs Lawers.'

Jane Hinton smiled. 'Oh yes, it was her way of letting off steam, if you know what I mean. Mrs Lawers was good and kind but a bit, well – eccentric. She had many bees in her bonnet . . .'

'Did she tell your aunt anything about her background?'

Amy put in, 'I always understood that your aunt and Mary were alone in the world.'

Jane nodded, thought for a moment. 'We gathered that poor Mrs Lawers had only the one relative, a bachelor living up in the Highlands, as she called it. There was another, but Aunty said she didn't talk about him because he wasn't really family. He had been adopted . . .'

This was interesting, I thought, a new lead, a new suspect, as she went on, 'He was a distant nephew, and we guessed that reading between the lines, or between the sheets,' she giggled, ' – if you ladies will pardon the expression – he was a by-blow from the other side of the Lawers family. Mrs Lawers and her husband were first cousins, you know.'

'Did this nephew ever come to visit her?' I asked.

'Once or twice, I believe, and there was a great to-do according to Aunty, who guessed he was hoping to be left everything in her will. Although "everything" didn't amount to much more than the house – and a package of old papers which she guarded with her life.'

And lost it because of them, I thought sadly.

Jane's statement had cleared up some of the issues, but I was still no nearer finding out the identity of the bogus Miss Hinton. The only plausible reason was that this unpleasant nephew had a female accomplice.

At the kitchen table I made a note in my logbook of the meeting with Jane Hinton and noted certain vital theories, including the somewhat obvious connection with that missing nephew.

If only John Lawers in Lochandor had been amenable and not met such an unfortunate end, he might have been able to shed some light on this family scandal. Certainly Mrs Lawers believed him to be a bad lot and, according to Molly Hinton, after her money. This doubtless included possession of the legacy resting in my sideboard drawer.

I threw down my pen. So where was this mysterious nephew lurking now? Was he still in Edinburgh?

I now identified him as Amy's 'bullying man', whose threats she had overheard, determined to obtain the legacy. Threats being to no avail, he had finally lost his temper and knocked them to the ground. Two frail old ladies, one of whom was lame, would have put up little resistance. He then smothered them and, arranging the murder scene to look like a faulty gas connection, began a frantic search of the premises.

The only other person who seemed interested in the house, apart from the morbidly curious, was the Frenchman. Not being on speaking terms with Mrs Lawers and being despised by her was hardly a motive for murder. Regarded by everyone as an eccentric and a recluse, he must have hated those policemen prying into his affairs. An unlikely suspect, I felt a sneaking sympathy for him.

But where did I come into all this, what was my

role in this scheme of things? It had all happened in a short space of time and when I returned ill from Lochandor the two women were already dead – but for how long had they lain unobserved before Amy Dodd made the grim discovery? There were conceivably times unaccountable for even to the police.

Perhaps rifling through the drawers had revealed that Mrs Lawers had been a client of mine. Had he guessed that she might have entrusted the documents to a lady investigator and, with his victims already dead, engaged his female accomplice to relieve me of the legacy on the train journey?

And from my angle, the most important detail was missing. Not the present whereabouts of the chief suspect, the villainous nephew, but the chilling thought that lurking somewhere in the district was the bogus Miss Hinton.

Wherever she was, she now knew that I still held the vital package. Having uncovered its contents I decided that the safest place of concealment was the secret room until Mr Hayward, the historian, produced the other half of the torn map left by a refugee or a spy in his flight from Solomon's Tower.

Uneasily, I wondered: how did she know that I was living in that ancient dwelling at the foot of Samson's Ribs? Did she even know of DI Macmerry's existence?

Hardly a consolation that he was at present disabled, lying in the infirmary. Of course, I had Thane to protect me, but I had now added the precaution of keeping the derringer loaded and close at hand, and I certainly wasn't afraid to use it if necessity arose.

I still had my letter of authority from Jack and accordingly set off next morning to call on Mr Hayward at his home in the west end of Edinburgh. Despite the library being unable to give me his details, finding someone when armed only with their name is an important skill for a lady detective and some gentle enquiries at the university had produced the professor's address. Parking my bicycle, I walked up the stately steps of number 7 Melville Crescent.

Alas, I was out of luck. There was no reply, so I scribbled a message that the map was urgently required by DI Macmerry. When would it be convenient for me to call and collect it, or could it be delivered as soon as possible to Solomon's Tower?

With that unsatisfactory arrangement I had to be content. There was nothing else I could do, staring helplessly at the line of windows in the grand terrace all gazing down coldly upon unwanted callers. Their lofty regard and closed shutters on Mr Hayward's house hinted at a lengthy absence.

This terrace was not a place that encouraged nosy or even friendly neighbours and I could hardly imagine myself instigating a door-to-door enquiry. However, fortune decided to shine on me. As I was walking down the steps a solemn bespectacled young man briskly approached. I mentioned Mr Hayward, he shook his head and pointed to the letters he was delivering.

'Away from home. Off to Aberdeenshire for the shooting – we're expecting him back any day now.'

With no indication as to who 'we' referred to and a stern expression which forbade any further enquiry, at least I now had a time gauge.

I returned home to find a message had been left for me. Mr and Mrs Blaker had returned. They were now in residence and would be delighted to make my acquaintance. One cheery light in the gloom. I was about to meet Meg at last.

CHAPTER EIGHTEEN

She stood at the door at Mrs Nora Blaker's side. I went forward, extended my hand, and a lot of thoughts rushed through my mind as I gathered that small chubby hand into mine.

Relief flooded over me. She was so obviously Jack's child, a small female edition in his image, with sandy hair, bright hazel eyes and a wide mouth. When Jack saw her again, infancy vanished into a little girl, his misgivings that he had been trapped into that short loveless marriage could be stilled for ever.

I smiled delightedly but she was not prone to smiles.

As we assessed each other in that first cautious encounter, she regarded me solemnly. Was the next move up to me? But I was at a disadvantage. True, I had nephews and nieces from my stepbrother Vince in London and my sister Emily in Orkney, distant and therefore rarely, if ever, met, but this was a new experience, making the acquaintance of a three-year-old.

Gazing at Meg I knew better than to rush forward and seize her in a fond embrace that would embarrass and terrify both of us. Children, I realised, should be left to make the first overtures after careful contemplation and cautious consideration of these monuments of humanity towering over them. Smaller than average, nearer the ground with my four feet ten inches, was that in my favour as she looked at me so gravely from the side of the two tall people who were to be her new parents?

Her eyes wandered to my wild yellow curls and less-than-elegant appearance. A flicker of comparison perhaps.

Meanwhile I had no idea what was expected of me, as we stood statue-like for what seemed a very long time, both, as it were, considering the next move.

Mrs Blaker's gentle laugh broke the silence. 'This is Mrs McQuinn, Meg. She is a friend of your pa.'

I gave the tiny hand a gentle squeeze. 'Rose – please call me Rose.'

She was interested now. A quick glance at the tall couple for their approval, then she left them and came to me.

She smiled and I choked, for even in miniature that smile was Jack's.

'Rose,' she said, and stretching up a hand she touched a curl of my hair. 'Pretty.'

It was a bond; I gulped. Only her father ever called that unruly mop 'pretty'.

'Did you like the dolly your pa sent?'

She looked away, nodded vaguely.

'Oh, she loves it, don't you, Meg?' said Mrs Blaker encouragingly, leading the way through the hallway and up a splendid oak staircase into a handsome drawing room well appointed with soft sofas, plump cushions and an assortment of small tables made childproof by the removal of their precious ornaments to lofty shelves and mantelpiece.

Still holding Meg's hand I said, 'What a lovely room. Do you like your new home?'

Another nod, frowning, evading eye contact. Mrs Blaker invited us to sit down and Meg hitched herself up on a sofa next to me.

Mrs Blaker knelt down beside us, stroked back childish curls. 'Meg needs a little time to get used to things,' she said softly. 'She has the prettiest room in the house. Why don't you show your room to . . . er, Rose, Meg dear?'

A polite nod, a thoughtful glance in my direction; her tiny hand in mine, she led the way across the corridor.

Mrs Blaker opened the door. The room was pretty, plenty of lace and satin, and pink everywhere, as befitted a small girl. There were dolls too – lots of elegant dolls, many dressed in the latest fashions. My heart failed me; small wonder she had been uncertain with Jack's gift perched alongside the richly garbed aristocrats of the doll world and looking like a poor relation.

The Blakers lingered by the door. Piers Blaker, who had followed us upstairs, watched silently, having said not a single word beyond the polite bow at introduction. I wondered if the fostering idea had been his wife's, or maybe he was just overwhelmed by all this femininity.

I caught his eye, smiled. Mrs Blaker touched a bell pull, and as he bowed and left us to it, a maid appeared.

'Bring Meg some milk and a biscuit please. It is time for her tea, and her afternoon rest.'

Meg darted an anxious look at me and sensing dismissal I said, 'Your pa will be coming to see you very soon.'

A frown – she didn't understand very soon – and I added, 'In a few days.'

I could hardly explain the delay as she still looked doubtful, frowning, and I wondered how much she remembered of Glasgow and who this man called 'Pa' really was.

I followed Nora Blaker downstairs and the room seemed strangely empty without Meg's small presence. Mr Blaker was now sitting at his desk, busy with papers, and turned round to join us in the talk about Meg's adoption.

I explained that her father was in hospital at the moment.

Anxious looks, murmurs, was it something catching? I felt that fears of the dreaded consumption haunted the middle class.

'He had an accident, nothing serious,' I lied. 'He will be delighted to know that I have seen Meg and he will certainly be pleased to know that she is to have such a lovely home with you.'

There wasn't much more to say and Mrs Blaker escorted me to the front door, with assurances that I must come again and any time.

As we shook hands, she said, 'You have no idea, Mrs McQuinn – having this lovely little girl at last means so very much to me.' She sighed. 'I can't believe it is going to happen at last, after these long years of waiting and hoping.' She frowned. 'We have been married five, nearly six years, you know, and we had lost hope of having a child of our own.'

'It could still happen.'

'You really think so?' she said anxiously.

I smiled politely but didn't add that Danny and I had been married ten years before a baby arrived.

I walked down the steps, glad to have met Meg and heartened by the awareness that I had somehow established a bond with Jack's child.

He would be pleased. But there were vague misgivings stirring, threatening confidence in the glowing future for Meg promised by the Blakers, and all this talk of adoption.

There was a reason for my unease and it had nothing to do with Meg. I kept remembering how Mr Blaker kept in the background, said little, and then I knew the reason why.

Piers was an unusual name and this was not our first encounter. A couple of years ago he had been involved in a particularly nasty and spiteful divorce action by one of my clients, who needed the services of a private investigator because of her own husband's high profile in Edinburgh society. Mr Blaker had been threatening to make matters worse by making public love letters sent by her.

It was not a comforting thought that one of Meg's prospective parents hid an unpleasant past as a blackmailer.

CHAPTER NINETEEN

Before I could go down to the hospital and console Jack with the outcome of my meeting with Meg, I had an unexpected visitor. I opened the front door to a distinguished silver-haired elderly gentleman.

He bowed, looking embarrassed. 'Pardon me for applying so vigorously to the doorbell, but it seems to be out of action.'

'A little rusty, I'm afraid.' Another of Jack's repairs for when he had time on his hands that wasn't urgently needed by the Edinburgh City Police. I was making up quite a list.

'I am Trevor Hayward,' said the newcomer. 'Is Mr Macmerry at home?'

'Not at present, I'm afraid. But do come inside.'

So this was the librarian-cum-historian who I hoped was now going to produce Jack's map. As I introduced myself, he said, 'Ah, the young lady who left a message at my home.' He paused. 'Then you know why I am here. I apologise for the informality of the visit, but I had someone to see in Blacket Place and on impulse, to save a second journey, I took a chance on Mr Macmerry being at home . . .'

So he was unaware that Jack was a detective. As I led the way across the Great Hall he looked around, shook his head and smiled. 'I have not set foot inside Solomon's Tower for many years. It belonged to an old friend – long before your time.' And with a rueful glance, 'He was a bachelor, and the house is much improved by a lady's hands, better than I ever remember it,' he added candidly.

Thinking of the doorbell that didn't work, creaking floorboards as well as an uncertain roof, I said, 'There is much work to be done, inside and out.'

He smiled. 'That is to be expected considering that it has been bravely standing here on Samson's Ribs facing all manner of weather for three hundred years.' Another wry glance. 'At least it does not smell of cats.'

Leading the way into the kitchen, I laughed. 'Now there is a very large dog.'

Thane was nowhere to be seen, absent on one of his daily forages.

'A species I much prefer. May I?' And laying his case on the kitchen table he opened it and took out the map Jack and I had found. 'This is definitely part of a rather crude map, a plan of battle manoeuvres. Note the roughly torn edges. Not giving away much helpful information I'm afraid, but my researches suggest that Mr Macmerry's theory was right and that it was drawn in 1745, possibly on the eve of the Battle of Prestonpans.'

Pausing, he looked at me and asked, 'How did Mr Macmerry come by it?'

Reluctant to mention the existence of a secret room, I said, 'Among some old junk in the upstairs regions. We thought it might have been left by a soldier or an officer from that time – billeted in the Tower.'

He rubbed his chin and said eagerly, 'That is a perfectly logical explanation. The prince, we are given to understand, was in a house in Duddingston. His highlanders camped hereabouts on Arthur's Seat, but presumably those in command might well have been billeted here.' Looking at me, he tapped the map. 'This, of course, is only speculation – a fragment of the original map on its own is merely of historic interest.' I decided to show him Mrs Lawers' piece of the map and the letters which I had brought down to study that morning, explaining that it had belonged to a lady recently deceased.

Eagerly he spread it out alongside Jack's map. I watched as he studied the two pieces minutely.

'There is certainly a similarity in the parchment – only an expert could tell if it was from the same roll.' He shook his head. 'If you look carefully, you will observe that the edges do not fit together and might well be from two different maps.'

Taking out a magnifying glass, he examined the edges and gave a nod of satisfaction. 'The similarity of the writing, however, illegible and faded as it is, suggests that these two pieces were part of a larger map, but for some reason, the middle section linking them together has been removed.'

Straightening up, he said, 'Why, or indeed by whom, is a mystery.' And shaking his head, 'Alas, I can tell Mr Macmerry no more than that, but I have a large collection of maps of the period – and if he would wish me to investigate further I will do this immediately and return with my deliberations.'

I did not want to part with Mrs Lawers' map, even knowing it would be in safe hands. I needed to discuss it all with Jack but time was short. Perhaps that missing section held the clue to Mrs Lawers' murder and for that I must leave no stone, or map, however improbable, unturned.

Mr Hayward was looking at me, obviously waiting for me to say 'Yes, please take it', and I did so.

He smiled, placing the two maps carefully in his case. 'Mr Macmerry may rest assured, they are in safe hands.'

I offered him tea, and in a mood to linger, he accepted. Sitting at the table, he looked round and asked, 'May I enquire how Mr Macmerry came by the Tower?'

'It doesn't belong to either of us. My stepbrother, Dr Laurie, was left it by a grateful patient, Sir Hedley Marsh.'

He gave me a look of triumph. 'My old friend!'

This was my chance to find out more about that formidable old man, who scared us as children playing on Arthur's Seat. When he emerged and shook his stick, that was enough to send us rushing away in mortal fear for our lives. No nightmare story or threat for disobedience from our housekeeper at Sheridan Place could equal the terror of the resident of Solomon's Tower.

Mr Hayward shook his head sadly and continued. 'Sir Hedley never married, you know. One of those tragic love affairs that went wrong. Heartbroken, never looked at another woman, all that sort of thing. Lonely and bitter, in a rare moment of confidence, he once told me that he believed his lost love had borne his child.'

I was astonished. Such a romantic story would never have fitted our youthful conceptions of this scary old man with all his cats.

Mr Hayward accepted a second cup of tea, and I remembered guiltily that although Vince had attended Sir Hedley during his last days, he had found it quite revolting, having always detested the old man; he recalled heading to the local golf course in his student days and taking the short cut past the Tower, and how, to his embarrassment and his friends' teasing, that wild demented-looking creature would emerge from the front door and try to strike up a conversation with him.

Vince was furious. He used to shudder and tell us, 'It's as if he's always lying in wait for me. Oh, how I hate him!'

Mr Hayward had been looking at the family photographs on the dresser while I was preparing tea.

Touching one, he smiled, 'Your father, Mrs McQuinn? The legendary Chief Inspector Faro? Well, well.' The photograph was of Pappa and Vince taken at Balmoral Castle seated by the late Queen in her carriage.

I answered that in retirement my father spent a great deal of time abroad, fulfilling his dream of seeing the world at the end of a long and distinguished career with the Edinburgh City Police.

'A pity they don't make policemen of his calibre any more outside the pages of fiction,' said the historian. 'Just think what he could have achieved with all these advances in the science of crime detection unknown in the past century.' Pausing, he examined the photo closely. 'The elegant young man? Is he a member of the royal family?'

'No, that is my father's stepson Vince – the present owner of Solomon's Tower.'

'May I?' And rising from the table he took the photograph to the window and examined it in the better light. 'Remarkable,' he said, 'quite remarkable.'

He prepared to leave with promises to return the maps as soon as he could, the hope that his researches might uncover some important information.

Whatever his revelations, Jack would be delighted and I had an instinct that this was a man to be trusted, so as I handed him the two letters I realised that a further explanation was needed. 'As matter of fact, sir, I am a private investigator—'

His head jerked up and he chuckled. 'Well, bless my soul. I might have guessed that. Your father's daughter, eh? I beg your pardon, I interrupted you . . .'

'These letters were included in the package with the map. The lady was a client and I believe they are of the same vintage as the map. Unfortunately, they are written in French, of which I have very little acquaintance.'

He studied them carefully and shook his head. 'The writing is fairly illegible and my French is also somewhat rusty these days. But I will be happy to have a look at them and perhaps find out if there is any possible connection.'

Leaving, he bowed. 'It has been a delight to make the acquaintance of such an illustrious member of the Faro family.'

Another bow. 'Please give my regards to Mr Macmerry, who I hope to meet on my next visit,' he added, either too polite or too disinterested in our connection for further comment. 'When is he likely to return?'

There was nothing else for it but to inform him that Mr Macmerry was in fact a detective inspector and at present in hospital following an accident while on duty.

He looked grave. 'Nothing of a serious nature, I trust.'

In return, I gave him the hearty assurance which I hoped was true and he smiled again. 'Then all is well. Excellent, excellent. And a detective? How interesting. I will look forward most eagerly to our meeting, since we have something in common. A lifetime of searching for clues, mine to the past and his to the present.'

And mine, I thought, to solving a mystery that had little concern with the Jacobites but all to do with the solution of a present-day murder just a mile away from where we stood.

CHAPTER TWENTY

Closing the door, I took out my bicycle and headed to the hospital, eager to tell Jack of the latest developments, not only regarding Meg, but also the possibility that the map from the secret room was part of the one in Mrs Lawers' legacy. That opportunity was to be nipped in the bud, for as I approached Jack's ward there were voices. Opening the door, I saw that he was sitting up in bed and he had a visitor.

I recognised that familiar voice and the familiar face that turned to greet me with a beaming smile.

Jack's father, farmer Andy Macmerry, jumped from his chair and gave me a great hug.

'Grand to see ye, lass. Got your letter this morning and his ma insisted that I come in and see the lad for ourselves. Jess is no' very great, a bit too frail for long travel these days.' And holding me at arm's length, 'Ye're looking just great, lass.'

Jack was watching all this, waiting for his turn in this exchange of greetings. I leant over, kissed him and he grinned.

'Good news, Rose. They're letting me out tomorrow if I behave myself. I'm so looking forward to seeing Meg. How is she?' he asked anxiously.

I said, 'She's fine, Jack. Such a lovely little girl, you'll be proud of her. And she's the very image of you.'

'That will do her no favours, poor lass.' A grimace, then he grinned and looked across at his father. 'I'll go and see her.'

'And I'll come with you, lad. I'm keen to meet this wee granddaughter I've heard so much about.'

I doubted that, looking at Jack, but I smiled anyway.

Andy put an arm around me. 'The lad's coming back home with me,' he said firmly. 'Just for a day or two – a wee rest. Get some good fresh Border air into his lungs, away from Auld Reekie. And some of his ma's cooking. He'll be right as rain in no time.'

Pausing to see how I was receiving all this, he patted my hand. 'I had a word with the surgeon mannie, and he says it's vital that the lad doesna' go rushing back to chasing criminals for a wee while.'

It took a little time for me to arrange my face at this news, and watching my expression, he added hastily, 'Why don't you come along. Just great to have you too, lass. You're always welcome and Jess is just longing to see you again. We both ken how busy ye are, what with one thing and another, but it's been a while now since your last visit . . .'

That made me feel guilty – so often Jack went alone. But I knew the surgeon's recommendation was right, it was the best thing for him. If he came back to the Tower he would be restless at this forced inactivity, longing to get back on the job.

I had learnt through our years together that police business often sent him to Glasgow, Aberdeen or elsewhere. I could deal with that, but since his accident I realised how much I had missed him, longing to have him home again.

I looked at him sitting in that hospital bed and could not deny that the gunshot wound had taken a lot of his vitality – he certainly looked far from the strong detective inspector ready to deal with any emergency. He had lost weight; thin and worn, he certainly was not up to the rigours of Solomon's Tower with my indifferent cooking compared to his ma's sumptuous feasts.

'Why don't you come, Rose?' he asked.

'Aye, lass,' said Andy. 'And bring that great

doggie with you. Thane! I well ken the last time you brought him. We got along like a house on fire.'

I thought of that 'doggie' and remembered that Andy had a local reputation for healing sick animals. Thane's injured leg had made a startling recovery. But memories of that visit were painful, of a wedding that never was, and Jack's mother would want to know as always why we weren't married yet. It bothered her, and Jack on his own would have to do some explaining to a woman whose upbringing had set down certain principles of respectable living, much simpler than ours. And that applied equally to Andy Macmerry, as both failed to understand why a couple who obviously loved each other chose to live together instead of tying the knot legally.

Andy was saying to Jack, 'I'll be back for you tomorrow. There's a sheep sale in Fife I'm mighty interested in – buying a new ram for my ewes. May as well take the chance of a gossip with some of the local farmers.'

A final résumé of arrangements and it was agreed that there was no point in Jack returning to Solomon's Tower to wait for him there.

Andy took out his watch. 'There'll be a train on the hour. I'll check in at the local hotel overnight with my farming mates.'

Both men looked at me for approval and Jack said, 'You don't mind me going, Rose?'

'Of course not.' And to Andy, 'It makes sense – far easier to meet here with Waverley Station just down the road.'

'Aye, there's a local train passes through Eildon every hour. Maybe I'll leave that visit to your wee lass until next time, eh?'

Jack nodded vaguely while Andy, giving me another bear hug, said, 'I'll be on my way, then. Leave you two lovebirds together.' He was away, firm footsteps echoing down the corridor.

Jack took my hand. 'I feel badly about leaving you, Rose. And I did want to see Meg in her new home. But . . .'

He stopped, shrugged. I was able to fill in what he was leaving unsaid. He didn't want to meet her alone, he wanted my support. And it would be much better for both of them if he waited until he was fully fit. If he went now, a possibly stressful emotional meeting would not be good for him and could cast a shadow on his future relationship with his young impressionable daughter.

'That's settled then. Pack a suitcase for me – you're good at that!' He grinned.

'I'll need time to do some laundry, Jack. Shirts to wash and iron and clothes to press,' I reminded him.

'In that case Wright can collect them.'

A bell had sounded. A nurse looked in and said, 'Time the patient had his rest. He's had an extended visiting time today,' she added reproachfully.

We kissed and Jack held my hand, looking anxious. 'Sure you'll be all right?'

'Of course,' I lied, feeling guilty again.

I should go with him, I knew. But I also knew that it was impossible. Everything in my life as a private investigator sternly demanded that I should remain in Edinburgh at this crucial time. There were too many things that Jack knew nothing about, too many unanswered questions that could not await delay and matters that had developed since his accident and that I must be on hand to deal with alone. I was glad now that he didn't know of my attack on that train journey, or of any of the stresses regarding the tracking down of Meg, and above all there was the investigation of the murder of one of my clients that was also of vital importance to me personally.

As I was leaving he said, 'Take the Jacobite file with you, I don't imagine I'll need it.'

'I had a visit from Mr Hayward – he brought back the map and had some very interesting observations.'

Jack smiled and stifled a yawn. He looked exhausted, his eyelids heavy. This wasn't the time to go into explanations about the possibility that the two maps were connected by a missing portion.

Besides, I hadn't finished with Duddingston. I wanted to have another talk with Jane Hinton.

Unexpected visitors weren't over for the day. I had hardly entered the kitchen when there was a knock at the door and Beth appeared, looking tearful and upset, no longer cheerful and radiant, a return to the Beth of our first meeting.

She came in and took a seat at the kitchen table, her shoulders dropped wearily. 'Oh Rose, I had to come and see you. You are my friend and I am sorry to be here without warning – perhaps it is inconvenient,' she added with a glance around, remembering her manners as a well-brought-up young person.

I shook my head. 'You're always welcome,' and taking her hand, 'tell me about it.'

She sat up straight, shivered and whispered, 'It's Adrian. He doesn't think we should get married after all. It's all Frederick's fault. He had called when I was out with some gifts, flowers and chocolates. Adrian was absolutely furious . . .'

That, at least, was understandable, a poor young man rivalled by a wealthy suitor.

'He doesn't care that I'm not interested in Frederick, that he is only a kind old friend – told me that I'd be better off marrying him, if he would still have me, if he still wanted me.' Tears began to flow, a handkerchief dabbed. 'He said he was leaving anyway very shortly for that audition in London, the one he's been hoping for after the Portobello Players perform their Prince Charlie pageant at the Pleasance Theatre. The same old story, Rose,' she added with a sob. 'He can't hope to keep a wife and child in London, not until he gets big roles, makes a name for himself—'

I was less concerned with Adrian's ambitions than the fate of the baby. 'What about Lillie?' I interrupted.

'I knew I had to tell him the truth about what happened. But he doesn't care,' she wailed. 'Said it was a relief that Lillie wasn't his after all. He didn't need to feel he had any obligations to either of us. Then he laughed – *laughed*, Rose! – reminded me I should realise that in my class of society our affair would be regarded as a fellow sowing his wild oats. So cruel – I thought he loved me. How could he say such things!'

More tears, then, 'Oh Rose, I don't know what to do. He seemed so fond of Lillie, I cannot believe he doesn't care for her either.'

I didn't know what to say; I couldn't find the right words regarding Adrian's conduct that would not be a lie.

I put an arm around her shoulders. She dried her eyes and sighed. 'I'm so sorry to inflict all this on you, but you are such a comfort. Besides, it's no use talking to Nanny, she agrees with Adrian.' And taking a deep breath, 'She thinks I should let him go and marry Frederick.'

This was no surprise, as Nanny had said as much to me.

'Frederick knows all about Lillie. He has told Nanny – not me, of course – that we should get married.'

I could see further complications looming on that horizon. 'I gather he's well known, and then there is your family and their circle of friends. Surely you appearing as his wife with a tiny baby would be hard to explain away – a local scandal.'

She shook her head. 'Oh, he's worked that one out. We would get married secretly at Gretna Green and go immediately to his estate in Argyll. No one would ever know that Lillie wasn't ours.'

As plots go this one seemed fraught with loopholes, but at least offered a more positive solution than the uncertainties of any future with Adrian. In fact, all things considered, once she could dry her eyes over losing him, it was a fortuitous ending indeed, one that most girls in her unfortunate circumstances would have leapt at.

I had one final question. 'Do you love Adrian?'

She frowned. 'I think so. And I truly believed in him, that he loved me. But since I came back, I am not so sure that he would make a good husband.' She paused, adding anxiously, 'What shall I do, Rose? What do you think?'

I took her hand. 'My dear, this is a decision that only you can make, especially as I have never met either of the men concerned.'

She frowned. 'But you are so wise, Rose. What do you think I should do?'

I shook my head. As for my thoughts, I was hardly the right person to advise anyone regarding marriage, considering my own lengthy indecisions regarding Jack Macmerry. And Beth was certainly taking me on trust, for she knew nothing about my life.

I took it that she was too involved in her own problems to show any curiosity about how I managed to live in Solomon's Tower or if there was a Mr McQuinn, and would have probably been surprised to learn that I was one of this new breed of women who had a career, a private detective at that.

She sighed and smiled wistfully. 'I would have enjoyed London, though, such an exciting prospect.'

I had no wish to disillusion her about the life she imagined she'd have lived in London – a life her parents had provided until recently – with wealth and a position in society, calling cards and dressmakers and balls, when, in reality, she would have been facing the very different prospect of scrimping and scraping to make ends meet as an actor's wife.

Our conversation ended as Thane came into the kitchen. She gave a great shriek and bounded to her feet.

I put a hand on her arm. 'This is Thane – my dog. He won't hurt you.'

Thane came over and she took a step backward, shuddered and said, 'But he is so . . . so huge!'

As she spoke Thane looked from one to the other, quite bewildered by this reception. He sat down at my side a little hurt and offended as Beth continued to regard him, wide-eyed, keeping her distance.

'He is gentle and friendly, Beth, I assure you. And he is my protector, aren't you, Thane?'

He looked at me gratefully, with that almost human smile.

Beth sighed, putting out a rather nervous hand. 'May I?'

Thane looked at her still with that gentle expression and she stroked his head. Then she laughed. 'We have lots of dogs – a beagle pack for the hunt, and my father has two Labradors and a spaniel, but they live outside in the kennels.'

Stroking Thane's head, she sighed wistfully. 'I have never been allowed a dog of my own. And I'm allergic to cats, they make me sneeze.'

She smiled and looked up at me. 'But he is rather lovely, Rose. So unusual. What kind is he?'

So I had to give a recital of the deerhound pedigree and the connection with the legend of Arthur's Seat.

'So romantic, Rose. What a lovely idea. Perhaps I could take him out for a walk on the hill sometime.'

I laughed and said 'Of course', though it would be more likely that Thane would be the one taking her for a walk. At least his entrance, so well-timed, had cheered her up for the moment and she left quite happily promising to come back very soon.

I watched her walk down the road with feelings of great compassion. So vulnerable and with such an uncertain future to deal with for one so young.

CHAPTER TWENTY-ONE

Closing the door, I got down to the domestic chore of Jack's laundry which I would have been tempted to take to the local 'steamie', as it was called, for the larger items of bed linen and towels. However, time did not permit. This was still a good drying day with a fine strong breeze, blowing down from Arthur's Seat. I was just pegging out the last shirt on the line, when Thane raced over to the gate.

I looked up to see a policeman approaching the garden greeted by Thane, who ran back to my side, disappointed, no doubt, that the uniform had not heralded another visit from Sergeant Wright.

'Excuse me, madam.' This constable was a newcomer, a stranger older than the sergeant, his features under the uniform helmet almost invisible apart from bright-blue eyes and a heavy grey moustache.

'Mrs McQuinn?' I said 'Yes' and he saluted me gravely. 'I have been sent by the hospital. Your presence is required there immediately.'

This piece of information was surprising.

'What is it they want me for?'

The policeman was turning on his heel to leave. 'I have no idea, madam. I was just told to deliver the message.' Touching his helmet he was away.

I wanted to shout after him. I wanted to know more. In despair I regarded the washing blowing briskly in the wind. And then sudden panic as I reconsidered that brief message.

Did it mean that Jack had had a relapse? Oh dear God—

I rushed inside, collected my cape, took the bicycle and headed down the road. I had never ridden so fast, my imagination out of control and running riot.

At the hospital I hurried along the corridor to Jack's ward.

His bed was empty, stripped of its sheets.

I put my hand to my mouth. A sick feeling of terror and dismay.

'Mrs McQuinn?' I turned. The nurse, who I recognised, had approached.

'Mr Macmerry – where is he?' I felt I was

yelling at her and she gave me a very odd look as I regained control and asked, 'Tell me, please – what has happened? Is he . . . is he . . . ?' And looking at the empty bed again, my eyes filled with tears.

The nurse took my arm very gently and led me into the corridor.

I started gabbling again and she said, 'Mrs McQuinn, please be calm, there is no need to upset yourself—'

'Upset myself—' I gulped and before I could say more, she shook her head.

'Mr Macmerry is taking a bath at this moment, preparing to leave us in the morning. He won't be sorry—'

'Taking a bath?' I whispered and sat down on the bench.

'Yes, indeed, we do try to provide such facilities when requested.'

I jumped up, regaining my composure. 'Oh thank you, thank you.'

Her eyes widened. She seemed to find such gratitude overwhelming. 'Would you like to sit down and wait for him? He should not be too long. Perhaps a cup of tea?'

The relief that had flooded over me receded. 'A moment if you please, Nurse. Forgive me for being in such a state, but a police constable came – oh, half an hour ago – with an urgent message from the hospital that I was to come immediately and I presumed . . . well, the worst.'

She stood very straight, looked at me, shook her head. 'You must be mistaken, there was no such message sent from us or from Mr Macmerry.' She paused. 'This policeman – was it Sergeant Wright?'

'No. I had never seen this one before.'

She continued to look at me, then said gravely, 'Then I can only conclude that someone was playing a practical joke – in very bad taste, if I may say so.' She paused a moment. 'Now, a cup of tea.'

I stood up. 'Please, don't bother. I won't wait after all. I shall see him and his father tomorrow. And one other thing, Nurse, if you please: no mention of my visit and the urgent message to Mr Macmerry. I'm sure you are right, it was a practical joke, but it might alarm him and I would not want that.'

She smiled and put a finger to her lips. 'Not a word, Mrs McQuinn. Not a word.'

Perplexed and angry, a little scared too, I rode swiftly back home. The washing, witness to the mystery, was blowing in the wind and drying nicely. I parked the bicycle and, opening the kitchen door – never locked, to give Thane, who had swiftly learnt how to lift the latch with his nose, easy access to the Tower when we were absent – went inside.

There was no sign of Thane. But listening, I heard faint but frantic barking from somewhere above my head.

I ran up the spiral stair. The barking grew nearer, from the master bedroom. I opened the door and Thane rushed out to greet me. He was excited, agitated. Trying to tell me something.

And I realised that although he could manage latches, he could not have turned the doorknob on a room we seldom used and always kept closed. Someone had shut him in there.

Patting his head, I leant against the banister. He must have heard my heart racing, for, whining gently, he came to my side, watching me anxiously.

And I knew the answer. Someone had been in the house while I was at the hospital. Thane had followed the intruder upstairs. There was only one answer to that too: the identity of the burglar must also be the messenger who lured me out of the Tower with a false message.

'Righto, Thane. We'll see what's missing.'

Beginning with the bedrooms, Thane at my side, I searched each one, although there was nothing portable to steal in any of them.

Leaving my bedroom to last, it looked untouched. There had been no random opening of drawers and emptying of contents. Not that I had much to steal – the contents of Mrs Lawers' legacy minus the documents given to Mr Hayward were in the secret room.

I wasn't surprised that my jewel box had been opened, the lock broken. But nothing was missing; my few pieces, of sentimental value only, had been of no interest.

Downstairs, the Great Hall. Again, nothing portable, other than Jack's rather unwieldy typewriter. So what had the burglar been searching for?

Into the kitchen. Again nothing. I opened the sideboard drawers – linen, cutlery, my derringer, some letters and bills, the note Mrs Lawers had written regarding the documents and the jewellery.

Here was a puzzle indeed. If he wasn't the usual kind of burglar looking for jewellery or money, what had been his motive?

And suddenly I had it – the answer.

His target had been Mrs Lawers' documents and I sat back, breathed a sigh of relief, glad of the instinct that had made me decide to entrust the map and the letters to Mr Hayward.

But with relief came another scaring thought: I had been tricked out of the house by a bogus policeman and this was no opportunist burglary, spur of the moment, but part of a very carefully thought-out plan.

I sat down at the table. Someone knew a lot

more about Mrs Lawers' affairs than I had had the opportunity to discover in our brief ill-fated acquaintance. I had unwittingly become custodian of that deadly legacy, and without knowing why or what for, I was in mortal danger at the hands of that same person who had murdered her and her maid.

Close to my side, Thane sat looking guilty and unhappy. He wanted me to understand, his eyes pleading. I hugged him and realised that although Thane was quite unique, he lacked only two desirable human attributes. If only he could talk – and make a cup of tea.

'It isn't your fault,' I said, his gentle whine an apology.

Who was this bogus policeman who had sent me on a wild goose chase to the hospital so that he could return and search the Tower? Thane would never have allowed a stranger to come through the kitchen door – the only access when we were absent – let alone climb the spiral stair to the bedrooms . . . unless . . . unless it was someone, or something, familiar. The police uniform – a familiar sight to Thane, particularly with Sergeant Wright visiting over the last few days.

That had to be the connection. Both men dressed identically. Thane had seen the bogus one speaking to me. Remembering how well he got along with Sergeant Wright, had the uniform fooled Thane into believing he was also a friend?

I would never know or hope to learn how much Thane understood of human communications, but he had let him in, followed him upstairs, and been shut into the master bedroom while this intruder searched the premises.

There was a disquieting agenda. The bogus policeman knew the secret of Mrs Lawers' legacy and therefore a link existed between him and the false Miss Hinton.

I shuddered to think that they might at this moment be engaged in an urgent discussion regarding their failure to get their hands on the documents – both ready and prepared to kill again if necessary.

I took in the damp shirts, ironed them and pressed Jack's best suit for the visit to his parents. Tired by my activities, sleep still evaded me except for a series of weird nightmares. Jolted awake, I searched the darkness, consoled by Thane's gentle snores from the rug at the bedside.

When at last I dozed off, I opened my eyes to hear the grandfather clock strike nine. Springing out of bed, I dressed hastily, packed Jack's suitcase, and with it firmly strapped on to the back of the bicycle, I hurtled down to the hospital.

Ten was striking as I ran along the corridor, hoping that I was in time. I was – just. I was met by two anxious faces, wearing expressions of ill-concealed impatience.

Andy, always an early riser, up and about at six, had arrived on the first train just after eight o'clock, I was informed, with a reproachful glance from Jack as I handed over the suitcase.

'We have to go, Rose, or we'll miss the morning train to Eildon.'

Andy nodded vigorously. 'Aye, and Jess'll be worried sick if we don't arrive. I sent her a wee note.'

I had no intention of worrying Jack with details of the break-in even if there had been time to do so, but I asked, 'What about Meg?'

Jack ignored that and repeated, 'We have to go.'

About to leave, Andy added, 'I would have liked to see the wee lass, maybe on my next visit . . .'

I gave Jack a despairing look and he said, 'We can't just arrive at the Blakers' door unannounced, Rose. Tell you what, I'll write from home letting them know when I'll be back and arranging to see Meg then.' He paused and looked at me, an appealing glance. 'Maybe we could meet there.'

I nodded vaguely, as I wrote down the address aware once again that Jack was dreading this encounter with Meg, relieved to delay it and hoping that my presence – having already established a passing acquaintance – would make it easier.

I went down to the station with them, pushing my bicycle, with Andy trying his best, even as the train stood at the platform, to persuade me to come along, insane and impractical as it was, with me totally unprepared to dash off without even a toothbrush on a visit to Eildon.

Kisses and hugs exchanged, I watched the train gather steam, Jack leaning out of the window, smiling and saying that he would miss me.

'We all will,' shouted Andy.

A final wave from Jack, a yell about writing.

'Take care of yourself!'

Chance would be a good thing, I thought as the train vanished, leaving me suddenly vulnerable, aware that I needed Jack's presence more now than at any other time. A man to listen to the dark deeds of the past few days and the dire situation I had found myself in, a man to protect and calmly advise me.

I walked out of the station, got on my bicycle and rode homeward feeling sorry for myself, very much alone and, even if I refused to admit it, scared.

CHAPTER TWENTY-TWO

Fate was smiling on me, even if from behind a grey cloud, for I wasn't destined to be alone for long.

Prayers for a man to protect and advise me were being answered in the handsome form of my stepbrother Dr Vince Laurie, arriving next morning, totally unexpected as usual.

As he alighted from the carriage I was delighted, even tearful, to see him. And so was Thane.

Soon he was sitting at the kitchen table and declining tea, taking a swig – at eleven in the morning, I frowned – from a silver flask which had been the gift of the late Queen.

Vince sighed. 'I do miss HM. I was very fond of her, but Bertie—' He grinned. 'Beg pardon, His

Majesty, is a vastly different proposition. And alas, from my point of view, he doesn't share his mother's passion for Balmoral and all things related to his father, Prince Albert. He's a bit contemptuous of the whole mourning business, believes in getting on with life. As for John Brown – that legendary figure – you should just see his eyes snap at the mention of his name.'

'So I gather you won't be stopping off on the royal train quite as often.'

Vince smiled wryly. 'If only . . .'

And I learnt quickly what I feared most. That his infrequent visits when the royal train stopped off in Edinburgh were likely to be even fewer, since the King did not consider it necessary that the junior physician to the royal household accompany a selection of children and grandchildren back and forth, up and down the railway line to Ballater.

'His only interest in Balmoral is for the shooting – which is why he is here. He vastly prefers London's bright lights, and his favourite indulgences – gambling and the society of beautiful women.'

Vince sighed. 'The reason for my visit is that there is a problem – a medical one – with his digestive system. It is playing him up, and regardless of advice about overeating and overdrinking, he refuses to curtail his social life. However, I am here because he has quarrelled with his personal physician. No reason given directly, except that rumour – never to be disregarded in royal circles – has it that he has been playing excessive attention to said physician's very beautiful young wife.'

As he paused to moisten his lips with another sip of very expensive whisky or brandy – my experience of both was minimal – I realised that this elevation to royal favour was primarily because the King could rely on Dr Laurie's discretion from experience while he was still Prince of Wales. On the only occasion when I had met the heir to the throne, Vince was accompanying him to the opening of a new bridge in Edinburgh, and Bertie, as he was then popularly known, was paying particular attention to a lady in the Lothian area.

Yes, Dr Laurie was definitely to be relied upon and he did not fuss. Fuss was something the King despised. And so Vince found himself spending a few brief hours in Edinburgh while his royal master visited the same Lothian lady, recently widowed and by whom – rumour had it once again – there was an offspring who bore him a remarkable resemblance.

Vince was sorry to have missed Jack and very concerned about the shooting. He demanded to know all the medical details.

'I can't tell you anything, Vince. You had

better apply to the surgeon Mr Wainland for such details.'

'Wainland,' Vince smiled. 'Then Jack was in good hands. I knew Wainland well in the old days here. He will have made an excellent job of patching Jack up.'

And that was good news for me too. When I said Jack had gone to Eildon, he asked the obvious question: why had I not gone with him?

I smiled. 'What – and miss your visit!'

He smiled wryly. 'I would have been sorry, especially now that I won't be coming on the royal train so often . . .'

'Often', he called it – I thought not more than twice a year, as he went on, 'You have no excuse not to visit St James's, see Olivia and the children, all three of them, growing up without a sight of you. You'll love London.'

I thought of Beth and smiled. 'It's on my list but Edinburgh keeps me busy. I have a career, if you hadn't noticed already.'

'Any interesting cases?'

'Just a couple of frauds and private shadowing of suspected cheating husbands,' I said. 'That was a month ago. Main concern now is Jack's recovery and Meg, his little girl, you may remember . . .'

He nodded and I went on, 'Her aunt died, her uncle by marriage remarried . . .' I decided to spare him the tedious details of tracking Meg down. 'She now lives with new adoptive parents in Joppa, conveniently near at hand for Jack to go and see her.'

Vince sat back and smiled. 'He will be delighted about that. His visits to and from Glasgow were rather like mine to Edinburgh, infrequent and unreliable. Has he seen her yet?'

'No. All this happened while he's been in hospital. He is to call on her on his return from Eildon, richly sustained on fresh Border air and his mother's cooking.'

Vince nodded approval. 'Knowing Jack, that was advisable in his condition.' I told him that Andy had come post-haste to escort him and Vince laughed.

'And you too, I dare say, if you'd been of a mind for it.' He paused, looked at me quizzically. 'But Eildon was never your favourite place, was it?'

I shook my head and we were both silent, back with the wedding-that-never-was, a nightmare that I preferred not to remember.

At least Vince, whether he approved or not, refrained from nagging me about Jack and I being still unwed.

'So what would you like to do? I have a carriage and driver at my disposal. Shall we go out somewhere? Joppa perhaps? I'd like a look at Jack's little Meg.'

I wasn't desperately keen on that idea and – as if on cue – it began to rain. 'Let's wait a while. Look at the weather!'

As we adjourned to the two comfortable armchairs by the fire, Vince looked at me critically. 'I have a strange feeling that you have a lot on your mind, Rose, that you need to talk about. It's confession time, so let's hear all about it.' He lit a cigar. 'Right from the beginning!'

So I told him about the ailing Mrs Lawers' legacy, how Jack had persuaded me to accompany her to Lochandor since Meg was now with her aunt and uncle nearby at Tarnbrae. How, on the day appointed, her maid Hinton arrived, saying Mrs Lawers was too ill to travel.

When I reached the train journey and the maid's insistence that she should carry my luggage, I noted that my scrupulous stepbrother had been concentrating on every detail with only an occasional interruption to make a comment or ask a question.

After I had described the attack on the train, he held up a hand and said, 'It's a wonder you survived such a fall, without severe or even fatal injuries.'

'Fortunately the train had slowed down at a bend and I fell down a steep grassy slope. I was rescued by the local doctor out walking his dog. Bruises and so forth but nothing broken, but he insisted on seeing me on to the next train back to Edinburgh.'

I went on to describe how I made the decision to return to Lochandor, how Mr Lawers refused to accept the legacy and of my failed attempt to see the Pringlesses. When I told him of my fever, Vince shook his head and said firmly, 'That could not have been the influenza, Rose. It is a serious illness and patients could never make such a rapid recovery.'

I thought of Thane's part but meekly agreed, as Vince was yet to be convinced of Thane's mysterious powers, as were all but Jack and I who had witnessed the evidence with our own eyes.

I described to Vince my shock and misgivings on being told of the deaths of Mrs Lawers and Hinton. 'I wasn't the only one to have grave suspicions. Amy Dodd, her friendly next-door neighbour, told me about a strange man who she had heard threatening Mrs Lawers. And from Mrs Dodd's timing I had a new piece of evidence. Both women must have been dead before I left on my second mission to Lochandor, in which case it wasn't Mrs Lawers who spoke to me through the door that day.'

'Where was Jack in all this?' asked Vince.

'Oh, he knew the police were involved and that this was a possible murder case.'

'You told him of your attack on the train, of course.'

I shook my head.

'Why on earth not?' Vince demanded. 'It was surely of great significance in connection with the deaths of those two women.'

'I knew that Chief Inspector Gray was involved and I suppose I had some thoughts – seeing that we are old enemies – of solving the case myself.'

It was Vince's turn to shake his head and sigh deeply. 'Not a very wise decision, Rose. Go on, what next?'

'If you must know, Jack was more concerned about Meg in her new surroundings than the fate of Mrs Lawers' legacy. So I promised to go to Tarnbrae and see her, which pleased him.'

'That was very brave of you, Rose, considering the circumstances, to set forth again—'

'Not brave, Vince, merely duty to a dead woman. I had been paid a substantial fee and I felt it was my moral duty to try to persuade John Lawers to accept the legacy, only to discover that any such hopes were doomed. He had died of a heart attack after a house fire, which left the fate of Mrs Lawers' legacy in my hands.'

'And if you were to do anything about that, you had to know immediately what this package contained,' he said.

I described the contents and in particular the map which I had recognised as similar to the one Jack and I had found in the Tower.

'In your possession?'

I told him how Jack had decided there might be a connection with the Battle of Prestonpans and had sought the opinion of an Edinburgh historian, who I had recently met and entrusted with the documents.

Finally I told him about the bogus policeman and the break-in at the Tower. 'Much missing?' Vince put in.

'No, and that is what is so curious. Thane had been shut in the master bedroom, the Tower carefully ransacked, but nothing was stolen.'

Our discussion was cut short by the arrival of the postman. Two letters: one from Mr Hayward asking if he could call in two days' time, when he hoped to have more information on the documents; the other was from Jane Hinton, letting me know that the funerals of her aunt and Mrs Lawers were to take place at Duddingston Kirk.

Vince looked at his watch. 'It has stopped raining, Rose. The sun shines – shall we go out to Dirleton for lunch? I would enjoy a sight of East Lothian again and time is so short.'

It was always a joy to spend precious hours with Vince, especially as they were to be even more infrequent in future.

CHAPTER TWENTY-THREE

After lunch we walked at Yellowcraigs, sat on a boulder in the sunshine, watching the lapping waves gently caressing the shore.

Vince, smiling, said, 'Now where were we? Why didn't you inform the police about the break-in, Rose – and this fellow Gray?'

'Think of it – who would believe me? Not Chief Inspector Gray, I assure you. Report a burglary with no evidence of anything stolen, a broken lock on a jewel case? Gray thinks little enough of my abilities as a lady investigator and would immediately claim that I was suffering again from an overactive imagination.'

Vince bit his lip and looked thoughtful. 'So we have evidence here that the searcher's interest lay primarily with the map and those letters.'

'Which I was unable to read. Besides being written in French, they were illegible. I gave them to Hayward.'

'A professor of history before he retired,' said Vince. 'I knew him well. Highly respected member of the community.'

'Trustworthy?'

'Indeed, yes. Absolutely reliable. Your documents will be quite safe with him.' Again he frowned. 'Let us hope from that letter you have just received that he has succeeded in making something of them.'

He leant across, took my hand. 'As for me, my only concern is you. I worry about your safety with Jack away.'

'There is no need. I have Thane.'

'Thane is a dog,' he muttered. 'And, may I remind you, a dog who let a burglar into the house.'

I explained the circumstances about the similar uniform and so forth, but he didn't seem convinced, merely shook his head and said, 'I'd be a hundred times happier with a strong man who had fists and could reinforce them with a gun.'

'I have a gun,' I said firmly. 'And I know how to use it.'

He grinned. 'I heard that you were quite a crack shot with a rifle in your pioneering days.'

We were both sad for a moment, as unhappy memories stirred. Then Vince straightened his shoulders, sighed and said sternly, 'You really should have told Jack, you know. It was quite wrong to keep it to yourself, carry this dangerous burden alone. Why on earth did you not tell him?'

'As a doctor,' I said slowly, 'you know the answer to that. If you'd seen him after the shooting – for those first twenty-four hours it was touch and go whether he would survive. Your surgeon friend did a marvellous job, but at each visit I saw how frail he was, even yesterday when I saw him off at the station with his father. It was too late then, and what was the point of burdening him with something he could do nothing about? He'd only worry.'

'He has influence in his position – he could have got you police protection.'

'Vince, you're confusing me with your royal employers. That doesn't happen to ordinary folk on such uncorroborated evidence like falling – or being pushed – out of a train, and a burglary with nothing stolen.'

Vince wasn't listening. He frowned. 'Tell me what you can remember about this map among those documents.'

'I have a very good memory, Vince, as you are well aware; I could draw it for you. The battle formations of the clans were probably drawn by the prince himself while he stayed at Mrs Lawers' house in the Causeway. Two opposing army lines drawn up facing one another. In the background, the shape of a mountain roughly drawn, the coast, Arthur's Seat and the Firth of Forth.'

Vince looked up. 'Obviously relating to Prestonpans.' He shook his head. 'But surely a crude map could not contain some secret never to be revealed.'

'What if it is only part of a larger map? Mr Hayward believed that to be a distinct possibility.'

'I still think that is extremely doubtful. More likely the truth must lie in those letters written a hundred and fifty years ago.' He groaned. 'And in French. How irritating.'

'But it does make some connection with the prince's campaign more certain. Perhaps he wrote the letters too. It was his native tongue after all, remember, not Scots.'

Vince sighed. 'Well, I wouldn't have been much use to you even if I'd seen the letters. Never was much good at French, or any languages come to think of it. Latin was hard enough, and once or twice failing exams put the possibility of doing medicine in question.'

The sun had fled, it was turning chilly, gloom had descended on the rocky shore, the ebb tide grey and uninviting. We went back to the waiting carriage, Vince thoughtfully silent.

In the Tower once more, while I made a cup of tea he hovered and said, 'I must confess the only likely suspect I have come up with from your evidence is Sergeant Wright.'

My eyebrows raised at that. 'Sergeant Wright?' I repeated. 'The most unlikely one if you knew him.'

He shook his head. 'But that's always the way of it. I shouldn't have to tell you that.'

'In this case, I'm sure you're wrong . . .'

'Perhaps. But let's face it, he is the only logical person from what you've told me—'

'He certainly wasn't the policeman who came to my door with an urgent message to send me off to the hospital while he searched the house,' I interrupted.

Vince was silent again. 'Do you know what I think, Rose?' And without awaiting a reply, 'I think, in your best interests, that you should abandon this mystery, leave the matter of the two dead women in the hands of the police, where it belongs. Declare the case of Mrs Lawers' legacy closed – unsolved, meanwhile remaining custodian of the documents and the trinkets until such time as someone claims them – such as Mrs Lawers' solicitors.'

'That's unlikely. From what I heard from Jane Hinton, or her friend Amy Dodd, she was the kind of woman who did not trust anyone, and certainly not a bank or a lawyer—'

'Hear me out, Rose. If you don't find someone to carry this burden for you, you are chasing shadows . . .' he paused and added grimly, '. . . but if there is something amiss and dangerous for the holder of these documents, then one of these shadows might materialise, knife in hand, from the darkness surrounding you.'

It was quite poetic the way he put it. Impressed, I said, 'Now you are just trying to scare me to death.'

'It's for your own good, Rose,' he said angrily, banging his fist on the table. 'Why don't you listen to reason for a change?' Watching my expression, he groaned. 'And if you'd had the sense to tell all this to Jack, I don't doubt for one moment that he would have felt as I do about it and utterly forbidden you to pursue it any longer.'

'Very well, I will tell him once he's restored back to health and strength after being spoilt rotten by his devoted mother.' I paused to see how he was taking this and added, 'Remember he has another problem waiting on the doorstep. A three-year-old problem which he has never managed to solve.'

'Meg?'

'Yes, Meg. And what he should do about letting the Blakers adopt her.' Over lunch I had confided my concerns about Piers Blaker.

Vince looked at me, considering, silent, as if searching for the right words. Then he smiled wryly. 'There is a very simple solution to the problem of Meg. So simple, I'm surprised that a lady investigator hasn't twigged it already.'

'And what is that?' I demanded sharply.

He grinned. 'I'm not going to put the words in your mouth, Rose. Just think about it, and the answer will come to you in a flash.'

He left soon afterwards with cheerful promises to meet again, *though God knows when that would be*, I thought miserably.

However, I did almost promise to visit St James's and see the family. But I knew that momentary enthusiasm would soon fade. The prospect of London did not enchant me; I found the thought daunting, even slightly scary.

There were other considerations. Would my sister-in-law Olivia have been changed by living within the royal circle? What would those three children make of their rarely seen aunt with the wild yellow hair and unconventional clothes? And what on earth would I wear, what kind of dress would be appropriate? Certainly nothing from a lady bicyclist's wardrobe in the wilds of Arthur's Seat. And I sighed, knowing this feeling of frustration and panic would inevitably provide another excuse for my not visiting London.

Almost before Vince was out of sight, watching

the carriage hurtle down the road towards Waverley Station, carrying him back to his duties as physician to the royal household and out of my life once more, the fleeting nature of our few hours together hit me. These visits, twice a year at best, so often left many important things remaining unsaid, forgotten in the moment – incidents to make him laugh or raise his eyebrows in despair, the ones marked aside in my mind with the tag 'must remember to tell Vince that when I see him'. Alas, none of the Faros were great letter writers, and these visits aside, we had no other means available to stay in touch, although the invention of the picture postcard had been a godsend to Pappa, enjoying his retirement by travelling abroad with his writer companion, Imogen Crowe.

I went inside, closed the door and reread the two letters that had arrived. The impending visit of Mr Hayward and a note from Jane, indicating that the bodies of the two women having now been released, presumably after the Procurator Fiscal had recorded his deliberations, there was a funeral for me to attend.

And I was not looking forward to that either.

CHAPTER TWENTY-FOUR

Arriving for a funeral at Duddingston Kirk by bicycle somehow did not seem dignified or appropriate. It might well raise eyebrows among the mourners – if mourners there were in any number.

So with my hair confined beneath a bonnet and instructed not to show one solitary wild yellow curl I set forth, accompanied by a brisk breeze along the road past the loch, and parked my bicycle at a discreet distance from the church, namely near the fourteenth-century Sheeps Heid Inn, still doing a roaring trade, especially when the working day was over.

Through the kirk gate, the bell tolling forlornly, I looked for recognisable faces awaiting the arrival of the two coffins. There were maybe twenty other mourners – mostly women and all strangers to me, possibly neighbours – sombrely attired, the men in tall hats, the women in black bonnets and bombazine.

Few to mourn Mrs Lawers and her faithful maid. In dying Mrs Lawers had indeed fulfilled her reputation to the very end of being a private person. I took in my surroundings: Duddingston's twelfth-century church, at the gate its 'loupin' stane' to assist worshippers to mount their horses, alongside the grim 'jougs', a forcible and public punishment for local transgressors, very unpopular with surprised fornicators.

A hand raised in greeting. Two figures extracted themselves from the small group, Amy Dodd and Jane Hinton. I joined them, and a nearby couple, whose name I did not catch, were introduced. Hands shaken, a solemn bow from the gentleman.

Amy was looking round for someone else to introduce me to when the hearse with its black-plumed horses arrived and we followed the two plain wooden coffins into the church. I looked around and wondered if the unpopular neighbour who Amy called 'the Frenchie' was present.

As the organ played dolefully I studied the interior of the kirk. Such an ancient building with its original Romanesque nave and chancel had known its days of fame. In the manse garden

Sir Walter Scott, kirk elder, had penned part of *The Heart of Midlothian*, while in living memory the kind and much loved minister, Rev John Thompson, gave rise to a new phrase for Scots: 'We're a' Jock Tamson's bairns.' A keen painter in his leisure hours, naming his garden studio after the Scottish capital meant that his housekeeper could quite truthfully inform would-be visitors or informal callers, 'The meenister is in Edinburgh the noo.'

The service ended, a procession to the graveside, ashes to ashes, dust to dust, the committal over, and as the small group dispersed I caught a glimpse of two familiar figures. Chief Inspector Gray and Sergeant Wright, hardly recognisable out of uniform, intent on studying tombstones and trying hard to look invisible.

Amy obviously had not seen them and said, 'Jane and I have laid on a little collation. Will you join us, my dear?'

I couldn't think of any appropriate words of refusal; besides, my curiosity was aroused for any further developments in the empty house next door and I still had questions to ask Jane.

I guessed there would be little chance of that since Amy's invitation seemed to have been extended to the neighbourhood, now being ushered into the parlour.

Jane, receiving the mourners, wiped away a tear. 'Poor Aunty, I'll miss her.'

Amy gave her a sympathetic hug, drew me aside and whispered, 'You'll never guess what's happened. The police came and d'y ken what? They took away the Frenchie.' A dramatic pause.

Overhearing her, Jane said, 'Just for questioning.'

'How do you know that?' Amy demanded sharply. 'They know he did it.'

Jane shook her head. 'Then why wasn't he in handcuffs if they were so sure?'

Amy nodded sagely. 'Aye, but they know he did it right enough. Just you wait and see. He'll not be back. That's the last we'll see of Monsieur Debeau, as he calls himself. Good riddance to bad rubbish I call it.'

And raising her hand in a gesture across her throat, eyes heavenward, she began slicing another loaf of bread.

The sandwiches were delicious and interesting – I wished I could have said as much for the company. Amy Dodd must have been a shining star among her neighbours, all of whom were agog that the Frenchie had been taken by the police, which became their sole topic of conversation. All of them full of hate and derision for no better reason than because he was different – and because he was French; although the Napoleonic wars were long distant, for many France was the enemy, still regarded with suspicion. There was one ancient chap who declared, incredible as it seemed, that he 'had been a lad at Waterloo'.

The other reason for their dislike was that M Debeau did not gossip, he kept himself to himself, and that was unforgivable. As I had earlier discovered with Amy Dodd, the neighbours liked a good gossip and in a small close-knit community anything that seemed faintly different to their conventional lives was seized upon and shredded very finely indeed.

I angled myself into a position close to Jane. She saw me, smiled and I said, 'I must leave soon.'

She glanced round the assembled mourners, now almost jolly with their post-funeral refreshments. 'I could do with some fresh air. I'll walk back with you.'

I explained about the bicycle and, unperturbed, she laughed. 'Maybe I can run alongside, work off some of those enormous sandwiches.'

As we left I wondered if I would be the centre of discussion once the door closed, and hoped that Amy would put in a good word for this strange woman who lived up the road in Solomon's Tower. Glad I had concealed the bicycle from prying eyes, I said to Jane, 'There are some things I'd like to know, if you have a minute.'

She nodded. 'Then let's have a seat by the loch

– at least the swans are mute. I'm leaving soon, nothing to stay for now.' And I got the feeling that she would not be sorry. She waited for me to speak.

'Was there anything in your aunt's letters about Mrs Lawers that might give some hint about – about what happened to them both?'

Jane was silent for a moment, studying the geese who, after a flurry of interest, had decided that there was no food forthcoming and had grumpily retreated to the water's edge.

'She said Mary was getting a little odd. Blamed it on age – that sort of thing.' Turning, she looked at me. 'She said she hoped Mary wasn't going barmy because she was so scared – "scared of her own shadow", she put it. And she had never been the nervous kind.'

'When was that?'

'Oh, in the last letter I had a couple of weeks before . . . all this happened.'

'Did she ever mention why she was scared – for instance did she mention any strangers calling at the house?'

'Not directly, only that she was in some kind of danger.'

'Something to do with a legacy?' I suggested.

Jane shrugged. 'I never heard that she had anything of value to leave.'

I was almost tempted to tell Jane the whole

story then. I might well have done so had not the sky, which had been clouding over and steadily darkening, decided to unload a heavy shower.

Neither of us were prepared for it – Jane had no coat – and we both leapt back up the road, bade each other a hasty farewell and I rode back swiftly homeward. The conversation with Jane had been disappointingly vague and my thoughts had taken a new turn regarding Mrs Lawers' legacy.

The police arrest was an unexpected development. What did they suspect? Were the killings of the two women linked with M Debeau? Would Mr Hayward's researches reveal some connection with the unpopular Frenchman that Mrs Lawers perhaps had reason to suspect and fear?

Was the presence of Chief Inspector Gray significant, lurking about the kirkyard, in company with Sergeant Wright? Had the pair slipped into the back of the church during the service, finding it necessary to attend the women's funerals in search of clues to their murders?

I had just removed my wet cape when I heard the sound of a carriage followed by the front doorbell. To say it rang would be an overstatement; the sound was more like a rusty croak. Wondering if I had got my times mixed up and this was Mr

Hayward, I opened the door to Mrs Blaker and, holding her hand, Meg Macmerry.

Full of apologies about the informality of this call, Mrs Blaker said, 'I am taking Meg into Jenners to buy some suitable clothes, and as I was passing the door, I thought we might call and see if Mr Macmerry was at home . . .'

It crossed my mind that coming from Joppa via Arthur's Seat would not have been my chosen route or even a direct one to Princes Street. But as Mrs Blaker responded eagerly to my invitation to come inside, I guessed, as she looked around, that curiosity regarding where Meg's father lived was the main reason for the visit.

I smiled down at Meg, who was regarding her vast surroundings wide-eyed and critically, with almost grown-up caution.

'Mr Macmerry isn't at home. He is away for a few days—' And I remembered Jack had promised to write a note saying that he would call on them on the way back. 'Have you not heard from him?'

Mrs Blaker shook her head and I felt a moment's wrath with Jack as they followed me into the kitchen.

Thane rose from his rug politely and waited to be introduced.

'Big doggie,' Meg chortled and rushed towards him while Mrs Blaker cried, 'No, Meg!' and added a shriek of terror.

I put a restraining hand on her arm. 'That is Thane, he is good with children.' A lie, I'd never seen him with children, but it was the best I could think of as Meg had already thrown her arms around him as if she had encountered a more-than-life-sized toy. Thane regarded these overtures politely from under those magisterial eyebrows, with what in human terms would be regarded as a fond smile. He made no move, no licking, nothing. Thane knew his manners.

Mrs Blaker shuddered. 'You're sure?' she asked me. I nodded and she whispered, 'He is fearsomely big for a pet dog, looks as if he might swallow her in one gulp.'

Thane darted an injured look in her direction that said clearly to me 'pet dog, indeed', as she eyed me up and down and added, 'Why, he is almost as big as you, Mrs McQuinn.'

I couldn't deny that.

Meg had lost all interest in the grown-ups. She had found a soulmate and was chattering away to him, twenty to the dozen. Mrs Blaker relaxed, shook her head and looked amazed.

'We have a wee Pomeranian called Posie.' And I remembered having heard distant barking when I called on them. 'But Meg has never shown the slightest interest in Posie.' She shook her head regretfully. 'I fear they will never be friends.'

And that did not surprise me. Doubtless Posie

had been suitably spoilt before this new interloper invaded what she regarded as her territory and became one of the household. She had been there first and doubtless was consumed with resentment and jealousy.

Mrs Blaker refused the offer of tea but had taken out a fan and was applying it vigorously.

This surprised me, as the temperature of Solomon's Tower on an autumn day hardly merited such action, although she did look quite pale and said, 'May I trouble you for a glass of water?'

I produced one. Sipping, she said, 'I was feeling a little faint.'

I looked at the richly corseted shape and realised this was a common affliction of highly fashionable ladies that, after my long years as a pioneering woman, had fortunately passed me by.

I asked, 'Are you sure you feel able to continue your journey into Edinburgh? Perhaps you would care to rest for a while.'

She straightened her shoulders, the corsets giving the faintest of creaks as she handed me back the glass. 'Thank you, but I am quite recovered and we have the carriage. We are meeting a friend in Jenners. She also has a small girl, called Teresa, and we hope the two little ones will become firm friends, and my friend's advice will be invaluable on what to buy.' Regarding Meg critically, 'What colour do you think would suit her best?'

I had not the slightest idea but ventured, 'Blue perhaps?'

Mrs Blaker nodded eagerly and said, 'We must go or we will be late.'

I looked across at Meg, so involved with her new live toy, and longed to talk to her. We had never exchanged more than the few words when she had made a flattering reference to my unruly curls.

I realised that I desperately wanted Jack's little girl to like me too. Perhaps Mrs Blaker recognised that wistful smile.

'I am sorry this is a short visit, but please come and have tea with us one afternoon, perhaps with Mr Macmerry when he returns.' She stood up. 'Come along, Meg dear. Time to go.'

Another hug for Thane, a whisper in his ear and Meg came obediently to Mrs Blaker's side, took her hand and stared up at me.

Mrs Blaker put an arm around her. 'Would you like a doggie like that?'

Meg grinned from ear to ear, nodding vigorously. Both looked at me and Mrs Blaker said, 'I don't suppose we could borrow—'

'No,' I said sharply, and although I didn't expect her to understand I added, 'Deerhounds need a lot of space, we have it here and on Arthur's

Seat. I would never recommend Thane's breed as a domestic pet. Besides, he is more than that. He is a member of the family.'

She frowned and said, 'Yes, of course.' And to Meg, 'Perhaps Mrs McQuinn will let you come often and see your new friend.'

An eager look and I said, 'Of course, Meg. You come at any time. And your pa will be delighted to see you too.'

That brought a shadow across Mrs Blaker's face. 'Please tell Mr Macmerry we are hoping to get the adoption business completed as soon as possible.'

I opened the door. The carriage was waiting.

'Goodbye, Meg,' I said and held out my hand. She regarded this doubtfully.

'Aren't you going to give Mrs McQuinn a kiss, dear?'

Poor Meg, I thought. Mrs Blaker knew even less about the feelings of small children than I did, or guessed, seemingly unaware that they perhaps found such demands unpleasant and quite embarrassing.

However, Meg rose to the occasion. I knelt down – I didn't have that far to go to be on her level – and she put her arms around my neck and kissed my cheek. It made me want to cry – I have no idea why – but I hugged her, kissed her forehead and said, 'Please come again, Meg.'

Thane had accompanied the departing visitors and she darted a longing look in his direction and blew him a kiss.

'Bye, Thane.'

If dogs could bow in a gentlemanly manner, Thane would have done so. We watched them go and looked at each other.

'Well, what do you think of that?' I asked, and as Thane had no human words available, there were volumes that had to remain unsaid.

CHAPTER TWENTY-FIVE

Mr Hayward arrived punctually for his appointment next day, and following me into the kitchen he walked over to the sideboard, and saying, 'May I?', he again took up the photograph of Vince with Pappa and the Queen at Balmoral that had fascinated him on his previous visit. Replacing it, he sighed and shook his head.

'This house is full of memories.' And turning to me he went on, 'There is one other interesting fragment of information regarding the previous owner of Solomon's Tower, my old friend Sir Hedley Marsh.' And from his pocket he withdrew a framed photograph which he handed to me.

'This is Hedley, as a young man.'

I looked at it, looked again, stared. The resemblance to Vince was unmistakeable.

Hayward smiled wryly and said, 'I can see what you are thinking. The same thought struck me on my earlier visit.' Taking a seat at the table, he said, 'I told you Hedley believed he had a son. Tell me about your stepbrother, if you please.'

'Vince was illegitimate; his mother was a servant in a big house in the Highlands, seduced – raped – by one of the guests. She bore Vince, who never forgave or forgot the blight of his birth—'

Hayward held up his hand, shook his head and interrupted. 'He was not the child of rape, or of seduction. Hedley, even as a young man, had high moral principles. This was no philandering middle-aged gentleman; he was the kind who loved only once in his life and that love, if lost, was lost for ever.'

Again he paused, shook his head, his face full of sadness. 'Poor Hedley. He fell deeply in love with that servant girl, came back for her, but found she had left and, as happened with extra servants acquired for the shooting season, no one knew where she had gone. He wanted to marry her and continued his exhaustive search over many years without success, disappointment turning him into a recluse, an embittered old bachelor.'

He stopped and smiled. 'I thought you would wish to know the truth about the previous owner.

Whether you tell your stepbrother or not is up to you. Now, I must not detain you further. With your permission, shall we proceed to the reason for my visit?'

And so saying, he opened his case and spread out the documents for my appraisal with a restrained air of triumph that hinted at some success.

'I have been diving into the depths, Mrs McQuinn, and have come up with some interesting facts, some acquired from the National Archives, in fact. The Jacobite Rebellion was a troubled time in our history and there are some facts which have gone unknown to general researchers.'

He paused, sighed. 'Fortunately I have friends in high places.' He produced a pen and tapped the papers. 'First of all let us regard the map, drawn, most likely, by the prince himself, at a table, perhaps something like this one, in the house at Duddingston.' He spread the two pieces side by side, leaving a gap of some six inches between them.

'If you will recall, I believed they were both part of the same map, and indeed, searching my historic map collection, this speculation was correct. Here is an identical-looking map.' And unrolling it he spread it across the table. He then placed next to each other the two portions he had taken away to examine – the right-hand piece the one Jack and I had found in the secret room, and the left included in Mrs Lawers' legacy.

'If you look closely at these two you will see there are some words scribbled across the base, almost illegible and almost certainly in the prince's own hand. But most important perhaps, as you will observe, is that the middle portion is missing. And that portion, Mrs McQuinn,' he said with a triumphant look, 'if you will regard my similar map of the period, encompasses a section of Arthur's Seat which includes Samson's Ribs and indicates Solomon's Tower as it looked originally, a mere pele tower.'

He leant back, smiled and I asked, 'But why had someone removed it?'

He wagged a finger at me. 'Do not be too hasty, Mrs McQuinn. That is something we still have to find out – the crux of the mystery. However, there is a piece of history which may not be known to you which concerns Prince Charles's sojourn in Duddingston prior to the Battle of Prestonpans.

'From the proceedings of the Court of Enquiry, there is a document from Lord Tweeddale, Secretary in Charge of North Britain, or Scotland, and resident in Pinkie House – you may know it, in Musselburgh and near the scene of the Battle of Pinkie fought in the time of the prince's great-grandmother, Mary Queen of Scots.

'Lord Tweeddale offered thirty thousand

pounds for the capture of Prince Charles Edward Stuart on the 17th of August 1745. A week later, on the 23rd, the prince offered the same sum for the capture of Lord Tweeddale. A mocking gesture perhaps, but how did the prince come by this sum? The answer lies in the archives of the Court of Enquiry, Tweeddale's report of the disappearance of thirty thousand pounds and his valet, one Simon Reslaw, a Frenchman who my lord realised too late was a Jacobite spy.' He paused. 'The prince was at that moment preparing to lay siege to Edinburgh, cannons trained on it from Arthur's Seat. The city mercifully fell to him without bloodshed on the 17th of September, and the prince proclaimed his father James VII as the rightful king.'

Mr Hayward chuckled. 'There is a story that it was on the same day the prince acquired his nickname. A lady watching the ceremony from her window reported "ladys who threw their handkerchiefs and clap'd hands show'd great loyalty to ye Bonny Prince".'

That was all very well but my interest lay with that thirty thousand pounds. My eyes widened at such a sum.

'A fortune, yes, even in our own time, but in the eighteenth century – impossible to envisage its significance.'

Mr Hayward shrugged expressively. 'How

and where did he get the money, have such a fortune available, when he was at the start of a campaign with Highlanders and loyal adherents all desperately in need of cash?'

And taking a drink of water from the jug on the table, 'You are a good listener, Mrs McQuinn, are you still with me?'

I laughed. 'I'm intrigued, please go on.'

'The answer lies with Simon Reslaw who had infiltrated himself into the Tweeddale household. His Lordship was something of a dandy and liked the idea of a French valet. Anyway, the letter indicates in strong words that Reslaw left in a hurry, discharged for theft.'

Again he paused, looked at me. 'You think he went off with the thirty thousand and carried it to the prince,' I said.

Hayward nodded eagerly. 'I do indeed. That is my interpretation. But there is a flaw. I don't think it ever got that short distance that separated Pinkie House from Duddingston or Prestonpans. Something happened en route and either Simon changed his mind, or lost his life. Anyway we lost track of him. His name was among the wounded after the battle when they were taken care of – both sides, English and Scots, for the prince, whatever his faults, was a humane man. So it was unlikely that he was at the disaster of Culloden—'

He stopped, made a grimace and sighed. 'The money was never heard of again.'

'Perhaps he hid it in the house in Duddingston.'

Mr Hayward shook his head. 'I think that is unlikely. I suspect that he hid it in that missing section of the map. Here – somewhere on Arthur's Seat. Consider the hundreds of caves, secret places where a man might leave treasure, intending to come back for it. But our Reslaw never came. Something happened to him. He died or fled.'

Hayward sat back, smiled. 'And that is all I have to report to you, Mrs McQuinn, just a fraction of the story, but it perhaps explains the two pieces of the map. I am sure Mr Macmerry will be particularly interested in the portion you told me was found here in the Tower.' He paused. 'I trust that Mr Macmerry is well?'

I explained that he would be returning within the week and as Hayward took his leave Thane came loping down the hill towards us, leaping over the garden wall.

The departing visitor regarded this huge apparition with apprehension, as might any stranger to the district, and I said reassuringly, 'That's Thane – he belongs here.'

'Your dog?' Mr Hayward was taken by surprise, and glanced from my slight shape to the huge deerhound who came and stood at my side. 'More like a pony than a dog, if I may say so.'

And I could feel Thane wince as he continued, 'A small dog like a pug would have seemed more appropriate.'

At that Thane shook himself and with a haughty look in Hayward's direction made what would have been in human fashion a dignified exit in the direction of the kitchen.

Mr Hayward watched him and sighed, 'Better than a houseful of cats, though. Yes, a definite improvement. Can't stand the creatures, smelly brutes. Place for animals is outside, not indoors.'

I wouldn't have gone that far, I thought, closing the door on him and avoiding the creaky board which so irritated me as I entered the kitchen.

His visit had given me much to think about, particularly Hedley Marsh. Now I had a clearer picture of the old man, the recluse taking solace for his loneliness by surrounding himself with an army of cats, investing in qualities of loyalty and devotion above human frailty and betrayal.

Tomorrow I would visit Duddingston. Amy would be agog with news, and I thought of the Frenchman who had doubtless been taken only for questioning, dramatically interpreted as an arrest by Amy. But even returned as innocent, untold harm would have been done to his already damaged reputation. Poor fellow, shy and retiring, stripped of dignity, questioned, perhaps even threatened, for no other crime than preferring his own society to that of gossipy neighbours who wanted to know all his business.

Perhaps he was Mrs Lawers' killer, but I doubted that; my money was on the bullying man Amy had seen and his accomplice, the bogus Miss Hinton.

My thoughts turned to another Frenchman, Simon Reslaw. A Jacobite spy living in Lord Tweeddale's household in 1745. John Lawers had mentioned an ancestor who had served with the prince. Could Simon Reslaw and Justin Lawers be one and the same?

A feeling of triumph. Someone in that family had passed down the secret of the Lawers legacy and generations of them had been searching for its whereabouts in vain ever since.

And that led me to the intriguing question of the fugitive in the secret room of Solomon's Tower one and a half centuries ago – was his name Simon Reslaw, aka Justin Lawers, and where had he hidden thirty thousand pounds?

But as I climbed the stairs that night, I touched the panel that operated the door to the secret room, which I had not mentioned to Hayward. It wasn't my secret, somehow, and I was cautious, even nervous about imparting that information to anyone. Ominous, even scary by night, I had never been anxious to cross its threshold even in daylight, where so little penetrated the gloom from the long narrow window invisible from outside, unlike in my cheerful room next door.

Preparing for bed, I wondered if Hedley Marsh knew of its existence. Mr Hayward had given me plenty to think about regarding Vince's lifelong bitterness, the inescapable blight of the stamp of illegitimacy, which had clung like a shroud through his formative years. How different it might have been, not only for Vince but for Pappa, who had married his mother and given her boy an education.

And for the rest of us. Had Hedley found his Lizzie, she would never have met Pappa. Emily and I would never have been born.

It made me shiver.

Should I tell Vince that he had wasted a lifetime's anger based on hatred for the unknown man who had fathered him and wronged his mother, when the truth was that his conception was worthy of any novelette? Not a sordid interlude but a tragic reality. He was not the result of rape but a love child whose father had, over the years, sought his mother in vain.

Hedley Marsh must have often seen Vince, first as a small boy playing near the Tower, then as a young man, a student heading towards the golf course with his friends, when a closer look had made him suspect the truth. Shyly, slyly even, he had tried to strike up a further acquaintance. But Vince hated and detested the old man who seemed to fawn upon him.

Would revealing too late the reason why he had been bequeathed Solomon's Tower merely add another surge of guilt for his treatment of Hedley Marsh? Glad now I had not heard this story before Vince's visit, I resolved to keep it to myself while wondering if Pappa, who had visited Hedley Marsh in his last days, knew the truth and had also kept silent.

Solomon's Tower, my home, was becoming a house of mystery – like the skin of an onion, revealing its secrets layer by layer, one by one. What others lay in store, patiently awaiting discovery?

CHAPTER TWENTY-SIX

We were in for one of our dramatic changes of weather. I awoke to look out of the window and discover that Arthur's Seat was enveloped in thick mist. I was trapped in a cotton-wool world. Nothing beyond the windows but a great white shroud. A silence that penetrated everywhere.

Opening the back door it was as if in that soundless world all life had been extinguished. Not even a seabird, a skein of wild geese or swans flying over to feed on St Margaret's Loch. The garden birds were mute. None of the usual daily noises, the echo of a train's whistle approaching Waverley, or horses' hooves on the way to Duddingston.

I always found this claustrophobic world quite

terrifying, with not the slightest notion of when Arthur's Seat would become visible again and I would breathe in the clear air, a captive released from prison.

This phenomenon fortunately only happened twice or thrice a year and I had it explained, my limited knowledge of science taking in only that it had something to do with cold and warm air meeting, in clouds sailing in from the Firth of Forth.

That sounded innocent enough until encountered first-hand. I knew people had been lost on Arthur's Seat, had stumbled on rabbit holes, lain for hours with limbs seriously injured, or had fallen to their deaths from Salisbury Crags, caught out in the sudden descent of such weather.

Normally Thane didn't like it either and showed no desire to leave my side, or the comfort of the peat fire, but today was different. Unperturbed for once, he let himself out by lifting the latch with his nose, to be immediately swallowed up by the swirling white mist.

I didn't like being left alone in the Tower and realised that this sinister weather added to my feeling of vulnerability, a condition that had worsened considerably since the break-in – the burglary that never was.

In a curious way I would have felt less uneasy

if he had stolen something, but the fact remained that he had come for a definite purpose and, having failed, he would come again.

With that in mind, I kept my derringer in the deep pocket of my bicycling garments, well adapted to conceal a small weapon. During the night I slept with it under my pillow.

Hoping that Thane would not stay out long, after tidying the kitchen I made up my bed. But he was still missing when I returned downstairs.

I opened the door a fraction, to stare into that eerie white blanket which threatened to engulf me. I was indeed a prisoner until the mist lifted or at least thinned enough to see my hand before my face. There was no way I could go anywhere. Bicycling would simply deposit me in the nearest ditch in this invisible world.

All I could do was find household tasks to employ my enforced idleness, avoiding that creaking floorboard which was getting worse.

I darted a moment's resentment towards the absent Jack enjoying the comfort and well-being of his parents' house while simple domestic matters in his own home went untended.

Taking out the two portions of the map Mr Hayward had left, I spread them side by side on the table. The missing piece intrigued me, especially as I knew from the map he had produced that it contained Solomon's Tower. And remembering

Simon, aka Justin, I decided on another search of the secret room.

Perhaps I would find that missing thirty thousand pounds, but I wasn't exactly hopeful as I carried an oil lamp and some candles upstairs and opened the panel into the secret room.

A grim and unprepossessing sight, hardly lighter by daytime than when I had abandoned the idea last night. The illumination provided by my battery of lights was minute indeed.

I persevered with my search, pushed aside an ancient chair and a table. There was no bed; whoever slept here had to make his own provision. The deserting Jacobite or Hanoverian had most likely slept on the floor – Jack and I had found the remains of a palliasse on first entering the room – wrapped in the uniform cape which he had left behind in his hurried departure.

I tried to reconstruct that scene from a hundred and fifty years ago as I walked gently across the wooden floor searching for a loose board, but, even down on my hands and knees, detected none that might be concealing thirty thousand pounds – that vast and unimaginable fortune.

I tried a quick calculation – and failed – of its present staggering value. Turning my attention to a set of shelves in a recess originally intended to house a fireplace, but abandoned for lack of a chimney—

I was interrupted. Suddenly I heard a muffled sound, a creaking board. I listened. The echo came from downstairs. There was someone in the Tower.

I panicked. I was alone. Where was Thane?

Extinguishing lamp and candles, I closed the panel and with my hand on the derringer went soft-footed down the spiral stair through the Great Hall and into the kitchen.

There was a man, a stranger, tall with his back towards me, leaning against the table, his deep breathing erratic.

An injured man.

But he wasn't to be taken by surprise. He heard my approach – damn those boards – and turned. 'Good day, madame.'

'What do you want?' I demanded.

He staggered forward, tried a bow, but without the support of the table, almost fell and I found myself face-to-face with the Frenchie, Mrs Lawers' obnoxious neighbour and the most hated man in Duddingston.

Alarms were sounding – was I now trapped by a murderer, a man arrested by the police but who had escaped? My hand tightened on the concealed gun, but wait a moment – Thane was there standing beside him.

Where were the threatening barks, showing

his teeth, leaping up at this stranger he had let into the Tower? I gave him a reproachful glare. He was certainly slipping of late. First the burglar, now an escaped convict. At this rate I'd soon be protecting him.

On second glance, the fugitive didn't look as if he would be capable of attacking anyone. He looked quite awful, his jacket torn, clutching an injured wrist. His right hand bleeding.

Thane came over, whimpered gently. He was trying to tell me something.

The fugitive tried another bow. 'I do beg pardon, madame, for intruding on your property. I am afraid it was necessary.' He pointed to the window. 'I have been out on the hill all night.'

I thought of him lost and bewildered in that mist-shroud as he paused and indicated Thane. 'Your fine dog here found me this morning and led me here.' He shook his head. 'He seemed to know my distress; my wrist – I fear it is broken. I fell several times. The mist, you know. I had no idea.'

He stopped again, his eyes on Thane, and I thought of the police station at Central Office. Imagined the alarm, saw him followed by armed police, hunted down as he slipped from their grip, escaped, trying to reach safety. Where was that? Home to Duddingston with those angry neighbours thirsting for his blood.

'You must have walked some distance,' I said. I'd take a chance on him. He certainly did not look threatening, nursing that wrist, hardly able to stand with weariness and certainly no match for a deerhound and a woman with a gun.

As I put on the kettle, started the porridge, cut bread, I went back and forth to the table, but he never moved, statue-like, staring in front of him. A man in late middle age who was younger than the straggling beard implied, hair too long, unshaven, one cheek grazed and sore-looking, from a fall no doubt. A pathetic sight, too weary to put words together.

'Please sit down and I will give you some refreshment.'

He almost fell into the chair. As for Thane, he had retreated to his rug but was taking it all in, contemplating the scene. I was safe enough; one word from me, one hint and he would have had that poor shivering creature by the throat down on the floor.

'I will take a look at that wrist while we wait,' I said.

He stirred. 'Please, madame, do not exert yourself on my account. It is nothing.'

I ignored him and filled a basin with warm water, took out ointment and a bandage. He made no resistance as I took his arm gently, rolled back a shirtsleeve grey and much frayed. He winced as I took his wrist very gently.

'It isn't broken, sir. The cut isn't deep. It will soon respond to this salve and should no longer be troubling you in a few days.' The ointment was in constant use for my frequent bicycling bruises.

He nodded, a relieved smile. As I set the porridge before him, poured out cups of tea, he looked at me and sighed. 'You are so very kind, madame, the first kindness I have been shown for a very long time.'

And I saw through his tired eyes, those suspicious neighbours, even the normally kindly Amy Dodd, the whispering campaign he had endured for years, all because he was different – a foreigner. And I felt the loneliness, the desolation that Hedley Marsh had also known in this very house. But for M Debeau there was no solace of an army of cats to share his four-poster bed at night.

He ate eagerly, hungrily, accepting more porridge and bread.

'How did you come to be on the hill, sir? It is a long way from town.' I found myself talking with that careful enunciation as if he didn't understand English.

'The town, madame? You are mistaken. I left my own home just down the road to take a walk last night.' He stopped, frowned. 'There has been an unfortunate incident next door to where I live, two poor ladies died in what your police call "suspicious circumstances". We have all been questioned, but for some reason they took me to the station for more questions.'

And why was that, why was he selected? I thought angrily. Because his neighbours had voiced their suspicions, added fuel to what little fire existed.

'The police brought me home again, but those who live nearby were very angry at this. They are afraid of me and threw stones, knocked at my door and shouted.'

He paused. 'I was afraid of them. I could not stay in the house. I had to escape so I went out on to the hill. I walked and climbed; it was not until too late I saw the mist. It came on very quickly and soon I was lost. I could see no path, I stumbled, fell, hit my head. I thought I had broken my wrist and perhaps had a more serious injury, for the blow to my head knocked me unconscious for a while.'

He stopped, looked across at Thane.

'I was very cold and scared when this great beast appeared, I tried to shoo him away. But no, he came to my side, ran forward a few steps, turned, looked at me – as if he was beckoning – then he repeated this performance and I thought he might be trying to help me.'

He smiled, shook his head. 'I might have died out there, had it not been for that dog of yours. He saved me.'

I looked at the window. The mist was unlikely to rise immediately and it seemed that my unexpected guest would be trapped here for some time. Realising that I was in no danger from this harmless man, who I suspected was more sinned against than sinner, I wanted to know more about him.

Asking how he came to live in Duddingston, he smiled sadly. 'Ah, that is a long story. My late wife was Scottish. We met in Paris but she never liked France and always longed for home. We never had children but we were very happy, very close, and when she died I felt the need to be with her . . .' He paused, searching for the right word. 'I felt entirely lost without her and thought I might find her spirit . . . be close again . . . in the place where she had grown up and loved so dearly.

'For a while I stayed in Musselburgh but moved to Duddingston when the owner of the house I now live in, a much-loved old man, had died. I was prepared to be friendly, but alas!' Again he paused, sighed. 'I must confess that, being childless, I am not particularly fond of small children, particularly the ill-behaved ones. I am a gardener and I cherish flowers and neat lawns. Imagine my distress when my premises were being freely used by children who regarded it as an area for playing football.' A Gallic shrug. 'A few harsh words of protest from me and that was all that was needed. "How dare this foreigner who does not know his place tell us how to live our lives or raise our children? How dare he?" I regret to say, considering what has recently happened, the tragic accident, that Mrs Lawers was the main voice against me.'

He stopped, again smiled sadly. 'That is the story, madame, and I realise that I must leave my little home – reluctantly – as soon as I can find other accommodation.'

'Do you like living there?'

'Of course.'

'What about your neighbours, would you be happy to stay if they were friendly?'

Another shrug. 'Either friendly or indifferent. I just wish to be left alone and not . . . not persecuted by them.'

'Then stay – defy them. Don't allow them to drive you away.'

I went to the window again. I could now see as far as the garden wall.

'Good news, the mist is clearing and the road should be visible for you to return home in safety.'

He looked reluctant, almost scared, so I added, 'I will go with you.'

'No need, madame.'

'I have business to conduct with Mrs Dodd and I wish to see Miss Hinton before she leaves.'

He bowed. 'Then I will be grateful for your company. You have been so kind, I can never thank you enough for showing such kindness.'

As I put on my cloak I said, 'If life ever becomes unbearable you are more than welcome to drop in for a chat.'

CHAPTER TWENTY-SEVEN

As I headed along the Duddingston road with M Debeau, there were other travellers who had seized the gap in the mist to resume their daily tasks and I noticed that my bicycle was no longer an object of astonishment. Although still something of a novelty for women, it had become the accepted way of travel for many working men whose journeys lay outside of the local horse omnibus routes. Those who were better off were already considering motor cars to replace their carriages. What would happen to the horses, I thought, if all those hiring gigs became obsolete?

Turning into the Causeway, I saw Amy was in her garden. Her jaw dropped at the sight of the Frenchie walking at my side. He bowed, and unlocking his front door, vanished inside.

Amy stared at me. 'Well – of all things, that takes the biscuit. Never expected to see you talking to that creature.'

Ignoring that I said, 'May we go inside? I have come to see Jane before she leaves.'

'She's out at the moment. Shopping.' Amy's face remained a picture of shocked indignation. 'That man you were with. I'm surprised – we all are – that the police released him. We may now have a murderer on our doorstep. I don't know what they were thinking, threatening our safety.'

We were in the kitchen, and indicating a chair, I said, 'May I?' Still looking cross she sat down opposite and I continued, 'You very nearly had another killing on your hands – all of you good people.'

'What do you mean?'

'I mean, Amy, that by your collective hostility you drove Monsieur Debeau from his house out into a deadly fog on Arthur's Seat where he fell, hurt his wrist and a blow to his head knocked him out. He lay there for hours and could have died from exposure.' I paused. 'How would you all have lived with your consciences then?'

'I don't know what you're on about,' she said huffily.

'Well, listen carefully and find out, if you

please. You're a kind good woman; it isn't in your heart, or I'm sure in your good God-fearing neighbours', to be cruel to man or beast, but you have ganged up against a man just because of his objections to your children and animals ruining his garden.'

She gave a shrug at that. 'Mrs Lawers didn't like him either and look what happened to her.'

'Which had nothing at all to do with him.'

'The police—'

'Were questioning him as they do with all neighbours – indeed, like yourselves.'

'We weren't taken away – arrested.'

'And neither would Monsieur Debeau have been had you not given the police cause for suspicion – hints that he might have been involved.'

Her face reddened. 'Well, it seemed possible.'

'Thane – my dog – rescued him lost in the heavy mist. I bandaged up his wrist and gave him some breakfast – and in return he told me his story.'

She listened, frowning as I told her about the Scottish wife dying and so forth. At the end she said, 'Well . . .' And looking a little ashamed, 'It was his own fault, though. He should have told us.'

The door opened and Jane entered, unloading a bevy of parcels. 'All to take home. Edinburgh is such a good place to shop – I envy you.'

The conversation was general after that, and as I prepared to leave, she said, 'I'm sorry I couldn't be more help about Aunty's letters and all. The police returned them, and when I get home I'll reread and see if there is anything useful.'

Amy said, 'There's the pageant about Prince Charlie at the Pleasance Theatre on Saturday. The Portobello Players do it every year around the time of the Battle of Prestonpans. It's quite an occasion and the Duddingston folk support it. Will you be going?'

It sounded splendid and I promised to be there.

As I shook hands with Jane, she said, 'Such a pity I missed the chance to see your lovely Tower – I've passed by it so often on the road.'

I looked at Amy who had never been inside either. 'If you have time before you leave, why don't you both come over later and have the tour? Tea will be provided, of course.'

The invitation was eagerly accepted. We all laughed and Amy walked me to the door.

'Thanks for telling me about . . . him.' She gave a contrite glance towards the Frenchman's house. Shaking her head, she added, 'If he had told us all this in the first place, it would have been different. But he was always so aloof, seemed to think himself too good for us.'

I took her arm. 'For "aloof" read "shy", Amy. Make it different now. Try and make it up to him.'

She smiled. 'We could make a start by inviting him to the Jacobite play.'

'Good idea, a nice friendly overture.'

And I left her, wondering if Beth's Adrian, a member of the Portobello Players, would deign to take part in the village drama.

In the Tower I decided, as I was to have visitors, I might bake a few pancakes, the one domestic activity I excelled at. I had just completed the first batch when the rusty front doorbell rang.

I glanced at the clock – I hadn't been expecting Amy and Jane this early – and opened the door to Beth. As always, she was full of apologies for this informal visit, gabbling that her news was important and the next day postal service too long.

She followed me through to the kitchen, and declining my offer of tea said, 'Adrian and I have made it up, Rose. We are betrothed again. He is so sorry that he had doubts, all because he wasn't sure that he could support a wife.'

Her face darkened for a moment. 'I always suspected that he was influenced by Steven – his actor friend. As you know, he also boards with Nanny and I'm afraid he absolutely disapproves of me.'

'What makes you think that?'

She shook her head. 'It's not in what he says, he

is always polite, even a bit flirtatious sometimes. But I know what he is really thinking – that I am too young and silly for Adrian and his career.'

Pausing, she looked at me. 'It's quite an instinctive feeling one gets about some people, especially ones like Steven, who despite his good manners, objects to a baby in the house.'

She sighed. 'But now I'm sure Adrian's determination has overcome Steven's objections, especially as he is sure that his expectations are about to reach fulfilment. He is very excited but says it is still a secret – he wants to surprise me with it. Oh Rose, I just had to tell you. I knew you would rejoice with me at this change in my fortunes, this great news.'

I said I was happy for her and she took my hand. 'I knew you would understand, and I've arranged for Adrian to meet me here. I hope you don't mind.'

I said of course not. I was keen to meet Adrian.

'He is at rehearsals at the Pleasance Theatre just now. We will take the local train back home.' She paused, a relieved laugh. 'He knows all about you.' And wagging a finger at me, she said archly, 'You are a sly puss, Rose!'

'I beg your pardon!'

'Not telling me about yourself or your famous father and a stepbrother in royal circles. I am so impressed.'

That left me wondering how on earth she had come by all this information. I had not even told her that I was a lady investigator. Waiting a moment for my reactions, she went on, 'Adrian and Steven are friendly with a policeman who works with your detective.' She paused. 'When I heard that Inspector Macmerry was a widower with a little girl, I realised why you had such sympathy for my plight.' Touching my arm, she smiled sadly. 'As I do for your own – I mean, you not being married.'

I was embarrassed, taken aback and more than a little keen to know more about this overfriendly policeman who knew so much about Jack and me.

But it was not to be. A ring at the bell announced the arrival of my next batch of visitors. Amy and Jane.

Introductions were duly made, polite questions and answers exchanged and my batch of pancakes, buttered and jammed, ready to be demolished.

Feeling intensely gratified, I decided this unusual occasion was worthy of the grandeur of the Great Hall which Amy and Jane were keen to see.

Beth, keen to help, abandoned her pretty shawl and helped carry the trays through from the kitchen. All at once it seemed everyone was happy and getting on well, the atmosphere warm and cheerful, my pancakes duly praised and eaten, recipe demanded. Very domestic, the sort of things ladies talk about and I have always missed out on somehow.

It was all going very well, the last of the pancakes brought forth. I wished I had baked more. Thane would be sorry, shy of tea parties, that there were no leftovers, a rare treat.

A ring at the front door. Another arrival.

Beth smiled. 'That will be Adrian. Shall I?'

She rushed through the hall, opened the door to the tall young man whose exceptional good looks and attractive voice declared his profession as an actor. I could see him as Hamlet.

As I went off to the kitchen to refill the teapot, Beth was proudly introducing the newcomer as 'my fiancé'.

When I returned I discovered that the merry atmosphere, the laughter, had dissolved into silences broken by the occasional polite remark.

Amy was sitting very still, biting her lip and looking uncomfortable while Jane was endeavouring to engage a rather preoccupied Adrian into chat about the theatre, overlooked by Beth watching them narrowly and looking anxious. Everyone seemed ill at ease – all except me, blissfully unaware of the cause of this changed atmosphere, which I put down to Adrian's entrance and the ladies perhaps being a little overawed by an unexpected meeting with the handsome actor.

Adrian declined tea. He had just eaten, and smiling rather forcedly, said they must go or there wasn't another local train for an hour.

Amy and Jane exchanged glances, indicating that perhaps they should go too. Beth said, 'Please, ladies, don't let me spoil your party.' Farewells exchanged, she took Adrian's arm, and as I opened the front door, she said, 'Oh, I have left my shawl.'

'I will get it,' Adrian said.

I watched as Adrian headed in the direction of the kitchen and briskly retrieved the shawl from a chair. Returning to the front hall, where Beth was waiting to give me a hug, Adrian gave a smile and a bow and they both promised to come again.

I closed the door and returned to the Great Hall where Amy and Jane were waiting to depart.

'A handsome chap,' said Jane. 'Very interesting life. Loved his voice.' And to me, 'Did Amy ever tell you she used to teach elocution?' Amy's smile in response was somewhat strained. She looked at me very intently, opened her mouth and closed it again.

I gave them the promised tour. They were impressed by that, pronounced it great, lovely and all the other flattering adjectives which would make stones blush if they were capable of such emotions.

Downstairs again, the front door open, Jane said, 'Well, Amy, shall we go?' as her friend hesitated on the doorstep.

In answer Amy looked at Jane and at me as if something was bothering her and she didn't know how to express it.

Suddenly she straightened her shoulders, gave me a hug and thanked me for having them, and Jane said again what a pleasure it had been – Beth and Adrian, such a nice couple.

Amy looked merely bewildered and I got the impression she didn't share Jane's enthusiasm. Beth had talked so glowingly about her baby Lillie, perhaps Amy was shocked as, in her conventional way, she had presumed Adrian to be Beth's husband and was taken aback to have him introduced as her fiancé.

The afternoon was over. I wondered what had been bothering Amy, because something about that visit was bothering me too. I would very much like to know the identity of this policeman who had passed on to Adrian and Steven so much information about our very private lives.

It could only be Wright, recently new to Jack's team at the Central Office. This was a major indiscretion that would not readily be forgiven by his inspector, or overlooked when it came to recommendation for his promotion.

CHAPTER TWENTY-EIGHT

Alone once more, I decided to resume my activities in the secret room where those ancient floorboards didn't creak.

And that triggered another thought: a picture of Adrian gallantly retrieving Beth's shawl from the kitchen. From where I stood at the door, the offending floorboard could not be heard and yet I had heard it clearly from the secret room when M Debeau entered the kitchen far below.

This was strange; Jack and I had long since discovered, when trying to communicate with each other, shouting was of no avail when confronted by high ceilings and stone walls, and since it was impossible to hear anything from rooms on the same level downstairs, there must be a secret to this puzzle.

A hidden device. And I had the probable explanation.

A 'laird's lug'. This crafty installation, hidden by the chimney in ancient Scottish castles, enabling the laird to listen in to the conversations of his guests or enemies in the dining room downstairs, had possibly been intended by an early resident of the Tower. However, as no chimney had ever been installed in the secret room, there was no laird's lug or listening tube visible.

After a careful but futile search I gave up and returned downstairs. The house seemed so empty and echoing after my cheerful tea party. I heard a train go by on the nearby Innocent Railway – so named because no one had been killed or injured in its construction! – carrying goods and passengers to Dalkeith.

I hoped Beth and Adrian had caught the local Musselburgh train and wished I felt more confident about their future. It was interesting to know that I would see Adrian and his friend Steven taking part in the Prestonpans play.

With that in mind I sat down where the light was still good and spread Mrs Lawers' documents on the kitchen table, along with the two pieces of map, minus the missing middle section. With the use of a magnifying glass, it seemed quite definite that the whole map had been drawn by the same hand and detailed the rough grouping of the battle plans – the various clans involved and the possible placements of the Hanoverians, the latter provided by Jacobite spies like Simon Reslaw, who had infiltrated Sir John Cope's army.

The magnifying glass also made clearer the words at the base of both pieces of the map.

'Slow Moon Store' on the left hand. 'Simon's Brass' on the right. The former meant nothing, but the second was more meaningful. 'Simon' was the first name of the Jacobite spy; could 'Brass' refer to the thirty thousand he had stolen from Lord Tweeddale? My great sense of triumph rapidly faded when I realised that this plausible interpretation of 'Brass' did not bring me any nearer to solving the riddle. It merely added yet another dimension. If only we had the missing section and what decisive words, if any, it contained.

If only Jack were here.

The wretched mist had descended from Arthur's Seat once again, as so often happened, and I went to bed, my head buzzing with the day's events. Thinking of poor misunderstood M Debeau, it suddenly occurred to me that while we were in the realm of confidants he might have been the obvious person to interpret those letters, written by his fellow countryman a century and a half ago.

Then I went over my visit to Amy and the slightly vain hope that Jane's reappraisal of her aunt's letters would produce more clues to Mrs Lawers' odd behaviour other than the suggestion of approaching senility.

Another thought. Had her attitude to M Debeau been dictated by the fact that he was a Frenchman who had come to live next door and might have some sinister connection with the dangers that threatened her legacy?

I wasn't likely to find the answer to that one now that she had gone. I remembered that Amy had also had the vague impression that Mrs Lawers' confrontation with the bullying man involved him going on about his rights, which would suggest that he was no stranger and might be distantly related.

Next morning, after a restless night, I awoke to a balmy sunny day. The mist had lifted and I desperately needed fresh air and exercise. A quick breakfast, then with Thane loping along the verge of the road, we headed in the direction of the loch.

Suddenly he was rushing ahead, nose down. Ten yards ahead, he stopped, turned, looked at me.

'What's wrong? What have you found?'

I reached his side and on the steep slope down

to the loch, at the side of a small tree which had halted its descent into the sun-sparkling waters, a still, huddled shape.

A body.

Even before scrambling down for a closer examination, I knew what to expect.

There had been another death on the road outside Solomon's Tower.

While I was considering going back for my bicycle, riding into town to notify the police, a cart appeared labouring up the hill from the loch. I stopped the farmer, told him about the accident.

'I think he's dead.'

'Better have a look, might just be injured,' said the farmer, who leapt down the slope. I followed after and watched as he knelt down and turned over the dead man.

He was a tall youngish man. The farmer sighed, took off his bonnet and reverently closed the bright, clear blue eyes, still wide open in death.

The farmer shook his head sadly. 'Poor laddie. Probably drinking too much, got lost in that damned fog last night, staggered and missed his footing. I signed the pledge years since, but I've lads of my own.'

To my question he nodded, 'Aye, lass, I'm for the town. I'll let the police know, but first things first.' I waited while he went for a sack to cover the body.

I knew I had seen eyes like that before. The eyes visible below the helmet of the bogus policeman who had lured me to the hospital to ransack the Tower.

I felt suddenly very sick. I had met my burglar again.

I must have looked shocked for the farmer said, 'Don't upset yourself, lass. You go on home; the police will know what to do about this.' He had never heard of Rose McQuinn, lady investigator.

Still preoccupied with the identity of the dead man and his connection with the break-in, I returned to the Tower, alert for the arrival of the police. I didn't have long to wait.

A police carriage hurtled past and a short while afterwards I opened the door to a couple of uniformed policemen led by Chief Inspector Gray. He bowed politely.

'Have you a moment, Mrs McQuinn?'

I indicated that he follow me into the kitchen.

He sat down at the table, studied me with that intent gaze which must have disconcerted many an innocent man as well as the guilty.

'Just a few questions. I gather you discovered the body . . .'

Gray asked me to go through the details again.

When I finished with the arrival of the farmer, he repeated, perhaps for the benefit of the policeman who stood by with his notebook at the ready, 'A man's body found on the roadside, just at the corner where the road goes steeply down to the loch. I presume he was a stranger to the area.'

I wanted to say 'not quite', but bit back the words, utterance of which would have led into a long preamble. I shook my head and asked, 'Have you identified him?'

'Not yet. No papers or anything like that. But we'll soon find out.'

'Nothing in his pockets?'

Gray gave me a hard look. 'That's elementary police work, Mrs McQuinn.' A touch of scorn.

In defence I said, 'I just thought it unusual. He was well dressed; I would have guessed from my cursory look that he would be carrying money, a wallet perhaps.'

'Well, this gentleman had empty pockets, not even a watch chain. It was most likely an accidental death. Drunk perhaps, fell out of a carriage in the fog. Or walking, hit by a passing carriage.'

My mind was racing ahead. 'If it wasn't an accident, he could have been attacked, knocked unconscious, any valuables stolen and then pushed down the slope, his assailant hoping he would land in the loch. His body entangled in weeds could have lain there undiscovered for some time.'

Gray sighed wearily. He was not impressed. 'These are idle speculations, Mrs McQuinn.

Circumstantial evidence,' he reminded me, and I guessed, although he was being painstakingly polite, he found my questions rather irritating.

He nodded to the policeman, who closed his notebook. The interview was over. I wasn't a suspect.

'Anything else I can do for you?'

He stood up. 'You'll need to sign a statement. Your house is the nearest habitation and you were the first on the scene and discovered the body, down that steep slope to the loch. Surely a rather dangerous descent for a young woman.'

He gave me a quizzical look and I said, 'It was my dog here who discovered the body, not I. I only guessed something was amiss and went down to inspect in case the person was merely injured.'

Thane had sat by my side, a silent observer to this meeting, glancing from one to the other as if he understood exactly what was being said. Very polite and respectful, he had the measure of CI Gray and made no overtures of friendliness to this man who had so far ignored his presence but now gave him a sharp glance followed by a dismissive shrug.

Then to me a thin smile. 'Apologies for taking up your time, but as you will be familiar in your own work, the evidence of the first *person*' – he emphasised the word – 'on the scene is of vital importance.' Another pause, a quizzical eyebrow raised. 'If you have anything to add?'

He hadn't asked directly if I recognised the body and I certainly wasn't prepared to tell him that the dead man was the bogus policeman who had lured me to the hospital to visit Jack, then broken into the Tower but stolen nothing.

That was my investigation, mine to solve and I wasn't prepared to have him take it off my hands.

More significant, I thought of M Debeau's arrival – his distraught and dishevelled appearance – but closed my mind firmly on that. I had one more question. 'When did this happen?'

A weary sigh from Gray, eager to be gone. 'Our police doctor speculates sometime during the hours of last night.'

That let M Debeau off. This was Thursday. I did a quick calculation. It was on Tuesday that M Debeau staggered into the Tower lost and injured in the heavy mist on Arthur's Seat. It cleared during the day but came down again last night and set the stage for a further victim. And although M Debeau lived in nearby Duddingston and had been detained by Inspector Gray for questioning in connection with the deaths of Mrs Lawers and Hinton, it was highly unlikely that the Frenchman had recovered sufficiently from his ordeal to tackle the mist once again as the bogus policeman's killer.

I followed Gray to the door, where his two men were lingering by the gate. They were grinning at some secret joke but the approach of the chief inspector wiped the smiles off their faces.

They saluted him, turned and looked me over with an interest that suggested I had been under discussion and they knew that I was the woman who lived with Inspector Macmerry. I wondered what else was common knowledge and whether either of them knew the actors' friend who had passed on so many details of Jack's personal life.

Gray turned. 'Interesting old house, Mrs McQuinn. Wasn't sure whether you'd be at home. Thought you might have gone down to the Borders with Jack.'

I smiled. 'Not this time.'

'You'll have him home very soon. We had a letter, telling us to expect him back for duty at the beginning of the week.'

That was nice, I thought, closing the door, especially as I hadn't had as much as a postcard. To be truthful, business was business with Jack and I hadn't expected one.

CHAPTER TWENTY-NINE

That evening I was still battling with deciphering the map and the other documents spread out on the table in the Great Hall and making notes. Had it a connection with the dead man, my bogus policeman? Then from the kitchen a familiar voice. 'Anyone at home?'

'Jack!'

I rushed through and he had hardly time to put down his case before my arms were around his neck.

He grinned. 'You missed me.'

'Yes! Let me look at you. Well, you certainly look as if you've had a good rest; I'm relieved to see that.'

'Ma's cooking, good fresh air, that's the ticket – you should try it sometime.'

I promised to do so and he said quickly, 'She sends you her love, talks a lot about you.' I acknowledged this with a grateful smile and he added, 'Any tea forthcoming?'

In his favourite armchair stretching out his legs with a sigh of contentment that indicated he was happy to be home, he added, 'What news?'

'Just that there's been a body found near the loch – this morning.'

'Yes, victim of another of Arthur's Seat's seasonal mists, I gather.'

'You gather? You knew?'

He nodded. 'Looked into the Central Office on my way home. Just to keep up with events. I gather you were asked a lot of questions by Gray.' He grinned. 'Did they line you up as a possible suspect – first on the scene, that sort of thing?'

'Thane was first on the scene.'

He laughed. 'Well, you know the rules – always the person nearest or the one who finds the body.'

'So they think it is murder? I thought Gray was regarding it as an accident.'

He shook his head. 'They're just biding their time. What with the Duddingston business, perhaps being overcautious. And they have yet to find the man's identity.'

I looked at Jack; at that moment more than any other I wanted to tell him about the break-in, the bogus policeman. But I hesitated as I had with

Gray. Had I told Jack the morning he was leaving for his parents, he would have insisted that he stay. Worse, he would have insisted that this was police business. More questions from Gray. And there had been nothing stolen; my standing with the chief inspector, already one of scorn, was hardly going to improve with a tale of a break-in I couldn't prove, the burglar a bogus policeman I couldn't identify. I could see even Jack's reactions – his doubts, hints that I was becoming obsessive about the Lawers legacy.

After all, I had never been in any danger apart from that first train journey. I would tell him sometime, but not until I had solved the case. I said merely, 'I found the absence of a wallet or a watch chain in a well-dressed man very suspicious.'

Jack nodded in agreement. 'The absence of identity fits in with robbery and murder. The killer disposing of his body by throwing him down the slope into the loch, to be found, at some future date, drowned.'

He paused to eat the sandwich I had provided. 'Good this! Seen Meg, have you?'

I told him of Mrs Blakers unannounced visit with Meg when he was away and her invitation that we go and see them when he returned. He nodded approvingly but was quick to change the subject and said, 'I gather from the office there's absolutely nothing new on Mrs Lawers.'

I smiled watching him eat. There were quite a lot of new developments from my point of view. 'Mr Hayward's help about the map has been invaluable. When you've finished, it's all spread out on the big table through there.'

He put a delaying hand on my arm. 'First, all I've missed. Bring me up to date – right back to the beginning. When I was in hospital this business of the legacy and your attempts to deliver it – what really happened, Rose?'

So I told him then, somewhat reluctantly, about the attack on the train by the bogus maid Hinton.

He was even more horrified and concerned than I had expected.

'You are quite certain she drugged your tea in the station?'

'Well, it's very unlikely that I fell asleep on that short journey.'

Jack shook his head and said sternly, 'This is a police case, Rose. You should have told me—'

'And you would have told me to call it off.'

'Then you should have gone straight to Gray.'

'And faced his arch sneers about my imagination? No, thank you. This was my problem, it's what I do for a living, remember. You know me better than this, Jack. My case, and I was going to investigate it. Especially when both the women were murdered.'

'And you were likely to be the next on the killer's list,' Jack added grimly. 'Yes, you do thrive on danger – I've seen evidence of that with my own eyes. So you went back again, in spite of it all.'

'I was armed – with my derringer, this time.'

Jack sighed deeply as I added, 'To find that the relative who refused to accept the legacy in the first place had died of a heart attack. I fared no better at Tarnbrae. It will be news to you, but Meg's uncle has remarried.'

I told him about the new wife and the four children and said, 'Meg had been moved into the Lochandor orphanage and then to Edinburgh, just down the road at Newington. I felt quite heartened by that, so near to us. But no, another false trail; she had been moved once again, this time settled with prospective adoptive parents. You can imagine my relief when I met her happily installed with the Blakers in Joppa.'

Jack's head jerked up. 'That was your first meeting? What did you think of her?' he asked anxiously.

I took his hand. 'Jack dear, she's your image, I would have picked her out in a hundred children as your daughter. Same eyes, same smile, even your sandy hair.'

'Poor kid. Not destined to be a great beauty.'

'She's lovely.'

He grinned and I knew that he was pleased – and under it all, I sensed a feeling of relief. Babies all look alike, even to fathers, but a little girl aged three is a person, and when they met Jack would know now, without doubt, that he had fathered her. He said, 'We must go and see her.'

'I thought you were calling in at Joppa on the way back.'

'Wanted to see you,' he said quickly, but he was uncomfortable. It was a lie, a nice one specially for my benefit, but I wasn't the reason for his change of mind. He was on a cliff edge, scared of his possible reception by his little daughter. What if she didn't recognise him, turned away from him? No, he wanted – needed – support when they met for the first time in her new home.

Watching me pour another cup of tea, he asked, 'Any more adventures to report?'

I told him about the meeting with Beth and her extraordinary story about the switched babies. 'I was beginning to remember all those terrible tales about baby farmers in the eighties.'

'The police haven't forgotten, Rose. They are keeping a close eye on places like Lochandor Convalescent Home, especially where there is an orphanage attached for unwanted babies.'

I was relieved to hear that and we went through to the Great Hall with the pieces of the map spread on the table.

'They certainly seem to be part of the same map, with a piece cut out from the centre,' Jack said.

'I don't know if there are words on that missing piece, but look at this . . .' And I gave him the magnifying glass to study the words 'Slow Moon Store' and 'Simon's Brass'.

As he studied them thoughtfully I said, 'They must be significant. Simon was the first name of the Jacobite spy, according to the evidence of Lord Tweeddale's letters to the Court of Enquiry. And 'Brass' could refer to the thirty thousand pounds he stole from Pinkie House and carried to Prince Charlie.'

Jack put down the glass and I went on slowly, 'This might interest you: Reslaw was his second name. Rearrange the letters, and behold! You get Lawers.'

'Good girl – I'd never have thought of that and it's so obvious.' Leaning over he kissed me: my reward!

We both looked at the words again and I wrote them down.

'Slow Moon Store – wait a minute. That's Solomon's Tower.'

Jack was writing busily. 'Rearrange the letters of Simon's Brass and we get an anagram of Samson's Ribs.'

We hugged each other and looked at the map again.

Jack whistled. 'We've got it, Rose, the answer – the missing piece of the map. Samson's Ribs with Solomon's Tower. And that's here – where Reslaw hid the treasure.'

'So now we have a clue to the identity of our fugitive in the secret room. None other than Simon Reslaw – who had cheated both Hanoverians and Jacobites and made off with thirty thousand pounds.'

We stood up in one movement. Jack took my hand.

'It must be up there – in the secret room. Come on!'

We seized oil lamp and candles, raced up the spiral stair, opened the panel into that dark forbidding room and looked around. Stone walls, a chair and table, a few shelves in a recess, my hiding place for the documents the burglar sought in vain.

Jack set the oil lamp on the table. 'Thirty thousand pounds is a lot of money. What was it in – coin? No. Most likely paper, eighteenth-century promissory notes.'

'Then there is always the possibility that our fugitive took it with him.'

'I wonder. His hiding place in the tower had been rumbled. He was being hunted, his pursuers on the premises, literally at his heels. Left in a tearing hurry, without his officer's cape or the map.'

Jack paused, looked around. 'Didn't want to risk losing all that money by having it found on him. My guess would be that he hid it somewhere – in this room – intending to come back for it later. But where?'

There weren't many hiding places. And we got no further. Someone downstairs, at the kitchen door. A voice. 'Anyone there?'

Seizing the oil lamp and blowing out the candles, we closed the panel, and as we raced down the spiral stair, Jack said, 'How on earth did we hear that so clearly?' And I remembered he didn't know about the laird's lug.

Sergeant Wright was standing at the open kitchen door. He saluted us both.

'Chief inspector would like to see you, sir, down the road – at our investigation. If you have a moment.'

Jack groaned, seized his coat, realising it would take more than the promised one moment.

He kissed me briefly and was gone.

Deciding I had better return to our unfinished task, wishing I'd had time to delay Sergeant Wright and find out if he was the policeman friend of Adrian and Steven who knew so much about Jack and me, I had another caller.

This time I opened the door to Beth.

'Rose, I am sorry to call on you so informally

but I have two tickets for the Jacobite evening at the Pleasance and I decided to hand them in to you, in case we don't meet before the performance.'

'I'm sure it will be a great success, very popular.'

'I hope so too, but there are problems. Steven should be playing one of the major roles, but he has taken off to London. Left a note for Adrian, says it's very important, but it really is too bad. Poor Adrian will have all the responsibility if he doesn't get back in time. Typical of Steven, of course.'

She hesitated. 'I can't stay. Nanny is taking care of Lillie – I've been in town with Adrian, but he has rehearsals for the show all day.'

She didn't linger, refused to take payment for the tickets. 'They are with Adrian's compliments; actors always get one or two.'

After she left I considered the tickets, wondering if Jack would like to go, but as a keen Jacobite enthusiast he might be full of caustic comments on what was historically accurate, or, more to the point, inaccurate. And as always, whether he would be my escort on the night depended on the vagaries of Gray and the Edinburgh City Police.

I decided Amy Dodd a better prospect as a companion, although she might have tickets already, and if Jack was free and so inclined, he could accompany us.

CHAPTER THIRTY

I was looking forward to the Portobello Players' performance and in particular to seeing Adrian as the great actor, who Beth solemnly declared was just awaiting discovery and a great future in the London theatre.

Jack came home late that evening; it was past midnight and I was asleep. He crawled into bed trying not to disturb me. I stirred and whispered, 'Goodnight.'

We could talk tomorrow morning. I wakened early, went down and made breakfast. Jack appeared yawning as always after a late night. I told him about Beth's visit and, as I suspected, he wasn't madly interested in the prospect of the Jacobite play but gallantly offered to escort me if I couldn't find a more enthusiastic companion.

As he was singularly preoccupied, very thoughtful and not disposed to conversation, my attempts at resuming our discovery of last night were lost in a tide of words that drifted over his head. He was always like this at some crisis point in a case.

'Tell me about it later, Rose.'

A knock at the door, a brief kiss for me and there was Sergeant Wright waiting for him. I followed them out. At the gate I saw they were heading not towards Edinburgh but in the direction of the loch. Obviously developments of a crucial nature not to be discussed with the general public. In this case, including me.

A calm sunny day, vibrant autumn colours painting the garden. Too nice a day to miss – there wouldn't be many once the fierce icy winter winds blew in from across the Firth.

It really was too good to stay indoors and I wasn't lured by the prospect of a dark sojourn in the secret room. That could wait until Jack and I explored together.

So I got out my bicycle and headed towards Duddingston and Amy Dodd, pausing midway to look down again at the place where Thane had led me to the grim discovery of the still-unidentified body. But the scene was deserted of all humans; only the heron and the wild geese occupied the peaceful waters of the loch.

Amy wasn't at home. I hesitated about leaving the ticket and a note as the chances were that she would have one already, going with some of her friends. There was nothing else for it, Jack would go with me or I'd go alone.

With the extraordinary swiftness of weather changes in Scotland, and over Arthur's Seat in particular, the day turned cold and grey.

The Causewayside street was silent, the houses deserted. Mrs Lawers' house still empty and forlorn-looking, perhaps because of the tragic memories it aroused. There was no sign of M Debeau either, his door firmly closed, and I wondered if my stern talk to Amy had improved matters or if he was still the victim of his neighbours' prejudices and suspicions. I wished now that I had asked him to interpret those old letters written in French, perhaps by the prince himself.

As I cycled back, the police were down at the loch again, diligently searching the shore for clues.

A familiar figure, Sergeant Wright was leaving them, walking up the steep slope. I waved, and lingered until he reached the road. I wanted a word with him, but not about the dead man.

He greeted me, and nodding back towards the busy uniformed figures at the edge of the loch said, 'If that bush hadn't stopped him he would be right under the waters of the loch, lain there for ages with only the geese and the herons, and any murder trail long gone cold.' I followed his gaze. On a dull day it looked a dreary place, dark waters almost hidden under an entanglement of tall weeds.

'Still no idea of his identity?' I said.

He shook his head. 'We're working on it.' Any further conversation was interrupted by a shout from below.

'Maybe they've found something,' he said eagerly. 'Excuse me, Mrs McQuinn.' And he was off again before I had a chance to ask if he was the actors' policeman friend.

Jack came home early that evening and greatly to my surprise, having expected some reluctance, was willing, even eager, to go to the Jacobite play. I had certainly misjudged his reactions and I was now glad and relieved that Amy had not been at home after all.

Supper over, we decided to have another look for the location of the laird's lug. Upstairs, armed with our usual rather primitive means of illumination where some sort of searchlight would have been more effective for that dark, almost windowless room, we began a minute search.

I had told Jack that the first place of my search had been the alcove with its two shelves, but to no avail, so together in the manner suggested by Jack as that used in police investigations, we began testing the stone walls for possible crevices from floor to ceiling. We went over every inch of that ancient wooden floor for loose boards, which wasn't too difficult as the room was roughly the shape of a box or a large pantry, eight feet square.

We stood up, considered. There was no place to hide anything, but that laird's lug had to be somewhere, so we went back to the alcove with its two shelves.

'Here goes – our last resort.' And Jack produced a chisel and dislodged the shelves from the walls. A great flurry of choking dust and there, in one corner, an aperture. Jack brought the oil lamp closer.

'There's a deep shaft here.' And considering the geography for a moment, he added excitedly, 'This might well connect with the chimney in the kitchen. Hold on.'

He opened the panel and ran downstairs into the kitchen.

'Rose, are you there?'

I shouted, 'Yes, loud and clear.'

'Be right back with you.'

He came back and I said, 'I heard not only your voice but every footstep.'

'In the old days, what is now our oversized kitchen must have been the dining room of the old Tower.'

'We've solved that problem anyway.' And we grinned at each other, delighted with our discovery, but there was more to come.

The oil lamp raised again, I peered down the aperture. 'There's a tiny ledge, something lodged there.'

'Probably a dead bird,' said Jack.

'Well, in that case, you put your hand in,' I said.

Jack grimaced, sank his arm in up to the elbow and dragged out a black and ragged piece of cloth. We put it on the old table, and with growing excitement, shook off the gathered dust of times past.

It wasn't heavy, but we were almost afraid to open it.

Jack looked at me and sighed. I said, 'Go on.'

He pushed back the cloth to reveal paper. A huge amount of shredded paper.

Jack let some of it run through his fingers. A disgusting smell arose. Mice or rats!

Although I hadn't any desire to touch it, gingerly I gathered up a few pieces and quickly let them fall.

We stood looking down at what we had found, then we turned and looked at each other. The desire was there to either laugh or cry with disappointment.

'The treasure?' I whispered.

Jack nodded.

On the table all that remained of a king's ransom – thirty thousand pounds – in promissory notes once signed by the English Treasury and stolen from Lord Tweeddale.

'A king's ransom, right enough,' said Jack. 'A fortune today but in those days . . .' He scattered a few fragments with his hands. In those chewed-up papers there was barely one recognisable word.

Jack shook his head. 'Mrs Lawers' legacy – this is what it was all about, a treasure beyond man's wildest dreams.'

And I thought of the cost as he went on, 'This little pile of rubbish is responsible for at least three murders, that we know about. And there might be even more, a lot more, in the last one hundred and fifty years. Who knows?'

He paused, adding reluctantly, 'A king's ransom, all chewed into fragments, expensive bedding for countless generations of industrious mice.'

'Terrified mice,' I added. 'Scared up here to a safe retreat by Hedley Marsh's monstrous army of cats.'

We went downstairs again, threw the shreds on the fire. It burnt briskly and we watched thirty thousand pounds of Hanoverian money go up the kitchen chimney. Perhaps we even thought but did not brood upon what it could have bought, how it could have changed lives in the year 1901.

We had only the satisfaction of having solved the identity of the refugee who briefly stayed in the secret room in 1745.

Simon Reslaw had vanished, never to return and collect his stolen fortune. That task he had bequeathed to his ancestors. They too had failed. We had succeeded, but we still didn't know who had murdered Mrs Lawers and her maid, or the identity of a dead man by the shores of the loch.

Neither of us slept well that night.

CHAPTER THIRTY-ONE

A letter came from a prospective client requiring my services on a domestic matter of an indelicate nature, but such matters, the sources of my income and livelihood as a private investigator, were out of my province at the moment.

Jack needed me; there were murders to solve, as well as Meg's future with the Blakers. However, I replied immediately saying that I was heavily involved at present, which was true, but hoped that my services would be at her disposal the following week and suggested a date when I would call upon her. I awaited her reply, etc etc.

This was the evening of the Jacobite play at the Pleasance Theatre, according to newspapers and an abundance of posters in the area, their annual re-enactment of Bonnie Prince Charlie's local sojourn in Duddingston, including the Battle of Prestonpans and the Siege of Edinburgh.

It sounded like being an entertaining evening, and I was particularly keen to see Adrian Dyce on stage and whether he lived up to Beth's expectations and the high reputation she had built for him.

Relieved to see Jack home in time for a leisurely supper – for once – we both prepared to leave for the theatre. Jack was looking particularly good in his best suit and bowler hat, while I took out my best, and I must confess only, dress suitable for the occasion – turquoise satin, trimmed with lace, lacking only the tightly corseted fashionable hourglass shape which I resolutely refused to consider, regarding it as not only uncomfortable but utterly unsuitable for my bicycling activities.

For once unruly curls were persuaded into a velvet band with a sparkling diamante clip. White satin shoes completed the outfit to my satisfaction. And Jack's too. He was very complimentary and said that I should dress up more often.

The hiring gig he had ordered dropped us off at the theatre, where already the audience were being ushered to their seats. There is a never-failing excitement for me about waiting for that moment when the curtain rises and I had little time to study the programme, except to notice that Steven Sawler was playing Lord Cope, in charge of the Hanoverian army.

The backdrop had been carefully executed by clever artists and I settled back, prepared to be carried back to the autumn of 1745 and the story of Prince Charlie's triumph, depicted through the mouths of the actors as a battleground would have been beyond them on this relatively small stage. The audience had to imagine the scene of battle from the dialogue and a series of entrances and exits from one or two wounded soldiers, with bandaged heads or injured limbs.

Adrian made a handsome prince. He spoke with believable authority and I fancied he portrayed a far better commander than the real one. Watching his performance, which outshone his fellow actors, I was inclined to agree with Beth that he deserved better than a local repertory, with a magnificent voice well suited to the most difficult and varied of Shakespeare's heroic leads.

I was not alone in my opinion as the curtain fell, with tumultuous applause, on the first act and the audience gathered in the foyer for the interval.

There were familiar faces, some surprising, like Gray. I had not expected him to be a playgoer. He still had that sharp-eyed look and I suddenly wondered if he had completely abandoned his search for clues. Wright was there too, talking to Mrs Gray, and Jack whispered, 'Poor Con, in the wrong profession. Longing to tread the boards.'

I said, 'Thank you, Jack.' He looked puzzled but before I could explain, Beth emerged, radiant in a violet silk gown on the arm of a tall distinguished-looking man who at first glimpse could well have been mistaken for her father before she introduced him as Frederick.

So this was the noble Frederick, the man her family wanted her to marry. Introductions were exchanged and Jack listened politely to her exuberant comments on the performance before excusing himself to speak to an elderly fellow who looked suspiciously like a retired policeman. There is something about them, even out of uniform. Perhaps it was that ever-vigilant look they shared with Gray and never lost.

Beth murmured excuses to Frederick, took my arm and hustled me in the direction of the Ladies, where several other females were making use of the facilities.

Taking me aside, she whispered, 'It is just an excuse – I had to see you alone.'

As she seized a vacant mirror and attended to her hair, I thanked her once again for the tickets, and said how I was enjoying the play, particularly seeing Adrian giving such a splendid performance.

She looked at me eagerly. 'What do you think of Frederick?'

'Charming and very good-looking.'

She was pleased and gave a happy giggle. 'And so gracious. He would not consider my coming without an escort. Frederick is a keen playgoer, he attends all the most popular shows in London.'

'Adrian wasn't jealous?' I asked, wondering how her lover regarded her escort.

She shook her head. 'Adrian didn't mind in the least. He is so sweet, you know, and understanding. And between you and me I think he is hoping that Frederick will use his influence in the London theatre. He is on speaking terms with the most famous actors and managers,' she added excitedly, 'so Adrian particularly wanted him to see tonight's performance.'

She frowned. 'You have no idea how difficult it has been. Peter has done so well as Cope.'

I was wondering who Peter was when she said, 'Steven is down as Cope, one of the main roles, and there was no time to change the programme. I believe the manager was to have made an announcement but he forgot – or didn't intend to.'

I said consolingly that Peter was excellent and she nodded, then sighed, 'Poor Adrian. It is too bad. Steven's still in London, but no letter, of course.'

I asked after Lillie. She smiled. 'She is very well, thriving. And she has a companion at the moment. My Adrian has such a good heart, always willing to help, and how people use him! An actress who used to be in the company is in Scotland for a family wedding and wanted someone to look after her little girl for a few days. So now Nanny has the two of them.'

At that the bell rang, and as we returned to our seats I spotted Amy with a small group and I was glad I hadn't wasted the ticket. Hustled into our seats by the returning audience, she was several rows distant, saw me, waved and mimed 'meet later'.

The final act did not dwell on the disaster of Culloden, its climax providing the audience with the well-known story of Prince Charlie's flight, pursued by the Hanoverian army, and his meeting with his saviour, the brave Flora MacDonald. It was short and indicated a passionate tragic love affair, something of a liberty with historical fact, but making a satisfying romantic conclusion for the ladies in the audience.

The actress playing Flora was considering how best to persuade her prince to escape, reluctant as he was to leave her. He would have nothing of her suggestion that he disguise as her maid. She insisted and comedy was intended as he struggled with gown and petticoat, a bonnet and spectacles.

But for me this was no comedy.

This was a horrifying moment of truth.

We were in the front row and as the curtain fell, rose again, more applause, and as the actors took their bow, I was looking into the face of Adrian and knew that I had met the bogus Miss Hinton at last.

I wanted to tell Jack, longing to get him alone.

He took my arm. 'Gray has invited us to share their carriage. Wait here till I find them.'

I saw Amy at the entrance, looking round anxiously, obviously waiting for her friends. She saw me, waved and pushed her way towards me.

'Thank God, Rose. I've been trying to talk to you. It's been awful.'

I murmured politely that I was sorry she hadn't enjoyed the performance.

'No, Rose. Not this. I've been trying to tell you, ever since we had tea at your house.' She stopped, gulped, shook her head. 'That actor, Prince Charlie – the young girl Beth's fiancé . . .'

She paused dramatically. 'Rose, he's the man who was bullying poor Mary before . . . before . . .' She gulped, trying to stay calm. 'The man I saw outside her house. I tell you, it's the same man, that actor. And what's worse, Jane found some of Mary's photographs and although I never said a word to her, I'm certain sure that he's the ne'er-do-well nephew. He must have been trying to get money and the house from poor Mary. I was utterly shocked when we met him at your house that day with that lovely young girl. Someone should warn her – he's a villain.'

A feeling of chill and disbelief swept over me. It was my turn to stay calm. 'Surely not, Amy. How can you be sure? You could be mistaken; after all, old photographs and you only caught a glimpse of him.'

She shook her head. 'True enough. But his voice – very distinctive it is. Remember, I was an elocution teacher, voices are my business. I would have recognised his anywhere.'

Her friends were making urgent signs in our direction. 'I must go.' I was staring after her when Jack reappeared. In the shared carriage with the Grays, I tried to concentrate on polite conversation, my mind in turmoil.

We were set down at the Tower and had hardly closed the door when Jack turned to me, demanding, 'Well, what's wrong with you, Rose?'

I laid aside my cloak, shook my head, unable to think where to begin as he went on, 'You seemed very off-key. Didn't you enjoy the evening?'

He sounded disappointed and I sat down and told him all, finishing with Amy's revelations. He listened silently.

I had been fairly certain that there were two involved, that the killer had a female accomplice, the bogus Hinton who had tried to steal the legacy and push me off the train. But seeing him as Flora MacDonald's maid was my moment of truth –

and on top of that, Amy recognising him as the bullying man.

I looked at Jack sitting there saying nothing. I thought he would be very excited by this new information, but, being Jack, he merely shrugged before proceeding to tear my revelations into fine shreds.

'All very dramatic, Rose. Of course, I believe your story but alas, as you must realise, it is only circumstantial evidence. There isn't a single clue we could use as evidence in all this. We can hardly arrest Adrian because in female dress he resembles the woman who tried to kill you. Think about it, Rose—'

'But I am sure—'

He cut short my protests and went on, 'All I can say is that Gray would tell you that a dozen actors in that disguise would have looked like your bogus Miss Hinton, and insist that you imagined the whole thing – felt faint on the train, tried to open the window for air, opened the door instead and the woman was trying to stop you falling.'

He paused and sighed. 'As for Amy Dodd, Gray would want more than her claim that she recognised a man – whom she had merely glimpsed – by his voice, even if she was an elocution teacher.'

I knew it was useless to protest any further. And he was right about Gray's reactions, especially as I had an unhappy thought that Jack possibly shared them but did not want to hurt my feelings.

I didn't sleep much that night, troubled by nightmares. And when I lay awake afraid to go to sleep again my thoughts turned to Beth. If my suspicions and Amy's were true, and Adrian was a killer, where did that leave Beth? What sort of a future lay ahead, dispossessed by her parents, for this young girl with a baby?

Of course, she had said that Frederick wanted to marry her, but was that merely in her imagination too? Would he still want to do so when the publicity of her liaison with a murderer hit the newspaper headlines? What about his own reputation damaged by association?

I thought of Adrian, the splendid actor, remembering when he visited the Tower with Beth. He seemed such a nice pleasant fellow, he didn't look like a killer. But then Jack would say, and I knew also from my own experience, murderers usually looked no different to the ordinary fellows you met in the street on their way to work every day.

CHAPTER THIRTY-TWO

Jack arrived home earlier than usual that day. He had the afternoon off, kind permission of Gray, to compensate for having been on call since he came back from Peebles.

'I thought we might go out to Joppa and see Meg.'

I decided that was a great idea and he went on, 'And I have some other news. The dead man at the loch has now been identified. He is Steven Sawler.'

'Adrian's friend!' I gasped. 'The missing actor! Beth told me Adrian said he was in London.'

It was all becoming clear now as Jack said: 'He was identified by Con when he was in the mortuary with an accident victim's relative. He was very upset. Sawler had encouraged his stage ambitions, tried to get him bit parts with the Portobello Players.'

Jack paused, sighed. 'And since Gray thinks he was murdered, we're now looking for another killer and we're interviewing Adrian at that boarding house where they both lodged.'

It had all the makings of an open-and-shut case; considering my own suspicions of Adrian, confirmed by the play last night, and Amy's revelations, he must have invented Steven's London audition.

Again my first thoughts flew to Beth and Nanny Craigle. Police interviews were always an ordeal even for the innocent.

I looked at the theatre programme which I had read briefly at the performance: 'John Cope played by Steven Sawler.'

A sudden thought. 'For Sawler, read Lawers – both are variations of Reslaw,' I said, remembering how Beth said Steven was always going on about his ancestors. 'Perhaps he is the missing link with Simon Reslaw.'

'And thirty thousand pounds in chewed-up paper the reason for three murders,' Jack added grimly. 'With our prime suspect now conveniently dead. Oh, almost forgot, met our postman toiling up the hill. Here – he was delivering this letter.'

It was from Jane Hinton, thanking me for

tea that afternoon, saying how she had enjoyed our meeting and so forth. And adding that she had been rereading through those old letters, she wrote, 'Do you remember me telling you that Mrs Lawers had married her first cousin, Andrew Lawers, so she hadn't changed her maiden name?'

I put the letter down. Of course. It was all beginning to fall into place, the reason for this legacy being passed from one generation to another and reaching Mary Lawers who, either refusing to acknowledge the existence of a nephew of dubious parentage, or fearing she was not long for this world, her memory fading, believed that the distant cousin in Lochandor was the last of the line and became obsessed with the idea of getting the legacy to him.

As Jack read the letter, I told him my own theory. That it was the nephew, Steven Sawler, or Reslaw, who had heard the story of the missing thirty thousand. Beth had been so excited about Adrian's expectations – perhaps Steven had realised help was needed if he was to be successful and confided in Adrian, who had not been unwilling to come to his aid. So the two of them had set about recovering a fortune hidden in 1745 in the region of Arthur's Seat by Steven's ancestor, certain that the secret of its whereabouts must lie in Mrs Lawers' legacy. 'Thinking about it,' I concluded, 'the reality seemed a forlorn hope, but to two impoverished actors it doubtless promised a lifetime of ease and luxury, the world indeed becoming their oyster.'

This was a new twist. I knew from Beth that Adrian would do anything for Steven, his hero. Had the latter realised that, since Adrian had a dubious kinship, he was the perfect person to help him achieve his dream?

If I expected congratulations in having unravelled the mystery, I was disappointed. Jack's reality at that moment was meeting Meg, who he shamefully admitted he had not seen for far too long an interval in the life of a three-year-old child.

As we went to Joppa, I could see that Jack, although nervous of this encounter, was impressed by the exterior of the handsome villa where the Blakers lived.

The housekeeper opened the door and ushered us into the sitting room. A moment later, Mrs Blaker appeared. She recognised me immediately but regarded Jack in some surprise.

Not waiting to be introduced, he stepped forward eagerly, held out his hand. 'We have come to see my daughter Meg. I hope this visit is convenient.'

Mrs Blaker stared at him, opened her mouth, shut it again and sat down heavily on the nearest chair. 'That cannot be,' she said, shaking her head, her voice trembling; she looked pale, ready to faint.

'That cannot be!' she repeated, staring up at Jack. 'Mr Macmerry called for Meg last Thursday. He wished to take her to visit her grandparents for a few days. We could not refuse this request. Oh dear God,' she groaned.

It was Jack's turn to go pale. Rigid at my side, I clutched his arm for support while he took out a police card, the proof of his identity, and handed it to the distraught woman on the sofa.

With the two of us trying desperately to be calm and Mrs Blaker now in tears, sobbing, the housekeeper appeared wondering what the disturbance was about, and seeing her mistress's distress immediately applied the much needed smelling salts, murmuring, 'There, there, madam.'

Mrs Blaker looked up at her. 'Mrs Robb, this . . . this gentleman is Mr Macmerry . . . the man who took Meg— Oh dear God.' And collapsed again.

The housekeeper was clearly shocked but remained calm and Jack decided he would get more sense out of her.

'Do you mind if we sit down?' he said. 'You opened the door – can you describe the man?'

Mrs Robb said, 'Oh yes, he was about forty, clean-shaven. I never doubted him, sir – you see, he was wearing a policeman's uniform, carrying his helmet.'

That shook me – the bogus policeman again.

Mrs Robb looked ready to join her mistress in tears. 'I brought him through here to the mistress, went upstairs to collect Meg from the nursery and pack a few things.'

Jack, with admirable calm in the face of such dreadful news, turned to Mrs Blaker and said quietly, 'And how did Meg react to this man?'

'When he said "I'm your pa, Meg, come to take you on holiday" Meg looked as if she wasn't quite sure what a holiday meant and I said, "You'll be coming back home, dear." The man was holding out his hand. She looked at me – bewildered, a bit frightened – and . . . and then she went over and took his hand.'

Mrs Blaker began to cry again. 'I watched them leave. He had a carriage waiting. Oh Mr Macmerry,' she wailed, 'what have I done? I should have been protecting her, and I've let some vile man kidnap your little daughter. Who could have done such a cruel thing to a little girl? What can we do?' she repeated helplessly, looking ready to faint, Mrs Robb at her elbow.

There was nothing we could do. We were days too late, the trail already cold. I felt awful but my heart went out to Jack who looked dreadful, his face white, set in stone, trying his best to console Mrs Blaker that it was not her fault – never having met him anyone could have made the same mistake – and assuring her, which I wanted to believe but couldn't at that moment, that all would be well and that Meg would be found.

We left the two women, and in the carriage I took Jack's hand. He grasped it tightly until the pressure made me cry out. He apologised, and leaning back, he groaned.

'What next – what will we do?' I asked. And echoing Mrs Blaker's words, 'Who could have done this, who could have taken her? And why your child, Jack? I don't understand.'

Jack shook his head, stared out of the window, seeing a grimmer prospect than the passing street.

'She's been kidnapped, Rose. We don't know why – yet. But maybe this has nothing to do with me personally, maybe I'm just a link in the chain. We'll soon find out,' he added grimly.

And I knew he was thinking of the thirty thousand pounds when he said, 'There will be a demand for a ransom. In fact, I'm surprised they've delayed contacting me. In these cases usually it's the next day – why the interval? What are they waiting for?'

I didn't want to be left alone, but I had Thane and Jack needed to report straight away to the Central Office.

He held me briefly at the door and said, 'I know you're worried sick, so am I. But I've handled kidnap cases before; there's a definite pattern.'

I tried to be consoled, but those kidnappings were not personal cases and this one was his own daughter.

'We'll maybe need money, so I'd better see what I've got in the bank,' he said shortly.

Then he was gone and I was left with Thane, who had been regarding us with the anxious expression that said his humans were in trouble. And because there was no one else I told him what had happened and he moved closer to my side, a gesture meant to be reassuring. But what could a deerhound do against kidnappers?

Jack knew the procedure but so did I. Kidnapping was a hanging offence, and if the kidnappers didn't get the ransom they were demanding, they were quite likely to kill the child and disappear. They could not risk their victim falling into police hands and telling all. Not even a small child. No trail must be left.

This was one of the worst days in my life, and I did not dare to leave the Tower just in case. I hoped the ransom note would not be delivered while Jack was absent. But that was exactly what happened.

There was a knock at the kitchen door and I opened it. A man stood there, hat pulled well down over grey hair, eyes invisible under heavy eyebrows. A muffler to his chin completed the disguise, making certain that he would never be recognised again.

A hoarse voice. 'Afternoon, madam. I have a message for Mr Macmerry.'

There was no use pretending otherwise – I felt certain that he knew I was alone in the house.

'I will not beat about the bush. Give Mr Macmerry this message. If he wishes to see his daughter again, alive, he is to take a thousand pounds and leave it under a loose stone on the rim above the Wells o' Wearie.' The ancient well was half a mile from the Tower. 'Meanwhile I will accept a package from you, madam, a package containing documents given you by the late Mrs Lawers, just for any trouble and as a goodwill insurance that no ill will befall the little girl while her father assembles the required ransom.'

'I haven't any idea what you are talking about,' I said.

He moved forward menacingly, with a gun pointed at my heart. 'Don't try my patience, lady.'

As I backed away from him, moving further into the kitchen, I touched the derringer in my pocket. I could kill or wound him severely. As if he knew my intentions he said, 'Remember, if anything happens to me, the child will be disposed of immediately. So, the package if you please.'

I shook my head and at that moment a floorboard creaked at his heels. No human footfall, no other presence except for Thane and myself. But the noise was so loud that it completely threw him off guard.

He swivelled round. And Thane leapt, knocking him to the ground and pinning him to the floor.

He yelled. 'Call your dog off. Remember, if I die the girl dies too.'

Suddenly the door opened, and there was Jack with Gray, and never had I been so glad to see a bevy of uniformed policemen surging into my kitchen.

As Jack called Thane off, the man was dragged to his feet and Gray stepped forward. Pulling off the bonnet and grey wig he arrested Adrian Dyce on suspicion of committing three murders.

It was my turn to feel rather ill as they led him away, cursing his captors. Jack put his arm around me.

I said, 'Thank God you got here in time.'

He nodded. 'Gray has had his eye on Adrian for some time on suspicion of drug smuggling, and we're pretty certain he killed Steven.' It fitted what Nanny Craigle had said and my theory that, far from being friends, Adrian was heavily under Steven's influence, as Jack continued.

'As you so rightly worked out, we'll find that he was Sawler's accomplice. Together they hoped to find the treasure. But thieves fall out. Maybe Adrian got greedy, decided he could go it alone, pretty certain that there was thirty thousand pounds hidden in the Tower here.'

I hesitated for a moment and then said, 'Jack, I haven't told you before, but the policeman who lured me to the hospital to break into the house. I'm pretty sure that it was Steven.'

Jack looked at me. 'How do you know?'

'Well, it was one or the other of them. Adrian was the bogus maid, but he's smaller and slimmer than Steven.'

Jack frowned. 'And he could have known I was in the hospital. It was in all the local papers.'

He paused and then said gently, 'Why on earth didn't you tell me all this at the time? About the burglary? I certainly would never have gone to Eildon and left you on your own.'

'Which is precisely why I kept it to myself. And there had been no damage done. However, I thought I recognised the dead man at the loch as the policeman.'

'And you still didn't mention that important fact.'

I shrugged and he said sternly, 'Withholding

vital information, Rose, which would have been of considerable help, as well as saving precious time while we were trying to establish his identity.'

'If I had told you, then Gray would have wanted a lot more information.'

'For a murder you intended to solve yourself, of course,' Jack said mockingly. 'Rose, that was a chronically wrong decision. You must know that.'

'With hindsight, I suppose so,' I admitted reluctantly. 'All I knew was that I had solved several murders on my own.'

'And may I remind you, several times almost lost your life.' Jack shook his head. 'You must have used up more than a cat's nine lives.' He took my hand. 'This is all about Gray – your own personal feud, isn't it? A matter of female pride, not allowing him to catch the criminal, beating him to it because he refuses to take your role as a lady investigator seriously.'

Ignoring that, I said, 'There are some questions I want to know the answer to. You say they could have known you were in hospital, but where did Sawler get the uniform?'

Jack laughed. 'That's easy. He was an actor, and the Portobello Players have mystery plays on their repertoire and must have a costume hamper full of police uniforms.' Pausing, he looked at me. 'What's on your mind, Rose?'

'Where did they get all this information – us

and the Tower, I mean?' I didn't want to end Wright's brief career in the Edinburgh City Police and added quickly, 'I mean how widespread is your personal knowledge about each other in the Central Office?'

'It's all there, in the files; Gray and those above have it all on record. My career, my marriage, widowed, one daughter. And yours too, Rose – I'd be prepared to bet you have a dossier.' He paused, then added, 'And of course, ours.'

'Would anyone junior to you have access to this information?'

Jack thought about that. 'Well, we do gossip in the local pub. All lads together, that sort of thing, over a pie and a pint. We're only human after all.' A quizzical look. 'Is all this leading somewhere?'

It was, but I shook my head, determined not to incriminate Sergeant Wright, who I was sure held his inspector in high regard and had somehow allowed himself to be drawn into the Adrian-Steven conspiracy without the least knowledge of what dire crimes were intended.

'So Meg was no secret.'

Jack laughed. 'I don't go on about her like some of the doting fathers, but if any of the lads ask me, I say yes, I have a wee girl, living with her aunty. I dare say Adrian and Steven frequented the same local pubs, had the same acquaintances, and for their vile purposes, learnt that I had a little girl who might prove useful.'

Later he said, 'Don't worry, Rose, under pressure he will reveal Meg's whereabouts and all will be well.'

I wished I felt as sure as he did. I could not rid myself of that ominous feeling of disaster – one that I was quite used to and which, alas, often proved to be right.

CHAPTER THIRTY-THREE

Next day, in my role as a private investigator, I was to be present in the interview room in the Central Office while Jack questioned Adrian Dyce. This procedure had been approved, somewhat reluctantly, by Chief Inspector Gray, who poured scorn on the activities of female sleuths. However I had become a valuable witness, involved right from the start when I agreed to deliver Mrs Lawers' legacy, and gaining possession of it was the motive for her murder.

There was a policeman present and I wondered why it wasn't Wright taking notes, as Adrian began throwing all the blame on Steven, who, he said, had killed the two women because the legacy belonged to his branch of the family by rights – a lot of money, thousands of pounds stolen by his ancestor who was a Jacobite spy.

'I hadn't much faith in it personally but he persuaded me to go along with him. Said it would be easy, a sick old woman not long for this world. But she defied him, and when she refused to part with it by peaceful persuasion, he said he lost his temper and . . . well, he hit her – too hard. The maid tried to intervene.'

A pause; there was no need for further comment.

'And what about Steven's unfortunate death, did you have a hand in that too?' Jack asked.

'Of course not, that was an accident coming back from rehearsals. Birthday party for one of the cast. We both drank too much. Past midnight, we ran out of money for a hiring carriage. Nothing for it but to walk – took the short cut back by Duddingston. By that time, the fog was so bad over Arthur's Seat that we could hardly see our hands before our faces. We reached the turn of the road leading down to the loch. A carriage was coming up the steep hill. Steven tried to get it to stop and give us a lift. I didn't see what happened next. He staggered and fell down the steep slope to the loch.'

A pause. 'Naturally I went down after him, but I couldn't do anything to revive him. I guessed he was dead.'

He made the statement totally without emotion, and in the short silence I guessed that Jack and the other policeman present, who was taking notes, had also decided that this was an unlikely story.

Jack asked, 'Why didn't you go for help?'

Adrian thought about that. 'There wasn't any place nearby. That part is completely isolated.'

'What about Solomon's Tower?'

'In the middle of the night?' A sneering glance in my direction. 'A woman on her own with that great watchdog?'

That was significant, I thought, as he added huffily, 'Frankly I didn't want to get involved.'

'Why were you so worried? If you were innocent of your friend's death – an unfortunate accident – you had nothing to fear.'

'Indeed? I know what you lot are like.'

'Indeed you don't, Mr Dyce. We would be naturally suspicious of a man who callously left his friend lying dead at the edge of the loch and went home.'

I fancied that Adrian shrugged this aside. 'If I was detained for questioning, there was the Portobello play to be considered. It was imminent and I couldn't risk delays. Had the rest of the cast to think of, cancellations and so forth. We couldn't afford that sort of thing – or to disappoint all those people,' he added piously.

'All, in your opinion, more important than Steven Sawler's dead body? And, of course, wasting police time trying to discover his identity by emptying his pockets, removing any possessions.'

'Don't know what you're talking about.'

'I am talking about means of identification, a wallet, watch – the sort of thing you carry yourself, but all were missing from Sawler's body when we found him.'

A grim laugh. 'Then some of your lot must have helped themselves. It certainly wasn't me.'

A pause and Jack went on, 'Now, tell us where the kidnapped child is.'

'Can't help you there. Haven't the slightest idea. Steven arranged that and kept it to himself, as he did a lot of things. I was only the messenger.'

'The messenger?' Jack interrupted. 'With Sawler already dead, I think you invented this role – didn't you?'

Adrian was trapped, a note of desperation in his voice. 'I tell you this was all Steven's fault, right from the beginning. He wanted those documents Mrs McQuinn had been given by Mrs Lawers to hand on to some relative in the Highlands. That maddened Steven, said he was a closer relative by descent. Reslaw was his real name.'

'Did he know what these documents contained?'

Adrian laughed. 'Of course. He was obsessed

by them. The key to the whereabouts of a missing treasure – called it a "king's ransom".'

'And presumably you were to have a share in this vast fortune.'

'Yes, that was the general idea. But I would never have willingly become an accessory to murder. I was an actor, his best friend, and he needed my help to get hold of this hidden money that was to set us both up for life. He thought it might have been hidden all these years in the house where the prince had lodged.

'So he sent me to have a look around as a prospective buyer for this historic house and a distant relative of the Lawers family. But I refused to kill the old lady and the maid – he did that accidentally he said, and then he tried to make it look like a gas leak. He was desperate, and because I was shorter and slimmer than him and had played female roles, I was to pretend to be the maid and get the documents from the McQuinn woman over there on the journey.'

'Attempted murder,' said Jack grimly.

'Prove it, Inspector.' He jabbed a finger in my direction. 'Go on, tell them. You felt faint, tried to open the window and all I did was grab you to stop you falling out. I saved your life!'

I merely shook my head and Jack continued sharply: 'After being an accessory to murdering two innocent women.'

A short silence. 'I've told you. I had no part in that.' He laughed. 'Where's your proof?' With Steven dead that was true.

He went on: 'It wasn't in the house, so he decided that this ancestor of his, the Jacobite spy, must have been billeted with some of the prince's men on Arthur's Seat, and as the only building was Solomon's Tower, the money might still be there.'

'So you went disguised as a policeman, lured Mrs McQuinn away, so that you could have a look for them.'

'That wasn't me. That was Steven.' And Adrian realised too late that he had just revealed that he knew all about the break-in.

Jack returned again to Meg's kidnapping but Adrian remained adamant in his denial of having anything to do with that, perhaps believing that this was something he could use – assisting the police – that would reduce his sentence.

I lingered by the door waiting for Jack, who was with the young policeman obviously going over the notes.

As we left the building, I asked why his sergeant hadn't been with him during the interview with Adrian.

'Con asked to be excused, on the grounds that Adrian would recognise him. He was very apologetic, mortified. The two actors had

338

befriended him over the past few weeks, finding out in the pub that he was stage-struck and admired the Portobello Players; they even hinted at the chance of some walk-on parts. When he recognised Steven's body he realised what was going on, that he was being pumped for information and had unwittingly aided them in their murderous intent. The kidnap of Meg was the bitter end.'

Jack shook his head. 'Poor Con was almost tearful, offered to hand in his resignation. I said no, he's got the makings of a good copper, we all make mistakes in judgement and I trusted that this indiscretion would make him more careful in the future not to gossip about his colleagues.'

He added, 'As Dyce was taken down to the cells, Gray came over and said, "All that murder and mayhem for a mythical thirty thousand. After all that time, the idea of it still existing is preposterous. Sawler must have been insane to believe it."'

Jack laughed, 'I said nothing.'

'You didn't tell him that at home we had a souvenir?'

'An envelope full of mouse-chewed shreds?' Jack added. 'No, I think we keep that piece of information to ourselves.'

But we had more to think about; a king's ransom wasn't worth the life of a child, at this moment in deadly peril.

The terrifying question remained: where was she?

And the dreadful reality was unshakeable. Steven was dead and, if Adrian hadn't lied, the secret of where she was hidden had died with him.

Who could we turn to? I thought of Nanny Craigle – she knew Adrian and Steven and possibly actors' favourite haunts. I would go and see her, trying not to think of Beth – of coming face-to-face with her terrible distress that the man she loved and hoped to marry was a ruthless killer. I thought of Lillie . . .

And suddenly I had an idea.

CHAPTER THIRTY-FOUR

'Jack, I think I know where she is.'

Hardly daring to hope we took a carriage and went to Portobello. Nanny Craigle opened the door. Very upset she was, gasping out that she couldn't believe all this about Adrian and Steven. It wasn't true, was it?

'Poor Beth, that lass has suffered so much.'

'Where is she?'

'Upstairs in her bedroom with Lillie and the other wee girl, Madge.'

Jack almost pushed her aside and raced upstairs.

The door was open; Beth sat on the bed, tear-stained, tragic, rocking the baby Lillie in her cot. The little girl on her knee saw us, jumped down and ran to Jack.

Laughing, she shouted, 'Pa!'

He swept her up into his arms and held her close to his heart. I saw his expression. He had not expected this since Steven claiming to be her father had taken her from the Blakers. And yet some instinct, some fragment of memory, had recognised that this man was her real father. Now he held her as if he could never let her go again.

We explained to Beth, as gently as we could, that there was no actress mother. Steven, or Adrian at his behest, had kidnapped this little girl and held her to ransom.

Beth ran to me. 'Oh Rose, I am so ashamed. Loving a man, giving my heart to such a vile creature. I never want to see him again. And I am so glad that my little Lillie is not his child.'

It was sad, for Meg's kidnapping was the final curtain on Beth's tragedy. We left her shocked and disillusioned, unable to offer words of comfort, and we were the only ones with even a crumb of joy in our hearts.

Except perhaps for Nanny Craigle, who whispered as we were leaving, 'Miss Beth will be all right. Sir Frederick will take care of her.'

Longing to take Meg home with us, Jack had a duty to her adoptive parents. 'To the Blakers first. The poor woman was distraught.'

At the house in Joppa, a happy reunion. Mrs Blaker took us into the sitting room, Meg frowning, holding on to her father's hand with both of her own, as if reluctant to be separated from him for an instant.

Mr Blaker was there, solid, quiet. Saying 'All's well that ends well,' he left the rest to his wife. Meg went over politely, sat on her knee, but all the time looking back, watching Jack with that anxious expression I had seen in the orphans, reminding me of stray dogs.

It broke my heart. I felt tears threatening.

'Welcome home again, dear,' said Mrs Blaker.

She was wearing a long pendant with a bright jewel. Meg toyed with it, not looking at her.

A clearing of the throat and Mr Blaker said sternly, 'You had better tell them, my dear.'

Mrs Blaker sighed, looked across at us. 'We have just discovered from our physician that after all these years we are to have a child of our own.'

Her husband interrupted quickly, 'In the circumstances, as my wife is somewhat delicate, I am afraid we must decline adopting Meg. It is most unfortunate, of course, but I am sure other adoptive parents will be found, and she is most welcome to remain with us until suitable arrangements are made.'

We waited no longer. We took her home with us. Thane was waiting with a joyous welcome. Almost asleep, Jack carried her upstairs to bed in the spare room.

Thane came with us, sat at the bedside watching as Jack tucked her into bed. Her eyes opened, she pointed.

'Want doggie,' she said firmly, 'Doggie stay.'

Jack was already carrying Thane's rug from our bedroom floor. I felt that he wasn't displeased.

There were decisions to be made. As for that legacy and the money which cost so many lives, we treasured our envelope of mouse-chewed paper. The historical documents, including the letters and map drawn by Prince Charlie, would go to the archives. The snuffbox and mourning ring might be valuable but I wouldn't lay claim to either of them, and we decided that their future lay in a glass case in the history museum.

Jack came in while I was writing letters.

'Hold on, you can post these for me in town,' I said.

He looked over my shoulder at the addresses and I explained, 'Two new cases, prospective clients, Jack, but I'm postponing everything to do with my investigations until we get Meg settled.'

He was silent, nodded, then said, 'You can't do this, Rose. It isn't right.'

I sighed. 'Meg's future is more important than a couple of new clients.'

He looked down at me. 'Listen, Rose, Meg is

my problem, I can't let you sacrifice your career. There must be some other solution.'

As he said the words, Vince's parting remark flashed into my mind – that the solution was so simple he was surprised it had taken so long for a lady investigator to work it out.

I handed the letters to him. 'And until we do, I will look after Meg.'

I cut short his arguments. 'Jack, Meg is your daughter but I have always felt that she is partly my responsibility.'

He frowned. 'How do you come by that, pray?'

'I know it is disagreeable for you to remember, but if you can bear to cast your mind back, her very existence is my fault – if I hadn't rejected you and sent you away, you would never have taken up with Maggie and married her on the rebound. And wee Meg would never have been born.'

'Don't be idiotic, Rose. I can't allow such sentiments. Now let's be practical.'

'I am being practical. I have thought of a way . . .' I paused, took a deep breath. 'We could get married – make it legal. Be proper parents.'

Jack stared at me and bit his lip. Not only angry but obstinate. He shook his head, 'No Rose, I will not marry you against your every inclination, just because of Meg. The idea is intolerable. I will hear no more about it. And that's definite.'

'Jack.' I put my arms around his neck and

he backed away, eyeing me coldly. 'It is not intolerable, because I love you,' I whispered. 'I think I have known that for a very long time.'

Silent for a moment, he said grumpily, 'You might have told me, then. What about your career, always so important?'

'It still is important, but I want you. There's plenty of room for you – and Meg.'

'No, Rose.' He held up his hand. 'You have consistently refused to marry me for years – only once did you agree, and, as I found out when you miscarried on the eve of our wedding, that was only because you were pregnant,' he added bitterly.

'Yes, I lost that baby, yours and mine, Jack. It seems unlikely that I'll conceive again; the Faro women are rather doomed in that respect, one child – if they are lucky. The old Orkney selkie curse.'

He gave an impatient shrug as I went on, 'So having your daughter is the next best thing.'

'I'm not listening to all this, Rose. Meg can stay with us till we sort something out that is best for her, meantime—'

'"Meantime" is for always as far as I am concerned. She is your daughter and this is her rightful home, here with you. As for marriage, if you won't have me, I really don't care. We are already married under Scottish law – by habit and repute, remember – and I am not greatly concerned about the legal documents, the church wedding or what people think.'

Jack looked at the clock. 'I have to go. We'll discuss this later.' He held up the letters. 'Sure you want me to post these?'

'Yes. I want a week or two to spend with Meg, get to know each other while I make some arrangements that will suit all three of us.'

'What kind of arrangements would those be, pray?'

'With the convent – the Little Sisters of the Poor across the way.'

'They have an orphanage?' It was a question, not exactly an eager one.

'I'm not interested in their orphanage. They also have a nursery for little girls. And Sister Clare is an old friend. When necessary, if I am working, I can put Meg there, and when she is old enough she will go to the convent school.'

Jack was listening now. 'You've worked it all out, haven't you?'

'With your approval.'

'Of course I approve.' Sounds on the stairs, an excited child's voice. Meg came in with Thane and rushed over to Jack who swung her up in his arms.

For a moment there was no thought of him rushing away and I went quietly about preparing

Meg's breakfast. I'd try her with porridge, see how we got on.

Jack kissed her again, set her down at the table. Pointing across at me, he said solemnly, 'This is your ma, Meg.'

And I wanted to cry as she looked at me and laughed delightedly – a wee girl who had been through so much in her three years, radiant, trusting.

Jack put an arm around my shoulders. 'We are your ma and pa, Meg. Your own family.'

She frowned, not quite understanding what the word meant. A moment later she touched Thane's head – he had moved to her side – and she nodded eagerly, saying proudly, 'And doggie too.'

And that's about all there is.

For now.

AUTHOR'S NOTE

Among the many historical accounts and material consulted, I am indebted to The Battle of Prestonpans Heritage Trust for 'The Prestonpans Tapestry 1745' published by Prestoungrange University Press with Burke's *Peerage & Gentry*, 2010.

If you enjoyed *Deadly Legacy*,
read on to find out about the latest case
in Alanna Knight's Inspector Faro series . . .

To discover more great fiction and to
place an order visit our website at
www.allisonandbusby.com
or call us on
020 7580 1080

MURDERS MOST FOUL

1861. When the body of an unknown woman is found in an Edinburgh close, Detective Constable Faro assumes the killing is a random act of violence – until he finds a playing card, the nine of diamonds, planted under her corpse.

His superiors scoff at his suspicions of a serial killer, but days later a man is attacked in the street, and left badly bruised and battered with the nine of diamonds in his pocket. Faro believes there's a connection. Could the sudden disappearance of a servant also be linked to the playing-card killer?